My Perfect Family

Melanie Price

Books by Melanie Price

The Mother-in-Law's Secret

My Perfect Family

For my dad, Geoff Price.

Forever young.

Published by Wendlebury Ltd in 2024

20-22 Wenlock Road
London N1 7GU

ISBN: 978-1-7384652-3-1
eBook ISBN: 978-1-7384652-2-4

Chapter One

I wake with my heart hammering and an insistent buzzing beside my ear.

Where am I?

Blinking my eyes open, I try to take in the room through a hazy blur. A plush grey rug runs across the wooden floor towards a heavy white curtain, and an assortment of clothes are strewn along a cream sofa.

My heart rate begins to steady itself.

Ah, that's right. No need to panic.

I'm in a hotel room on Sydney Harbour. Today is my final morning here after closing a deal yesterday for my London law firm and judging by the pounding in my head, I'd made the most of toasting my hard-won success.

I groan, sinking deeper into the soft sheets. I know it's all my fault that I'm feeling terrible – but when I saw my best friend, Addie, she convinced me to have a bit of a celebration. I'm only back in Sydney briefly, and I hadn't seen her in so long. I should have known better, though. I don't really drink much anymore, having experienced a few too many blackouts in my early twenties. But I'd obviously got a little carried away in my excitement.

And now I'm suffering the consequences: my brain feels like it's gone through a washing machine, and my memories are all blurry. *What exactly happened last night?*

Squeezing my eyes shut, I burrow deeper into the large king-sized bed. I wish I could hide here and recover all day. Especially because I don't want to face where I'm supposed to be staying next: 8 Merton Street. My stepfamily's house.

I stretch my arms under the silky-smooth covers, wincing at the movement. There's a sharp pain across my back, and when I wiggle my legs, they feel like lead. I try to ignore all my problems and settle back into sleep.

But it's impossible, as the continuous buzzing starts again, making me jump at the sound. Whoever wants to talk is being very persistent.

I roll onto my side and reach a hand beneath the pillows, trying to ignore the ache that runs up my shoulder. When I pull out my phone and bring it towards me, I notice some scratches in the dim light across the palm of my hand. I must have fallen somewhere. Though when and how is a total blank.

I frown as I glance at the caller ID, blinking in confusion.

Because it's someone who *never* calls me.

For a moment, I consider not answering. But a reflex kicks in, and I end up sliding my thumb across the screen. I press the phone to my ear as I whisper, 'Hello.'

A shrill Australian accent comes thundering down the line.

'Emiiily, it's Jennifer.' An unnecessary disclaimer: I know who she is. My step-aunt, who I haven't spoken to in at least a year.

Before I even have a chance to respond, her words start to tumble out thick and fast. A cold sweat breaks out across my body as I try to follow.

'Emily, look, I've been trying to reach you all morning. I'm sorry to have to be the one to tell you this... but there was an accident at the cliffs... and your mum... your mum, she's...' Her voice cracks.

With my heart in my throat, I croak, 'She's what?'

'Your mum. Lovely Suzannah... she's dead, Emily. She's dead.'

The phone falls from my hand.

I feel like I've been punched in the stomach, and I turn my face into the pillow to let out a guttural scream.

This isn't possible – my mother *couldn't* have been in an accident at the cliffs.

She *cannot* be dead.

Because if she is, then I think it's all my fault.

Chapter Two

My skin feels like bugs are crawling all over it, and my insides lurch. I throw the covers off me as my mind furiously tries to piece together the disconnect between my night and Jennifer's words.

She can't be dead, she *can't* be dead.

It's not possible.

Because I swear I saw her last night.

I have one clear memory of my mum's face as I said goodbye to her yesterday after lunch. But after that, from when I met up with Addie, my recollections become a blur.

I know I promised Mum that I would stay with her at my late grandparents' house last night. My grandparents' house in Dover Heights, overlooking the cliffs...

And yet, here I am – in my hotel room. Did I still go and see her?

Hazy images of my mother's face flash through my mind, so I'm sure I did. But the order of my night won't come back to me. I can't get a grasp on the full picture.

I put my head in my hands. My thumping headache continues as I attempt to force my brain to retrace my footsteps. But I can't – it's a kaleidoscope of mismatched memories.

'Emily?' I hear Jennifer ask from a distance.

I'm speaking aloud, mumbling, *No, no, no* through my fingers.

'Emily!' she tries again, shouting down the line. 'Listen to me; come on over, we'll talk it all through. We can explain properly what happened – or what we think happened.'

I scoop the phone back up. 'Wait, Jennifer, tell me now – I don't understand. It *can't* be true!'

I grasp at that explanation; maybe this is a ridiculous joke. I leap out of bed now, even as my body screams at me in pain. But I have to move around. I have to do *something*.

A sad sigh follows my outburst, and I stop myself from throwing the phone across the room. Jennifer can't be this resigned to doing nothing.

'I'm so sorry, Emily. I know this is a huge shock... we're still piecing everything together. Hopefully, when you come over, Glenn can tell you more. All I know so far is that a dog walker spotted something on the edge of the cliffs where they meet the water very early this morning – just below your grandparents' house – and they called the police. Glenn was alerted and taken over there; he's been there for hours. Then, well, it was a bit tricky because of how she fell, but he's now identified the body as your mum's... I'm *so sorry*.' She's silent before she adds in a small voice, 'But you know how dangerous it is up there.'

I pace up and down the small room as I try to process what I've heard. My long, lightly freckled legs cover the distance in a matter of steps. I turn and start again.

I picture those exact cliffs that make up Dover Heights, my grandparents' house one of many nestled above them. I'd always loved that their back garden beyond was wild, and that there wasn't a fence blocking the incredible natural view of the Pacific Ocean, unlike many of the other newer houses that had started to pop up. But I knew, we *all* knew, the danger of venturing too far out towards the edge. It leads to a sheer, unforgiving drop – an impossible fall to survive.

A bubble of anger rises in my throat as Jennifer keeps talking. The police had called *Glenn*, my stepfather, over me. *He* identified the body – not me. Not her only daughter.

'So what are they saying? How did she end up there?' I'm shouting, and I know I sound nearly hysterical. But I don't care – I can't believe these words are even coming out of my mouth.

'I don't think I'm the right person to tell you everything, Emily. But the police are saying it's most likely a terrible accident. Please come over and speak with Glenn. He can properly explain what he's been told—'

But that's the last thing I want. If Glenn tells me, I'm certain I'll break down in front of him. And I won't let that happen. I can't see him until I'm more in control of my emotions – and my memories.

'No,' I interrupt. 'Tell me what you know *now*.' I'm gesturing wildly even though no one can see me. But as soon as the demand is out of my mouth, a flash of a scream flies into my mind. It's unclear. But it's there. And I'm certain it's a memory of last night.

I freeze, still as a statue. I hold onto the moment, bringing my free hand to cover my eyes as though that will help me. But it's gone before I have a chance to grasp it. I let my hand peel back, and that's when I notice the scratches again. The scratches all down my palm. They send a shiver down my spine as I recall that earth-shattering cry.

I fall with a thump onto the sofa as my legs give way. And that's when I see them: the angry red marks all over my knees, a light purple bruise blossoming like a flower in early spring over my pale skin. My stomach twists.

I have no idea why I'm hurt and no idea how or why Mum could have fallen off the edge of the cliff last night. But I do have a memory of a scream and cuts and scrapes on me as though I fell in some scrub.

Scrub that could have been at the edge of my grandparents' house.

As soon as I brush on the thought, I shove it away hard. I couldn't have had anything to do with this...

But then again, I know I'd promised Mum that I *would* come and see her yesterday evening. And I've never let her down before.

I'm breathing in and out in shallow puffs, my heart thumping faster than I've ever felt it as these frantic thoughts race around my mind.

Jennifer's voice echoes down the line, pulling me out of my spiral.

'Emily, I don't know why she was there. This is as much as I know right now. So please, come over. Glenn can tell you more.'

My body is going into shock. I have to get off this call. So even as a thick tightness in my throat threatens to choke me, I manage to say, 'Okay, Jennifer, I'll be over soon.' I don't give her a chance to respond as I end the call.

The instant it's over, I hurl my phone across the room. It thwacks against the wall with a resounding thud.

I don't care if it's broken. My heart has already shattered into a thousand tiny pieces.

A shuddering howl escapes from the very centre of my chest, and sobs wrack my aching body. The words *she's dead, she's dead* echo around and around my mind.

I fall sideways on the sofa and roll my thin body into a tight ball. I try to make all five foot ten of me as small as possible, tucking my knees into my chest as though curling up will protect me from my awful thoughts.

But it's not a soft pillow I land on.

My face makes contact with something wet and slippery, the shock of it halting my choking tears. I slip my hand out to pick up the cold, soaked item. My stomach plummets to the floor as I realise what it is.

My top from last night.

Completely soaked in water.

And blood.

Chapter Three

My mouth goes dry at the horrific sight, and I just make it to the bathroom in time. Afterwards, I lie on the cool tiles of the sparkling marble floor, trying to breathe in and out. In and out. I need to calm my shaking body and breaking heart.

But when I close my eyes, all I can see is dark red splatters across my white top. As my hands press into the tiles, I can still only feel the coldness of the wet fabric. I crawl towards the walk-in shower, manage to stand and wrench the tap on. A jet of hot water erupts from the waterfall ceiling. I'm only in my underwear, and I want to wash away every inch of me.

As the flowing stream floods my senses, I stare into space, allowing myself to feel nothing except the warmth on my skin and the roar of the water pummelling on top of me. I don't want to feel – not after what I've been told.

But when what could have been hours pass, I know I can't ignore this any longer. I can't pretend like something hasn't happened. Because my mother is dead. And I'm terrified I might have something to do with it.

I massage my fingers through my wet hair, trying to get my brain to work. I need to think through the wave of grief that has taken over my mind. I start by picturing my mother's face and replay the last time I properly remember seeing her.

After completing my client deal yesterday, we'd met for a late lunch at one of the restaurants that look out onto Sydney's Darling Harbour. At that time of day on a hot Friday in mid-summer, when most Sydneysiders are on their summer breaks, there had only been a handful of tourists eating al fresco along the open strip connecting to the bustling wharf.

I'd been late after my meeting overran and had arrived a hot, sweaty mess. My thick black work dress had been a bad choice. I'd forgotten how hot the Australian summers could be. I hadn't returned to Sydney for a year, not since the big fight between my step-sister Zara and me. I'd thought it was no bad thing to give Zara a bit of space. To give *everyone* a bit of space.

But our fight hadn't been the only reason why I hadn't returned home in that time – I'd also been desperately trying to find my feet in London. I'd always wanted to move overseas on a big adventure to prove that I could make it on my own. Though, if I was being honest, the reality hadn't been living up to the big dreams I'd worked hours at law school to achieve.

But I didn't want to admit to anyone that I'd been struggling. I could picture the smug look on my stepfather Glenn's face if I fessed up. I knew he thought I'd become too big for my boots. He's an Australian bloke through and through – and couldn't understand why I'd ever want to leave this sunkissed country.

I'd missed my mother, though. She'd been put in a tricky position in the middle of our blended family dynamic. I hadn't meant to punish her by staying away so long, but I hadn't quite been able to forgive Zara for what she'd done. It's not every day you catch your stepsister making out with your long-distance boyfriend, after all.

'Emily!' A bright, excited voice had called to me as I rushed into the restaurant's outdoor seating area. It was a voice I would have recognised anywhere.

I'd whirled around, and there she was: my larger-than-life mum, Suzannah, smiling so broadly it left me in no doubt that even though I hadn't seen her for a while and despite my complicated history with her husband, Glenn, and stepdaughter, Zara, I was still her little girl. She jumped out from behind the table and raced over to me as I rushed over to her. We caught each other in a huge hug, and I leant in to smell her familiar scent of lavender mixed with the fresh salt of the ocean. It had been like I was five years old again, wrapped in her arms. Except, of course, I was a fully grown thirty-year-old woman, and I towered over her in my sensible corporate heels.

'Let me look at you!' Mum pulled back and beamed at me, taking in the little details of my face that might have changed in the last year. I did the same and wondered if I appeared as different to her as she did to me. She still looked like my mum, but her normally meticulously shiny auburn hair was full of new grey streaks, and the laughter lines that had been growing the last time I'd seen her had stilted. Instead, she had a series of new frown lines across her forehead, as though for the last year, something had been consistently bothering her rather than making her laugh.

And her eyes – I'd never noticed how bright her light blue eyes had always been until that moment outside the restaurant when I saw how tired and grey they looked instead. But I realised with a jolt that I'd seen that look once before: when my dad vanished all those years ago.

'Oh, darling.' She squeezed my arms tight. 'I still can't believe that my little girl is a powerhouse lawyer now. You look great!' She let go of my arm, and I beamed at her words. 'But you also look extremely tired,' she added as she took her seat once more. 'Do they ever let you sleep?'

I deflated with a sigh and took my seat. Of course, there would always be something for her to pick at. But I tried not to feel irritated: I knew it came from a good place.

'Don't worry, I'm fine,' I replied with an attempt at a winning smile. I knew she could see through it – she'd always been able to. But she thankfully let it drop.

As lunch got underway, and we reverted to normal like no time had passed, I thought that all the little problems and arguments we'd had about the rest of the family were finally in the past. That, for once, it could just be about me and Mum – no other complicating distractions. But that would have been too good to be true.

'So,' she said after taking a sip of her coffee, the froth of her soy cappuccino threatening to spill out over the edge. 'Glenn and I are *so* happy that you're coming to stay with us for the rest of your time back home. We're going to have so much fun!' She beamed across at me, and I tried to reciprocate, but I'm certain it looked more like a grimace.

Since arriving back last week, I'd been starting to regret saying I would stay with Mum and Glenn for some of my time in Sydney. I'd agreed over the phone months ago, in a moment of weakness. I'd been feeling guilty about how long it had been since we'd seen each other. And don't get me wrong – I *wanted* to spend time with Mum, but it was easier for Glenn and me not to be in the same house for too long. After I'd left home to go to university, we'd learnt that we got along much better when we lived apart, and I'd been keen to keep it that way. Especially seeing as his daughter and I were not speaking at the moment.

'Oh, you know,' I began, clearing my throat, 'I've been thinking about that, and I don't want to get in the way. I can get another hotel or Airbnb nearby for the next week.'

'Don't be silly – what a waste of money! You're staying with us.'

I repressed a sigh and smiled back. 'Okay, if you're sure!'

I'd grin and bear it. It had been a pathetic attempt to get out of it, but I knew that once Suzannah Olsen had an idea in her mind, there was no way to get her to change it. Dad had always said so. And then I felt that familiar twinge of sadness – technically, she was Suzannah Olsen-*Archer* now – having changed her name after marrying Glenn. At least I'd always be Emily Olsen. Wherever Dad was, I'd always have that connection to him.

She cleared her throat and tapped her spoon on the side of her mug, derailing my train of thought.

'Besides, it will be great for you to see Zara again because she's staying with us for a bit too...' Her eyes flicked up from her coffee to meet mine, bright and hopeful, even as I felt an instant flash of anger rise to the surface.

There she goes again, I thought. Mum was always trying to get us to play happy families. She could never admit defeat. I knew that she would never quit trying to make us become the perfect nuclear family that she'd always wanted. It was her nature.

So, I took a deep breath to stay calm. I was a thirty-year-old woman with a successful career. I would use all my lawyer training and face this rationally. What *was* it about this family that always made me descend into the old, chaotic and wild version of myself? The one I'd worked *so* hard to bury.

'Look…' I clasped my hands around my mug. 'You *know* Zara and I haven't spoken in over a year now. I've been trying to forgive her like you said, but it's so hard… I'm all for trying to see if we can build a bridge now if it'll make you happy… I'm just not sure if it will work. And I definitely don't think us living together is the first step back to repairing our relationship.'

'No, please, Em… That whole mess was so long ago, and things have changed since you left. She knows what she did was wrong, and I think we all need to put it behind us. She's had *such* a tough time of it as well, trying to find work and her place in the world. Acting isn't an easy path, you know. But she's your little sister – she's only twenty-four, and she needs you. It's time to forgive and forget!'

Her expression was as open as a book. She really believed it would be fine, that what had happened could be so easily swept under the carpet.

I knew the truth, though – it couldn't be reversed. Zara *had* become like the little sister I'd never had over the years. But as soon as she'd had the chance, she'd thrown our relationship away like it had meant nothing to her. All for a guy.

Besides, we were *not* one big happy family. We had *never* been, as much as Mum had always wanted us to become one. And so, despite my determination to remain cool, calm and collected, the heat of the day, the stress of my morning, and the two glasses of wine I'd had were getting to me. I'd had enough of all the pretending.

'Mum!' I snapped. 'You know what happened last year when I visited. I literally walked in on the two of them kissing. She *never* apologised to me. And when I tried to talk to her about it, she had the nerve to basically say that it was *my fault* that they'd got together in the first place. That when I'd left six months earlier, they'd "bonded and fallen in love!"' Rolling my eyes, I leant back in my chair and crossed my arms. 'She's an *adult* – she has to learn about consequences. Also, she's my *step*-sister anyway. What does it matter if we don't talk!'

'Come on, Em. You know that's a bit of a simplification of the story,' she said quietly. 'You and Harry had been on a break for a few months... You'd said it yourself that you weren't sure about him anymore.'

My mouth fell open. Was she seriously defending Zara over me?

'That still didn't give her the right to get with him at the very first chance!' I shuddered involuntarily, trying not to remember the image that flashed into my mind of tongues and clashing teeth. 'If she's my *sister* as you insist, she shouldn't be getting with my long-term partner, whether we were on a short break or not. Seriously, where is this coming from?' I spat out. 'I thought you were on my side!'

Mum leant back in her chair too, mirroring me. 'Emily, I can't take sides. She's my daughter too...'

'Your *step*-daughter!' I knew I sounded so childish, but I couldn't help it.

'Stop it! Can't you be the bigger person? You're doing so well in London, with a successful career. Zara is still finding her way, and she's always looked up to you. I'm certain she'll apologise the moment she sees you again. She just didn't know how to, with you leaving so suddenly and being far away for so long. Or that's what Glenn has told me anyway.' Mum looked up at me with hope in her eyes. But I was tired. So tired of it all.

And it wasn't only this latest situation between Zara and I. Ever since Glenn and Mum had got together fifteen years ago, a slow sizzle of resentment had grown below the surface. And it had always come back to Glenn.

Glenn said this, Glenn said that. Sometimes, talking to Mum felt like navigating a delicate precipice when it came to him. If he made her happy, that was great, but he was also controlling and opinionated. If I ever remotely suggested that she'd shut the conversation down completely. For a long time, it felt like she'd kept putting her new family first.

So, the hopeful tone in her voice only made me angrier. Years of resentment simmered to the surface – all the anger I'd felt over the last fifteen years since I'd been unwillingly dragged into the Archer family orbit bubbling up.

I wasn't one of them. I'd never be one of them. That much had been made abundantly clear to me over the years. And it all came flying out like poison from my lips.

'STOP! I'm *so* sick of this. You've made me feel guilty for *years* for not properly fitting into your perfect little family. But I'm sorry. They are *not* my family – they never can be. Look, I'm happy that you've moved on, but I couldn't forget Dad as easily as you. I've never been able to, and I've never given up on that small sliver of hope that he might still be out there – I'm his daughter, after all. And so wherever he is in the world, whatever happened, that will always be true. Mum, I've never stopped searching or hoping. I just – I just can't...' My voice had broken on the last word as I'd whispered low under my breath. 'Maybe he's still alive – maybe...'

Chapter Four

My words had run dry, and my face had crumpled.

Across the table, Mum had stared at me in shock, her eyes filling with tears. She *never* cried, and I'd realised in an instant how awful my angry words had been. And that they'd cut deep.

Because twenty years ago my dad – Luke Olsen – had gone out for a swim and never come home.

Everyone else had assumed he was dead. Even my mum.

But I'd never been able to give up that tiny sliver of hope.

Because his body was never found.

Too late, I'd seen that I'd failed in being the good grown-up daughter that I'd always tried to be since Dad's disappearance. I should have intuited how much pain Mum still kept hidden away, even though she seemed so happy with her new family. I guess I wasn't the only one keeping my heartbreak under lock and key. But I was exhausted. So exhausted.

'I'm so sorry,' I stood up in a rush, my chair scraping back loudly across the wooden decking as I raced around to kneel next to her, pulling her forcefully into a hug. 'I'm such an idiot. You know how I can say things without thinking. I'm just stressed and tired—'

I was about to go on when she pushed her chair back too, causing me to awkwardly let her go and hop upright with a stumble. She stood to face me, and I looked down at her. All I could see was pain.

Then she gulped as though to press down the threatening tears. I thought for a minute she was going to finally say something about Dad. But instead she said, 'Look, it's been a tough year for all of us, okay. Me included. Your grandfather's death has left me with a lot to deal with, on top of everything else at work and the family. So I think it's time we all sit down together and clear the air. Once and for all. Can you do that for me?'

She looked so small, so defeated, as the tears still swam. Even if there had been a grain of truth in my words, I'd been a monster to her. She was hurting from Granddad's death six months ago – and I needed to put everything aside and be there for her now. I knew that, even though so many years had passed, she still couldn't face all the unanswered questions from Dad's 'death'. It was easier for her to push them away. I had to be more understanding. She'd made a new life and family for herself. I knew deep down that she'd tried to keep going for us all those years ago.

I pulled her into a firm hug, whispering into her hair. 'Yes, of course. I'm so sorry for upsetting you.' She let her arms drop and nodded, a glazed look still in her eyes when I pulled back.

'Look,' I said, 'I'm going to go and pay and then let's get out of here. Go for a walk.' She nodded again. I'd never seen my mother so mute. It was strange. Had it only been my words? Or was there something else going on – what was it exactly that had cut so deep?

I was going to ask her this, but when I returned, she had a smile plastered to her face and her sunglasses on. All traces of her previous devastation were erased. She was back to her upbeat self.

'Thank you, darling, for a lovely lunch!' She looped her arm in mine and set us off along the boardwalk away from the restaurant, determined to start afresh.

I turned to look at her more closely. I felt as though I'd missed something in the moments I'd been gone. 'Mum...'

'Mmm.' She didn't pause and kept us at a marching pace, weaving in and out of the milling tourists.

'What's going on? Something I said touched a nerve.'

We reached the edge of the busiest section of the harbour and paused, looking out for a moment across the waterway of passing ferry traffic towards Balmain on the other side. The water sparkled brightly in the sunshine. I felt like it was mocking us.

She turned to face me, pulling her sunglasses onto the top of her head. 'Don't worry about me, it's just been a tough year, that's all. With you and Zara falling out, your granddad passing away and having to start clearing out their house in Dover Heights alongside sorting all the paperwork that comes with that... And, well, then the business has been struggling a bit too...' She trailed off, facing away from me and out towards the everyday harbour traffic.

I nodded slowly, trying to understand. I'd known about Granddad, of course, but I hadn't realised that Mum's advertising business, Imaginate, had been struggling too. She co-owned it with Glenn's brother-in-law, Mike. It was how she'd met Glenn. Mum was the creative lead, and Mike was supposed to be all about the commercial and financing. I wondered what had gone so wrong since I'd left Sydney.

But I didn't believe that the business was the only reason.

I took her hand and squeezed it. 'I'm so sorry, Mum. I should have been here to help you with Granddad and Dover Heights – but I'm here now, and I can do anything you need.'

'Don't worry, sweetheart, I've had John to help me. He's been so great – I really couldn't have got through it all without him. Especially with Dad at the end – but because of John, it was as painless as it could be.' Her eyes shone, and I pulled her into a fierce hug.

'I'm so glad you had each other,' I whispered into her ear. John was Mum's younger brother and a trained doctor. When they'd received Granddad's diagnosis, John had moved his entire life back to Sydney from Adelaide so he'd be there. I knew he had been a huge help to Mum looking after Granddad this past year.

'Still, I'm here now to help you *both*.'

She smiled at that. But there was something else that she'd said that was weighing on my mind. 'I didn't realise about Imaginate, though – why has business been tough? What does Mike reckon?'

She shrugged. 'We've had a lot less work coming in, I guess. In all honesty, I've been off for a bit and a little distracted the last few months because of Granddad. Mike says he's working on some analysis now.' She looked away, then added, 'It feels a bit like everything has all come at once – with Glenn losing his job too.'

'Glenn's lost his job – again?!' Glenn had been in and out of work constantly over the last few years. He'd been an IT manager, but he kept getting turfed out either by general redundancies or younger talent. Or so he'd always said.

I'd started to become suspicious of all these far-ranging reasons. Especially since it had been taking him more and more time to find anything new, meaning all the responsibility for bringing in any cash had started to rest solely on Mum's shoulders. And I knew they had a big mortgage on their house to pay as well as Zara's costs. Mum always said they were okay so long as the business kept steady. But if it wasn't doing so well right now...

I opened my mouth to say something along these lines, but Mum put her hand up to stop me. 'Please, Emily, let's not go down this path again. He's been very unlucky, and he's trying. He's assured me he's trying,' she added for clarity, as though trying to convince not only me but also herself.

Not wanting to cause any more arguments, I just nodded, accepting her request. But I promised myself I'd return to it at a later date. I was worried about her having to deal with financial stress on top of everything else.

'Anyway...' She sighed, looping her arm into mine once more to start walking further down the sun-drenched pier. 'That's why I've so been looking forward to us all being together. Last year was difficult – I'm determined that this one will be the start of something new for all of us.' She squeezed my arm even tighter, as though to physically stress how much she needed that to happen.

I decided to support her. I didn't need to make her life any more stressful than it already seemed, did I? 'I understand. And I'll be there tomorrow, I promise.' So I let the conversation drop – even though a dad-shaped hole still loomed large. It always did, though – and it wasn't the time to go down that path again. But I didn't think it would be the last chance I'd ever have...

'Thank you, darling. Now, you should go off and have some fun with Addie. And I,' she glanced down at her watch, 'need to get over to Dover Heights and do a bit more packing away of Granddad's things. The estate agent is coming early next week, and there's still so much to do – I even left my laptop in the office and my iPad back home to make sure I wouldn't get distracted! And I told the team assistant, Arabella, to only call me if an *emergency* happened.' She forced a small smile and tucked a strand of hair behind her ear, pulling her bag tighter over her shoulder as though she was about to dash off in a sprint.

'Oh, I didn't realise you had to go and do that now! Let me come over and help you.'

'No, no, you said you had plans with Addie. I'll be fine.'

'She'll already be on her way into the city, so I can go and see her for a bit, but then I could come over to Dover Heights later on tonight.' I wanted to prove that I was here to help – plus, I still felt guilty about everything I'd said earlier.

'If you really want to. I'm going to stay over because I'll be on a cleaning roll ahead of next week. So if you want to come join, that would be great. But see how you go – I want you to have fun while you're here!'

By this point, we'd reached the fork in the path that headed either towards the hotel where I was staying or back to the rest of the city. I knew I had to go, that I was already running late to get ready for meeting

Addie, but there was a part of me that didn't want to leave. Didn't want to say goodbye to my mum with so much still left unsaid.

She must have seen these thoughts etched across my face because she placed a hand on my cheek and said, 'Don't worry about earlier, darling, honestly. I've been having a wobbly day, too. We'll get everything sorted out between us all – you'll see. After all, we have to remember to live in the present – we can't always hold onto the past.'

I nodded and gave her a last tight hug. 'I know, Mum – so I'll see you later, okay? I'll get an Uber over to help.'

She pulled back, her now bright smile sparkling in the sun. 'Sure, honey.' Then she turned around and began to walk down the sidewalk, the black tarmac glistening from the heat of the day.

And that's when I noticed it: one looming dark cloud in the very far distance on the horizon.

Mum turned round once to wave and then busied herself, taking her phone out of her bag to check her messages. Her smile disappeared in an instant, replaced by a small frown as she began to type a quick message. She'd looked up to wave once more and then walked on out of sight, the thunderous cloud hovering in the far reaches of the sky.

And now, in my hotel room, as all the memories I can grasp from yesterday whirl around my mind, I can't help but think: who had sent her that message?

Surely, it was no coincidence that her whole expression had shifted in a matter of seconds.

And then, less than twenty-four hours later, she was dead.

Chapter Five

I eventually stumble out of the shower and manage to wrap myself in one of the hotel's large, fluffy white robes. I catch my reflection in the mirror and do a double-take. Because all I can see is a tragic combination of my mum and dad. Suzannah and Luke Olsen. They were the perfect high school sweethearts. And all that's left of them is me.

My long, auburn hair is a tousled, soaking mess and looks almost black as large droplets of water drip onto the floor. It reminds me of all those times I'd seen my mum's hair look the same as she'd leap out of the ocean, fresh after a swim. Her favourite thing had always been the sea and saltwater. But now... now she's dead, found on the edge of the ocean she'd loved so much. The irony was too cruel.

From this distance, I could be her double – with the same round eyes and oval face shape – but as I lean in closer to the mirror, I know what I'll see. My dad's dark chocolate brown eyes and a small, straight nose. My lips are the only part of my face that is not definitively one or the other of them: a combination of wide and full. But now, as I stare into the reflective glass, they are pressed into a tight, thin line. Is this my reality? Will I really never see either of my parents again, except through little echoes of my reflection?

My dad's death is already a mystery I'll never solve. And now my mum's... I can't bear being frozen in limbo, never knowing what happened all over again. I won't *let* that happen.

Even if the answer could have something to do with me.

I know I'll have to face my stepfather, Glenn, eventually to hear his story, like Jennifer had asked. But first, I *have* to try to piece together my night. I can't turn up on his doorstep with no knowledge of what I'd been up to.

Turning away from the mirror, I take a deep breath and head back out into the large hotel room. I start to think back to the blood-curdling scream I'm certain I remember hearing last night through the otherwise black void of memory. Had I been at Dover Heights too?

I find my phone wedged behind the TV, and luckily, it isn't smashed into a million pieces. I focus on trying to think objectively, pretending that I'm approaching a case, not this living nightmare. First step: look at my calls and texts.

I open up my phone and head straight to my message history with my mum. A creeping feeling begins to build up my spine as I find Mum's name near the top. It hasn't sunk in that I can't just text her and ask her. I swallow as the messages open, and I read our last exchanges.

Timestamped yesterday at five forty-seven, I see a selfie of me and Addie smiling wildly at the camera. God, we look drunk and happy. We'd met at about four o'clock for drinks down at the outdoor hotel bar, which ended up being *lots* of drinks. We'd sat in the late afternoon sun, and she'd helped distract me from everything swirling around my mind.

I bring myself back to the messages. Soon after I sent the selfie, about five fifty-nine, Mum responded:

Say hi to Addie! Don't worry about coming over. It's a dusty mess! I want you to have a fun evening. Xx

I'd responded about twenty minutes later with a:

Oh noooooooo. Are you sureee? I can defs comes. Xxxx

I cringe at my spelling mistake. But now I'm reading these messages, and those few hours are coming back to me. I'd stayed with Addie at the bar after that. But what could have happened later to give me these cuts and scrapes and a wet, bloody shirt?

Mum hadn't responded to the message. I scan the last message I'd sent her. It is almost unreadable.

At ten-forty:

OMGgggg. Imm s

Then at eleven-thirty:

Imm hrr

I shake my head, heat rising to my cheeks at my embarrassing and unclear messages. I chew on my lip and brace myself for what I must check next. My call log.

As soon as I open it, the bright red text jumps out at me. A missed call from Mum yesterday.

I check what time it was made, and my stomach drops. It was around eight-thirty in the evening. It looks like I'd tried to call her back at about nine-thirty but got no response, and then again at around eleven-thirty. So, I guess that's what my stumbling and nonsensical text had been about.

In between those last two calls, there was a call between Addie and me.

I put my head in my hands and rub my tired eyes. Why had Mum called me only at eight-thirty but not again? And then what did I do?

Standing up, I pace around and around the room again, my heart thumping louder with every step. I pause and look out the huge floor-to-ceiling window of this extravagant hotel room, which is so at odds with my current situation. Beyond the glass, Sydney continues on as normal, oblivious to the ripples of pain caused by its wild nature. The Harbour Bridge and Opera House are at the forefront, staking their claims on the ever-increasing skyline, but I try to look past them, far out towards where I know Dover Heights will be. And picture the stark and unforgiving cliff edge of the suburb perched on the edge of the Pacific Ocean, which points all ships towards the entrance to Sydney Harbour.

I see the hustle and bustle of the ferries and cruise ships, and below on the streets, the tiny movements of ant people and slow-moving cars and taxis. And that's when it hits me. A taxi. I could have ordered a taxi over to Dover Heights last night.

Rushing, I fumble with my phone, at last bringing up the Uber app. I race to open up my travel history.

And for a second, I can't process what I'm seeing.

Two new journeys. One at eleven o'clock from the centre of the city to the house in Dover Heights. And the next at eleven thirty-five from there to this hotel.

A whooshing sound escapes my lips as I sink onto the ground, clutching my phone tight. All I can do is stare at the two journeys in disbelief as three thoughts hit me all at once:

I *was* there last night.

I'd come from a random spot in the city.

And I had no memory of it.

I'm barely breathing. I can't believe it. But I have to. It's all there in black and white.

Now, I know without a shadow of a doubt that I *was* in the same location as my mother the night she died.

The question is, what did I have to do with it?

Chapter Six

I move around the dishevelled room, packing as quickly as I can. I need to start piecing together what happened last night. It's the only way I can make sense of this.

I would *never* have killed my mother. The thought is ridiculous. And yet, I remember that scream.

And I was definitely at Dover Heights last night. There's no denying that with the proof of my Uber trips. I can't believe I have to think through this – but what if I'd somehow caused an accident? I have to consider every possibility now and get to the bottom of it, before anyone else does...

I change swiftly, throwing on the first comfortable things I can find: some denim shorts and a loose white t-shirt. All the pretty dresses and work outfits I brought with me I continue to shove into the practical black wheelie suitcase. I don't imagine I'll have any need of them for a long while.

I wipe my palms on my shorts, a slippery sheen of sweat coating my body despite the cool air con. I pause to survey the remnants of the room. It looks sparse, messy and a little bit broken. Just like me. Part of me wants to crawl back into the bed, but I can't stay hidden away up here forever. I need to figure this out.

I've already confirmed some of my movements now, so I force myself to contact the only other person I can think of who could help me piece my night together. I call Addie. She picks up after a few rings.

'Hey, Emmm,' she yawns down the phone, slurring her words a bit. 'What's up?'

'Ads, you need to help me.'

'Anything at all,' she responds, her voice suddenly alert. She must have sensed the panic in my voice.

I'm about to tell her about Mum, the words on the tip of my tongue. But I can't quite say it yet.

'Please, can you come and get me from the hotel? I'll tell you everything then.'

'Of course,' she says, not missing a beat. 'I can be there in about thirty minutes.'

'Thank you,' I whisper back and hang up.

I feel my throat tightening and beginning to close again. She sounded so eager to help. But what would she think of me if she knew the truth of what I was beginning to suspect?

I have to speak to her, though. Because other than talking to Addie, there is only one other way for me to find out more about what might have actually happened to Mum last night, and that is going to see Glenn and Zara.

Before I can do that, I need to piece myself back together. I can't afford to break down in front of them and let them see my doubts.

Because if they know that I can't remember what I was doing last night, they might start suspecting me too. And I can't allow that to happen.

I finish the last of my packing, then turn on my heels, making a beeline for the door. I slam it shut behind me with a resounding thud and march towards the elevator to wait for Addie. I know I'll have to wait a little, but I can't stay cooped up for a second longer.

In my muddled state, check-out takes longer than expected, and by the time I emerge outside I see her familiar form. Addie must have made friends with the doormen so they would allow her to stay in this drop-off circle outside the hotel. She is petite and delicate, almost doll-like, and can twist anyone around her little finger. She spies me and rushes over to help with my bags, pulling me into a hug. Her shoulder-length blonde hair tickles my nose as my arms wrap around her tight. She doesn't know what's wrong yet, but her kindness hits me, and I burst into tears right there in front of everybody.

'Oh my god!' she says, jumping back from me in surprise. She ushers me into the car, throwing my bag into her boot. She sprints around to the driver's side as I get in the passenger's seat and squeeze my arms around myself, trying to calm my nerves and get my crying under control. She drives out of the circle of prying eyes and races down the street.

'What is it?' she asks. 'Did something happen last night after I left you? Oh god, I'm so sorry I left! I had to get back to help my flatmate...'

I shake my head quickly. I rub my nose, and she keeps her gaze fixed on the road as she hands me a tissue – always prepared. I think it's the schoolteacher in her.

I blow noisily. 'God, Addie. Mum—' I start, but then I stop, choking on the words. How am I supposed to get these out? I try again, 'I just got a call. From Jennifer – Mum fell off the cliffs. At Dover Heights. She's... she's dead.' I manage to stammer out.

'What!' she shrieks in shock, almost veering onto the curb. She corrects the car and screeches to a stop on the side of the road. She spins to face me. 'Oh my god, Ems, I don't understand – what – how?' She leans across the small space, pressing me into a tight hug. As she pulls back, I see that her normally tanned face has turned grey.

'I don't know!' I respond, trying to keep my breathing under control and stop a full-blown panic attack. 'I only spoke to Jennifer for a few minutes. But I know Mum was there tidying up yesterday. So I don't know. I guess she went outside at some point and fell. The police think it was an accident – but that doesn't make any sense at all! She knew how dangerous the cliff edge was. She's the one who taught me.' I rub my eyes with the tissue to dry my tears. My throat feels scraped raw.

Addie shakes her head in disbelief. 'Em, I'm so sorry... I guess there was that bad storm last night.' She adds, horror etched in every word.

I gulp. I have to say it – I have to confess that I can't remember much about last night. I need to hear her side of the story. But I can't bear to tell her what I know already about the Uber journeys... yet.

'Ads...' I begin slowly. 'I *know* I was planning on going to help Mum last night, but then she told me not to worry about it. Did I tell you that?'

'Sure.' Addie nods. 'I remember – I still can't believe you insisted we get shots. But I take the blame for how many we did... It probably wasn't my best idea in the world to do one every time we thought we spotted a first date.'

I groan. Oh yes, that sounds like one of our silly games. And, of course, the new hotel overlooking Sydney Harbour on a Friday night was the perfect impressive first date spot – so there would have been a *lot* of shots. 'Right... so I think all those shots gave me a bit of a hazy memory at that point... Remind me of where we went next?'

Her brow furrows, but she doesn't hesitate before answering. 'Well, remember, some friends from work texted me, and we went to meet them at the karaoke pub.' That must be those dark, loud flashes that are coming back to me. As she says it, the memory of laughter and caterwauling singing comes back to me. 'Then I'm pretty sure I ordered some food because they were about to stop serving, but the next thing I knew, you weren't there anymore.'

A spidery sensation crawls up my spine. So I'd wandered off somewhere. To call Mum back? Possibly. Or to go to Dover Heights.

'Oh right,' I manage to say in as breezy a tone as I can muster. 'So I just disappeared?'

She shrugs. 'I guess – sorry, I was so drunk too. I called, and you said you were going home.'

'Oh yeah.' I'd noticed a call between Addie and me after I'd tried to call Mum back, but I hadn't thought anything of it. 'And... how did I sound?' I hope she'll tell me if I sounded scared, angry, happy, delirious. Anything that could help me piece together my state of mind.

Instead, Addie looks at me, confused. 'Umm, drunk! To be honest, so was I, so it's a little hazy. But I guess I remember you saying you were going home. And honestly, that was a good call – all I had was some chips, and then there were more tequila shots.' She shakes her head, 'I'm feeling awful today.' Her face flushes bright red. 'I'm so sorry. Obviously, that's nothing in comparison to how you're feeling!'

I shake my head. 'Don't worry, I get it – I have a terrible hangover as well. Plus, I keep hoping that this is all a nightmare... that I'll wake up and it won't be true.' I stare into space as I say in a low voice, 'But I know it is...'

And Addie's words haven't reassured me. Not at all.

Not now I know that I was alone when I left her. And she doesn't know what I did next. All I said to her was that I was going home.

Addie will assume that by 'home', I'd meant where I was staying at the hotel, and I'll let her think that. But I know what I truly meant by home. I meant Dover Heights – the only house still in my life that I think of as home. Not my London flat, not Mum and Glenn's house. No, Dover Heights, where Mum and I had lived for five long years between Dad's officially ruled death and moving in with Glenn. It was the only childhood home I had left.

But there was one last thing I could ask Addie without sharing my fears about where I really went after leaving her. I clear my throat.

'Ads... I need to know one thing: did I trip over at all or something when I was with you?' I show her my scraped hands. 'It looks like I fell somewhere, and, well, I can't quite remember.'

She stares at them and takes one in her hand to look closer. I am hoping beyond measure that she says yes, but instead, she shakes her head. 'No, I don't think you did. That must have been on your walk home or something. It was raining hard out there. I guess you slipped?' She cocks one eyebrow.

I pull my hands back from her like they've been burnt and tuck them tightly across my chest. A puzzled expression flicks over her face as I say quickly, 'Yeah, that must be it.'

I feel guilty, but I can't tell her more.

She must interpret my dazed tone as grief because she says, 'Tell me what I can do. What do you need? Anything at all. I'm here.'

I look over to see the truth of her words written on her face. She means it; she'll do anything for me. And that makes me want to cry again – I've missed having a friend like Addie this past year. In London, I'd made a few close acquaintances – but nothing like this sort of fierce friendship that can only be built up over so many years.

Instead of feeling comforted, my stomach flips over at her words. Because she says she'd do anything to help me – but what would she think of me if she knew the truth of what I was now starting to suspect?

That I'd gone to Dover Heights.

That I'd seen my mum.

That we'd had a big fight.

And that, somehow, a horrific accident had happened. One that could have been my fault.

I can't help it as I begin to retch.

'Oh Ems.' Addie flips open the centre console between us and shoves a plastic bag towards me. I grab it, leaping out of the car.

I sit down on the burning hot tarmac and manage to get my breathing under control. The unused plastic bag lies deflated at my side.

Addie comes to hover beside me and puts an arm around my shoulder despite the heat.

'Right,' she says in a soft voice. 'You need food, and you need coffee – then it's time to face the dreaded stepfamily for some sort of explanation. So let's go.' She gently pulls me to my feet. 'I've got you.'

She picks up the bag, and I let her guide me into the car. When she smiles at me, I manage a weak one back as I dab the tissue again on my cheeks.

We drive off in silence, and I'm thankful that she leaves me to my swirling thoughts.

Thoughts that if I can't untangle soon, I know will destroy me.

Because what sort of person might have accidentally killed their mother but can't even remember it?

Chapter Seven

After a quick stop off for much-needed food and caffeine, Addie and I continue to drive in silence across Sydney towards the house I can't bear to face.

Too soon, we arrive, and Addie pulls to a sharp stop on the blinding white driveway, the sun dazzling off it. I don't even notice the tissue I'm tearing to shreds as I stare up at the house that always fills me with dread.

I know to the outside world, it looks like the perfect home. A symmetrical two-storey with identical two-up, two-down large bay windows on either side of the white-pillared entrance. A pebbled path leads up to the dark green front door, and the entire yawning lawn is mown flawlessly. Not a single blade is out of place along the box hedges dotting the front, and the entire house sighs out a calming neutral grey colour.

I'm sure it would be an estate agent's dream family home to sell. But to me, it signified the start of a life I didn't want.

When we first moved here, all Mum wanted was for us to start again. She'd thought this shiny house could replace the pain of our past, and we'd be able to become a happy family with Glenn and Zara. But it had never been that simple to me.

I couldn't let go of the hope of my dad, just like that. I couldn't accept that he wasn't coming back.

Perhaps it was as much my fault as it had been Glenn's that we'd had a tricky relationship from the start. I hadn't wanted to try. But as I'd grown up, I'd begun to realise that I'd only been a teenager; *he'd* been the adult at the time. Shouldn't he have taken more time to understand what I'd been going through?

Instead, he'd tried to deal with my acting out by becoming even stricter than he already was. In that first year, if I talked back, I was sent to my room. If I snuck out, I was grounded. If I went out underage drinking, I had my phone confiscated and had to listen to a list of all the ways I was screwing up my life.

My mum hadn't wanted to rock the boat, so she went along with Glenn's way of parenting. He'd said he had to try and curb my behaviour – it was setting a bad example to Zara. It infuriated me, and I'd escape back over to my safe space, my grandparents', as often as I could. It was my nana who finally helped me see a way through my pain and a path to moving forward.

'You know,' she'd said in a soft voice one day as we'd kneaded bread together in their snug little kitchen, the roar of the ocean our soundtrack in the distance. 'If you want to take control of your future, there's only one way of doing it.' I'd looked up at her in expectation, the dough melting into my hot fingertips. 'Making the grades to get it.'

That nugget of advice had blossomed into a consistent work ethic, which helped me get the grades to study law at the Australian National University down in Canberra, which meant being able to live away from home at last. By the time I'd realised what Nana had done for me with that advice, it was too late to thank her.

So now, I sit frozen in the driveway in front of the matching two-door garage. Of course, I've come back here many times over the years. Once upon a time, Zara and I had been extremely close. And more recently, Glenn and I had learnt to get along too – well, as much as was possible with our history – but we'd always got on much better living apart.

Then everything had changed because of Zara and my fight over the last year, and now, with Mum gone, I had no idea how we'd ever find a way back to anything resembling a family. Surely, all we were now was just a bunch of strangers.

But I had to face them. I had to hear what they knew about what happened to Mum – and at least for a time, we'd also have to work together to sort out all the bureaucracy that comes with death.

Addie breaks the silence. 'Do you want me to come in with you?' She takes my hand, and I squeeze hers in response but continue to stare straight ahead at this now-unfamiliar house.

Then I finally say, 'Thank you, but I think I need to face this alone.' With a deep breath, I open the car door, forcing myself out before I can change my mind. But another thought pops into my head, and I lean back in to see her looking up at me. 'Could I leave my bags with you for now, please? I'm not sure I can face staying here like I was supposed to. I'll see how it goes, I guess.'

'Of course, and if you need to, you can bunk in with me too.'

I smile back at her kind offer – I know she doesn't have any space, sharing with flatmates in a small apartment in central Sydney. If worse comes to worse and I really can't stand being in this house, then I'll find a hotel. I shiver at the idea of staying at the Dover Heights house, imagining it covered up with police tape.

'Thank you for everything, Ads – I'll call you later, okay?'

'Of course. Here for whatever you need.'

I nod for a final time and slam the door shut.

It's time I face my stepfamily at last.

I march up the steps from the drive and quickly press on the doorbell. A familiar chirrup echoes out. As Addie's car rolls out of the driveway behind me, my stomach does a flip. Seeing everyone without my mum will be the moment it all feels real. I try to prepare for the shock.

As the door opens, a whoosh of cool air rushes out to meet me, flickering up my skin. Goosebumps erupt at the impact, and it makes me realise how hot and clammy with sweat I am. But I'm distracted as I blink in surprise at the person greeting me.

A curly mass of light brown hair and serious dark eyes peek out from inside the doorframe, and the next second, I'm crushed into a tight hug by buttery soft arms. But the softness is deceiving, as it feels more like I'm being pinned in place by two pillows.

'Emily!' Jennifer cries. Her shrill accent threatens to burst my eardrums. 'Oh Emily…' she says again, pulling me in even tighter. I try to extricate myself, but she just holds on.

It's strange. I guess my step-aunt would care about me a *little* bit, but this reaction feels almost theatrical. She and Mum always had a *delicate* relationship, with Jennifer being the wife of Mum's business partner, Mike. A relationship that had become more complicated when Mum married her brother, Glenn. And after having quite a few blow-ups, Mum and Jennifer had agreed to disagree on a lot of things. So, it was confusing that she was not only the family member to tell me about Mum's death but also the first person to greet me at the front door.

'Oh, I can't believe you're here. I can't believe all of it,' she twitters as she squeezes. Then, stepping back at last says, 'Come in, come in.'

Being invited inside by her is like a bucket of cold water flying in my face. Where were Glenn and Zara?

I start to shuffle in, remaining silent as I hear Jennifer shut the door behind me.

Down at the end of the hallway, a distraction in the shape of a furry ball comes hurtling from the open-plan kitchen–living room and makes a bounding beeline straight for me.

It makes me want to smile and cry at the same time. 'Banjo!' I burst out, crouching down as our beautiful little fluffy, caramel-coloured dog crashes into my arms, his tail flying around like a helicopter propeller. I wrap my arms around him tight, trying to stop a sob from escaping. *This* feels like a normal greeting, and it is making my heart break.

I still remember the day Mum and I picked him up from the shelter. It had been after Christmas, another hot summer like this one, and I'd been back for the school holidays. We hadn't been planning on getting a dog, but Mum's friend who worked at the shelter had called her up to ask if she'd be interested in fostering a tiny little scrap in need of a home. He'd been found on the side of the road, clearly abandoned.

The intention was to only foster him for a little while, but Banjo ended up stealing our hearts. Even Glenn's. Banjo loved everyone, but Mum and I had always been his favourites.

I try to bury my face in his soft fur, but he wiggles out from my embrace, proceeding to tumble around my legs with excitement. Jennifer steps around us and starts to recede from view, down the long corridor towards the alcove that Banjo just ran out from. She's not a dog person, or a cat person, or any kind of pet person. I think she's too focused on herself.

Then I hear her announce to whoever is in the room, 'Emily's here.'

I gulp and walk on autopilot down the rest of the corridor. I ignore the framed family pictures that I know line the strip of wall to my left. I can't bear to see Mum's smiling face right now. Not when I know I'll never see it again.

I step into the kitchen, a room I have walked into a million times. But I was always greeted by the sounds of laughter and the smell of something delicious wafting through the air. Mum and Glenn loved to cook, and our love of food was the one thing that had slowly brought us together as a sort of 'family' over the years. But now the room is silent, and the stark smell of disinfectant greets me instead.

I look past the broad island bench, and that's when I see him. Glenn.

Or the back of his head. Because he doesn't acknowledge me, he sits motionless on the couch, staring out into the garden beyond. His brown hair is shaggy as ever, with patches of grey woven through his still-thick locks.

I intend to speak in a normal, calm voice, but instead, when I say his name, 'Glenn,' it squeaks up at the edges. Jennifer flinches, but I continue my shuffle forward towards him. His silence is unnerving. He doesn't even turn around at my approach. It's like he doesn't hear me at all. Or, in his mind, he's somewhere else entirely.

'Glenn,' I say again more loudly, placing my hands on my hips as I come around the couch to stand right in front of him.

This registers at last, and he glances up at me. He lets out a small groan, like he's had an electric shock, and I stumble back a step when I see the look on his face.

Because it's one I don't recognise. The Glenn I know is all mottled shades of suntan, brash expressive lines and intelligent slate grey eyes.

But this Glenn looks pale and waxy, his stubble masking the usual definition of his cheeks.

His eyes, I recognise at least – but not because they're sparking out their usual flecks of grey flint. No, it's because they have the same hollow look in them that I know I have in mine.

And now he's staring up at me like he doesn't even know who I am. It's like he's seen a ghost. He probably has. Mum and I look – looked – so similar after all.

But that's not the only reason why I've stepped back in surprise...

As for a split second I swear I see something else blinking out from those wide, haunted eyes: undiluted hatred.

Does Glenn already know something about me that I don't?

Chapter Eight

'Glenn?' I step forward, but my footsteps are light, as if I plan to dash away again at a moment's notice. 'It's me.'

He shakes his head to chase away whatever nightmare is playing in his mind.

My heart beats faster. Did I imagine the flash of hatred? Or does he know what I was doing last night?

But I'm not thinking straight. If he suspects me of being involved, wouldn't the police already be here, waiting to arrest me?

'I know, sorry,' he says, snapping out of his daze. It's like he's surprised to find me here.

He gets up and makes to hug me but stops himself and, instead, runs a hand through his dishevelled hair. 'God, Emily, I'm sorry. I'm a total mess. I just...' His voice breaks as though he's about to cry. 'I just don't know what to do.' It comes out strangled, like two hands are pressing around his throat.

I've never seen Glenn cry, and there's something in the complete devastation on his face that forces me to close the distance and pull him into a hug. As he lets me, relief tinged with guilt floods my body – he must not think I had anything to do with it after all. I have more time to figure that out for myself.

It feels weird hugging Glenn. We've only ever hugged a handful of times. Glenn has never been a touchy-feely guy. He's a classic 'old school' male, keeping his feelings locked away inside.

But this feels like the right thing to do. I know that Mum would want me to be here for him despite any differences we've had in the past.

His overlarge frame dwarfs my slight one, and when he squeezes tight, I know he needs this just as much. The squeeze verges on the edge of painful, but when I'm about to cry out, he lets go and flops back onto the sofa like the air rushing out of a balloon.

I rub the edge of my chin where it had been squished in tight. I don't know how to approach this conversation with Glenn. It's something I'd never imagined.

'God, Glenn, I don't know what to say... How did this even happen? What have you been told by the police?'

With those words, he stiffens up again. His hands ball into fists so small I can see the whites of his knuckles sticking out.

He remains silent. I know he's lost his wife, but I've just lost my mother, too. And I need some answers now.

I try again. 'Can you, uhh, tell me what exactly happened? All I've been told by Jennifer is that she was found by some dog walkers this morning. And that the police think it was an accidental fall.' I sit down next to him and try to be patient and understanding of his grief.

Eventually, he turns to face me. Defeat is etched deep in his stormy eyes. 'She fell,' he says simply, turning away from me again.

I shake my head in confusion, trying not to let the desperation take over.

'Yes, I know, Jennifer said on the phone. But I thought you could give me the full picture. What did the police tell you?'

Glenn remains mute.

'Glenn,' I try again and hear frustration tinge my words as I say, 'look, I know it's hard, but I deserve to know what you do. I'm her daughter.'

'Yeah,' he shoots back at me, 'so where have you been all this time, huh? Living it up in London with your fancy life. But not here. No, never here to help her. Not here to help her with that damn falling-apart house – and now it's been the death of her!' He propels himself off the sofa and storms towards the door that leads to the garden.

I stare after him, unable to process his words.

He wasn't accusing me of anything to do with last night, but he had insinuated that my going away had caused Mum's death as surely as if I'd pushed her myself.

'What the hell, Glenn?!' I shout after him, standing up. I'd tried to play it nice, and it wasn't working. 'What's that supposed to mean? And what about you? Why didn't *you* help her?'

He ignores me as he strides out the open glass door, not bothering to close it behind him. He kicks the pebbles along the path as he disappears out of sight.

I jump as I hear Jennifer say behind me, 'Please don't be too hard on him. He can't process anything right now.'

She is standing right next to the cream sofa, looking out at where her brother has disappeared.

'What sort of reaction is that?' I say, casting my arm out wide in total exasperation. 'I only want to know what happened to her!'

She shakes her head, and I see sorrow in her dark caramel eyes.

'I think he's blaming himself. What he said to you, he thinks that he should have been there to help Suzie more – with, well, everything, but especially clearing out that house to get ready for sale. She always insisted on going alone, mind you.' She folds her arms across her chest as though defending herself from any retort I might have to Mum's fierce independence. I hate to admit that she's not wrong – Mum was always so proud, and she never wanted to ask for help.

Maybe that's why we're all here now, my mind whispers traitorously to me.

Jennifer continues with a tired shrug. 'He's desperately trying to make sense of how such an awful accident could've happened. We all are. Most of all, I think he feels responsible for not going with her this morning.'

I nod. I guess that makes sense. In a way, I am also blaming myself – blaming myself for not remembering what happened last night and whether I have any knowledge of the accident.

But something Jennifer said drags me away from my thoughts.

'*This morning?* I thought Mum was there last night?'

Jennifer looks at me confused, and I clarify as my heart starts to thunder: 'She didn't come home last night, right? And that's how she got caught out after the storm? The accident was *last night*, but she was found *this morning*?' I suddenly realise that I hadn't been told any of this for certain – but I'd jumped ahead and pieced my own version together. Surely, the storm last night could have been the only way the police would think that Mum falling off those cliffs was an accident.

She shakes her head. 'Oh, Emily, no, I'm sorry if I wasn't clear on the phone. Suzannah left early *this* morning to go to the Dover Heights house. Glenn thinks it must have been about five-thirty in the morning – when it was barely light. The police think that the poor visibility and still-slippery conditions were a factor in causing the accident.'

I can't believe what I'm hearing. 'What – what happened then? Can you just tell me? Glenn obviously won't.'

Her shoulders sag in defeat when she sees my wild desperation. She continues. 'You're probably right. So I'll tell you what he's told me. As you know, Suzie was frantically trying to get the house ready for the estate agents next week. She was there last night but came back and told him she was going again early this morning to crack on. That's why he's now blaming himself for not going with her... as then the police found some large gardening pliers under some scrubs near the edge. Suzie must have decided to make a start on the garden as soon as she arrived around sunrise. But I guess she didn't realise how loose the dirt had become after the storm, and the police could see evidence of slipping around that area. They think she might have slipped when reaching for the tools or while using them and then fallen.'

Silence stretches out in the space between us for a matter of moments before she adds with a heavy sigh of resignation, 'We'll never know how it happened in its entirety as no one else was there, but it's the police's clear conclusion right now. And it does all make terrible sense.'

Her matter-of-fact tone makes it sound like it's all done. That there are no questions left unanswered – that when it comes to Mum's death, everything is now black and white.

Except it is not.

Because I know Mum would *never* have been so reckless as to risk gardening after a storm. The wild foliage that runs along the edge of the cliff-top garden needs regular tending, or it gets totally out of control. She knew the edge of that cliff like the back of her hand – when to venture out there and when to not. And this morning would *not* have been the time to garden.

And even if that wasn't the case, I know something else for definite: that Mum didn't stay here with Glenn last night. She'd told me so herself as we'd said goodbye yesterday. She'd said she'd planned to stay at Dover Heights. She was definitive. And that's obviously why I'd decided to still go over there at eleven at night.

I shake my head, trying to make sense of what I'm hearing.

'But... but,' I stammer, 'I thought Mum was staying at Dover Heights last night? She told me...' I let the statement hover in the air between us. I don't want to admit yet that I went over there myself. Not until I can be sure of my memories.

Jennifer shrugs as she turns to walk back into the kitchen. 'I guess she changed her mind and came back home. Glenn and Zara are certain she stayed here and left early.'

My stomach twists as I look out at where Glenn sits under the dark shade of the looming eucalyptus tree.

Mum had been absolutely sure she was going to stay at Dover Heights last night – why would I have got a late-night taxi to the house if she wasn't there? Would she have come back here, to Glenn, so late at night, only to leave again at dawn? It seems unlikely.

And if Mum had never come back here to 8 Merton Street, then it can mean only one thing.

Glenn is lying.

Chapter Nine

I try not to let my panic show on my face as I run through the options. Perhaps Mum *had* come back here to Merton Street last night. I could have got a taxi to Dover Heights, found it empty and left again.

But why did I have a memory of slippery tracks and brush underfoot? Maybe that was as innocent – I could have been trying to get into the house another way when I found the front door locked.

But what about the scream...

I frown as I think through this very possible explanation.

If Mum did go to Dover Heights this morning rather than staying the night, it does seem more possible that what happened was an accident. It would make me, along with Glenn, entirely guilt-free.

That would be easy to accept. The police think that's the case. But I can't ignore the growing knot in my stomach telling me that something doesn't add up.

And deep down, I know why.

Because if Mum *had* returned here last night, then she would have messaged me back. Even if she'd been asleep when my texts and calls had come through, she would still have responded to them when she'd woken up this morning. She has never ignored me before.

I don't know how long I stand staring into space towards the large glass doors that look out onto the expansive split-level garden beyond. Glenn is nowhere in sight – he must have gone down to the very bottom to cool off in the shade of the ginormous gum trees that hedge the edge of the garden. I watch them sway in the light breeze, then turn around to find Jennifer. I have more questions for her.

I stop short a few steps from the large island that frames the luminescent white kitchen when I see what she has thrown carelessly over her shoulder: Mum's self-proclaimed favourite tea towel. We had a bit of a thing about collecting one from every trip we did – and this was the one I'd brought her on my last visit over. It was only a little tourist print of a map of London, but she told me she loved it as it felt like every time she cooked, I was right there with her.

Pull yourself together. I berate myself and try to gulp away the lump that's risen in my throat by clearing it loudly.

'Jennifer.' I close the distance between us and lean over the island bench. She's started busying herself putting some lunch together, and my stomach turns at the sight of the dripping beetroots she's chopping on the board, staining it a deep, purply red.

As she looks up, I force my gaze away from the food and focus on her.

'What's happened to Mum's phone? Have the police said whether she had anything else on her?'

'Oh, I don't know,' she says, shaking her head as the knife continues to slice. 'You'll have to ask Glenn.' She pauses to look out to the distant trees where he's hiding. 'Maybe I can try asking him for you in a minute.'

'That would be great, thanks,' I say with a tight smile. I appreciate this small gesture of solidarity.

'Of course,' she says. 'Why don't you make yourself at home?' When she sees my small look of incredulity at being dismissed, she adds, 'I mean, lunch will be ready soon. Zara and Mike have just gone to pick up a chook. And your uncle John will be over soon.'

I raise my eyebrows at this. It sounds like she's organised a family party.

'I thought it would be good for us to all be together,' she continues, 'to help process this awful day.' She places the knife down. Some beetroot juice has dripped down the edges onto her hands, leaving a light maroon stain.

'Okay,' I say with a shrug. 'I'm sure that's a good idea.' I can't bear the idea of us all sitting around a table together without Mum. I don't think I'll be able to make it through. But I'm so tired, weighed down by my grief and anxiety, and all the fight is gone from me. So I turn to make my way towards the staircase.

This time, when I walk into the hallway, I stop and look up at the family portraits that line the walls. I glance up at the largest photograph of all, and a vision of the day it was taken shoots into my memory. I remember it so well – it was the first anniversary of Mum and Glenn's marriage, and apparently, all she wanted was a family photoshoot. The grimace on my awkward sixteen-year-old face says it all. I hated that day.

Zara and I stand side by side with our arms folded against our chests. We lean against each other in a ridiculously forced pose. Her blonde ringlets frame her cupid's face, and even in this two-dimensional photograph, I can see the sparkle in her bright blue eyes. She was only eleven years old, and she could have been a model. She was a natural that day, flashing smiles here, there, and everywhere – at one point, I thought the photographer was going to offer her a contract. And then there was me, a scowl across my spotty face whenever I wasn't forced to bear my teeth in a farce of a smile. In this blown-up portrait, my hair looks more copper red than auburn, and I can't help but think that I look like the ugly stepsister next to Zara's angelic Disney princess.

On one side of Zara is Glenn, and on the other side of me is Mum. Their arms are wrapped over the shoulders of their respective daughters, and they hug us tight as they glance over the tops of our heads back towards each other. Such broad grins ring their faces that it almost looks like they've won the lottery rather than just a complicated blended family.

I stare up at the sombre expression on the face of my younger self. How at odds it is with the rest of their happy faces. I sigh, thinking back to those days once more. Maybe the problem really was more *my* attitude to the new family than everyone else's. No one else appears troubled.

Shaking my head, I continue past the photo wall to the foot of the stairs. Reminiscing isn't going to help me today. I trudge up the wooden staircase, each step feeling like a mountain I have to climb. I should go straight to the room that used to be mine. But as though drawn by an invisible string, I turn left and walk straight to the end of the corridor to Mum's office. When it had been hard for me to adjust over those first few years of Mum and Glenn's marriage, I'd slip in here and do my homework as Mum worked. It felt like the only place in the house that was entirely Mum – with no trace of Glenn.

I take a deep breath and open the door, stepping inside, and shut it tight again behind me in one quick swoop. As I face the achingly familiar room, a fresh wave of grief and shock pour over me. The scent of lavender tinged with eucalyptus floods my senses, and for a second, I'm stunned. It smells like her, like she's stepped out of the room and will be back any second. I walk around in a daze, running my fingertips over the bookshelf lined with all our favourite books. I think of the new thriller I have in my suitcase that I'd planned to give her to read next. I can't believe that she'll never have the chance.

Sinking into the desk chair she has facing out towards the garden, I glance down at the tabletop. It's cluttered as usual, with candles, pens and notepads strewn everywhere. Mum was constantly jotting down ideas on scraps of paper or, more often in later years, on her iPad. *At least that is harder to lose*, she had said. Her laptop isn't here, but I spot her iPad. Its bright yellow case leaps out from under another mountain of books.

I pull it out on impulse. As I remove the slipcover, it flashes to life, and a sheet of paper flutters out of it across the desk. I almost drop it when I see the iPad background photo appear. It's a photo of us that I haven't seen before. I must be about four or five, and it's a classic bright summer's day. We have a large, misshaped golden sandcastle in front of us and the deep blue ocean behind us. I'm wrapped in a huge towel in Mum's arms, and we're both smiling broadly at the camera, my dad probably behind it. I squeeze my eyes shut as the tears threaten to pour out. My throat tightens. I don't even realise I'm sobbing until I hear my breath come out ragged and fast.

I swipe at the image, trying to make it disappear, and as I wipe my lashes on the back of my hand, I realise I've somehow opened the lock screen. Mum didn't have a passcode on it.

As I get my tears under control, the last thing Mum read on her iPad comes into view: an email sent from Mum to Mike. *That's odd...* Why would she be looking at her sent folder? The only reason I ever do that is to double-check something has been sent... I frown as I scan the screen.

From: Suzannah Archer

Sent: Friday, January 20, 2023 11:14 AM

To: Mike Cowper

Subject: Anonymous email

Mike – I just tried to call you. Call me back ASAP, okay – it's urgent.

This must be something to do with the work problems she'd referred to. But there doesn't seem to be any other intel to go on. Why would she have double-checked it had been sent?

And then, from the corner of my eye, I see the scrap of paper that flew out of the case. Glancing across at it now, I notice a wall of spidery text that doesn't look like her handwriting. As I reach across to snatch it up, I realise that it's not handwriting at all – but a typed and printed letter:

Dear Suzannah,

Please don't throw away this letter – I know it will be a strange one to read. But I had to warn you about something happening at Imaginate. You might not have noticed in your creative role, but there have been a series of dismissals in the financial team, the latest being Felicity Smith. And each person disappeared without a peep of complaint – why?

What I think they all had in common was discovering something that a certain person would want to keep hidden – you know who I'm talking about.

I don't know what that is exactly, and I'm not able to investigate myself – which is why I am letting you know. Because I am certain he's *doing something that* he *should not and that he's keeping secrets from you. But it will be hurting you and the whole business – so it's about time someone uncovered it. Before it's too late.*

I'm sorry I'm not brave enough to speak to you in person – but I hope this letter will give you the start you need.

A friend

I lean back in the chair, reeling at what I've read. No wonder Mum had been anxious yesterday – what a bizarre letter to receive. Why hadn't she told me about it? Had she told anyone? I guess she'd said there had been work problems. But she didn't say that she'd been sent a vaguely threatening note.

There was only one person it could be referring to: Mike. Even though the writer didn't seem willing to name him personally, I'm certain it could only be him...

I turn back to the iPad and exit the email application to navigate into the text messages. Even without Mum's phone, I should be able to read most of her recent communications on her iPad thanks to iMessage – except for her phone calls. I know it might be a violation of privacy, but I need to put together the full picture.

Scrolling down, I select Mike's name and scan through the most recent message chain – all from yesterday:

Mike C at 3.30 pm:

Suze – sorry I missed your email and calls. So hectic! I'll be in touch when I'm around.

Suzannah A at 3.45 pm:

Mike. Seriously, come on, you keep dodging me. We need to talk today. Away from the office – let's meet at DH.

Mike C at 7.15 pm:

Calm down, Suzannah geez! I'm on my way to DH now.

Suzannah A at 7.20 pm:

Okay. See you soon.

I run my fingers back through my hair. I know what that acronym means: Dover Heights. Which means Mike was with her at some point last night. What was discussed, and what had Mike been hiding from her? It might be nothing – or it might help explain why Mum was so distracted that she had fallen.

Or been pushed...

The awful, slippery idea pings into my mind before I can stop it. No. Nothing could have been so drastic that Mike would have *pushed* her. Then again, if Mum had confronted him about whatever this letter is referring to... then is it a possibility? I'm not thinking straight. The police are *certain* that Mum's fall was an accident and that it happened this morning. Shouldn't I just accept that?

But reading this bizarre note and knowing that Mum must have confronted Mike about it last night makes me pause. I might not be able to remember much – but I *know* I went to Dover Heights. And I heard a scream.

I push my hair back from my flushed face – my anxiety over what I've read makes my heart beat a little faster. I've always known that Mike has a tough, scary side. My mind flashes back to a huge screaming match I'd once witnessed between him and Mum in this very room. I'd come home early from high school one day and opened the door to screams, shouts and banging. Sprinting upstairs, I found Mike throwing books onto the floor like he'd lost his mind.

Mum had ushered me out, her eyes wide and terrified. She'd explained that it was nothing to worry about, that they'd lost a big deal, and this was Mike's way of processing. I'd accepted at the time that sometimes, at work, people get very stressed. I'd forgotten all about it. But when I'd gone into the workforce myself, I'd realised that what I'd seen from Mike hadn't been normal behaviour. I'd tried to talk to Mum about it once, but she said that she'd always known that Mike had some flaws, but he'd proved his brilliance time and time again. Besides, they were a family business now since she'd married Glenn. Her new motto seemed to be that where family was concerned, anything could be forgiven.

Thinking back now, I remember the look on his face, contorted in anger at losing that deal. Could he have snapped last night as well? And then turned violent?

I shake my head to clear the thought away – I'm being ridiculous. These messages were *hours* before I'd even arrived at Dover Heights last night. So, more than likely, Mike would have left by the time I arrived. The scream that I remember was probably nothing to do with him. Even so, a letter like that is hard to ignore.

I slip back out of Mum and Mike's text chain and see ours there – no further messages to what I have on my phone. I'm about to shut off the iPad when I notice Glenn's name. I chew on my lip. It would be an even bigger invasion of privacy to go into their message chain. But there is something in Glenn's story I'm not fully buying. I still *know* I heard a scream, and I'm sure it must have been when I was at Dover Heights. Where else would I have heard it?

As I scan through the messages, a sick churning fills my stomach.

Glenn at 7.45 pm:

You're being so ridiculous now!

Glenn at 10.15 pm:

Please come back home. I'm sorry.

Glenn at 11 pm:

Come on Suze, talk to me!

Glenn at 6 am this morning:

Where are you?

I lean forward onto my elbows and twirl the long auburn strands that fall in front of my shoulders as I try to process everything.

Glenn's messages confirm two things:

One, that Mum was out last night.

And two, she wasn't here this morning.

But could she have come back in between, making Glenn's story true? These messages make it seem unlikely but not impossible.

One thing is certain: these are not the messages of a happily married man. My mind whirls at all these what-ifs and unanswered questions. And I'm left with one overarching one: how does this letter fit into everything?

I spin my hair tighter and tighter around my fingertips until it feels like I've stopped the flow of blood. Then, I let it go in a rush alongside an exhale.

Mike and Glenn must know more about Mum's state of mind last night than anyone else. And so I need to speak to both of them to find out more.

I try to muster the energy to stand, but sitting in this room, surrounded by her presence, I feel almost suffocated. Every fibre reminds me of her – from the bright, vibrant prints of sunny beach days that line the walls to the feel of the soft, patterned rug under my bare feet. She chose every little detail in this room with such care. I breathe deeply, and the sweet scent of baked lavender and eucalyptus races up my nose. My head spins. I keep expecting the door behind me to click open and for Mum to burst in, my name a melody on her lips.

I try to imagine her walking in any second. But I know that she never will again.

Instead, I let a renewed sense of determination fill me. I will not rest until I know exactly what happened to my mum – and that includes retracing all my steps until I uncover what I did last night, too.

It may have been an accident, as everyone else has already assumed. But I will look into every potential red flag to find out the truth, no matter what – even if that means confronting that I might have had a part to play. I may never know exactly what happened to my dad, but I refuse to let that be the case with my mum. I owe it to her.

I slowly rise and try to take one last deep breath of the comforting scent, but it's too strong, an unbearable reminder of her. I race to the door, opening it quickly, intending to slip out unnoticed. But I stop short, locked in its frame, as my eyes fix on two blazing blue ones. They blink out at me from across the short, two-metre distance between us. But it might as well be an entire ocean. I flashback to the last time I'd seen them so piercing: when they were screaming at me.

Zara looks as shocked to see me as I am to see her. Her usual ringlets are straightened into a short bob cut that suits her petite face, emphasising her razor-sharp cheekbones and wide eyes. She looks different from the last time I saw her; she is older and more grown up.

My first instinct is to turn tail and slam the door back in her face. I don't know how to deal with seeing her again after what happened between us – and what's happened today.

Before I have a chance to speak, she is hurtling towards me. For a second, I think she's about to attack, but then her tiny body drags me into a tight hug.

'Oh Em,' I hear her muffle into my shoulder. I stiffen, but as she pulls back, I see that her eyes are twinkling with tears.

She wipes them away with the back of her hand, just like I'd done moments earlier inside the study. 'This is unbelievable,' she says. She opens her mouth as though to say something else but then stops short.

This is the first time I've ever seen a non-stop talkative Zara out of words to say. It's as though she is remembering the last time we spoke and how it had seemed like we'd never speak again.

And as I see the sadness etched across her face, the mirror image of my grief, I feel the urge to comfort her. I have to be the bigger person

'Zar,' I say, 'let's put everything behind us for now, hey? I know we have some stuff to figure out, but let's be here for each other today. Life's too short.'

'Em,' she says in a choked voice and wraps her arms back around me once more. 'I'm sorry for everything I said last year. And I'm *so* sorry about Suzie – I mean, your mum.' Her voice cracks a little at her last words.

I hug her tight and don't bat the tears away as they slip silently down my cheeks. And I realise that I might have lost my mum today, but at least I have my sister back.

So when she asks me why I was in the study, I can't help blurting out what I'd just discovered. I tell her about the bizarre letter and Mum and Mike's exchanges. We used to share everything before we fell out – and I can't keep everything bottled up. I don't mention my misgivings about Glenn, though – he's her dad, after all. And she's always been daddy's little girl.

When I finish my story, Zara frowns and shakes her head, telling me that she has no idea what that might be about.

'Suzie didn't mention that weird letter at all,' she says. 'But Mike is downstairs now. You can ask him yourself.' She interlocks her arm in mine, and as we traipse towards the staircase together, I feel a tiny bit lighter.

Because at least I have Zara back – the one person in this family other than my mum that I used to be able to trust.

But a shiver of doubt creeps up my spine as I think back to last year and everything that happened with Harry. The deceit and betrayal of it all.

Now, we're acting like nothing has happened.

And maybe trusting her is my first big mistake.

Chapter Ten

As we step onto the stairs, the far too cheerful chirrup of the doorbell blasts through the hallway. Zara and I exchange looks as we hear Jennifer cry out, 'I'll get it.' We continue our slow descent as she dashes into view. She doesn't notice us as she flings the front door open, her hair still bouncing behind her.

'Oh,' she says, 'come in, come in.'

By the time Zara and I reach the bottom of the stairs, I can hear the answering voice say, 'Thank you,' in a deep tone. I know that voice: it's my uncle John.

He steps through the door, and the four of us squished at the entry makes for a crowded first meeting since we'd heard the news. My heart lurches in my chest as John locks eyes with me, and I see Mum's bright eyes blinking back. My knees buckle a little, and I'm glad I still have Zara's arm to lean on.

'Emily,' he says without hesitation, 'I'm so sorry.' He has a bunch of white lilies in his hands, and though they're full to the brim, they look tiny in comparison to his tall frame.

'Let's go through, let's go through.' Jennifer bustles us on, herding him towards the kitchen before he has a chance to say anything else to me. I watch the back of his short dark brown hair disappear out of view.

'Well,' Zara says to me through gritted teeth, 'shall we go and join Jennifer's pantomime? Orrr, we could cut and run now?' She looks over her shoulder back towards the door.

Despite everything, a laugh escapes me at her suggestion. It comes out more like a strangled cough. 'Ah, I wish. But let's go through.'

She sighs as I drag her into the kitchen, where everyone is loosely gathered. John looks baffled as Jennifer hands him a tray of something to take to the table, and in the corner Glenn and Mike sit locked close in conversation.

As soon as we enter the room, Mike sees me and jumps up. I swear the last time I saw him he was going grey, but now his hair shines onyx black in the brightness of the sunny day. As he runs over, I notice that he's also in better shape than when I last saw him. There's an athletic spring to his step that contrasts with the mood in the rest of the room, and as he forces me into a hug, I feel his biceps crush into my shoulders.

'Oh darl,' he says, squeezing me tight, 'this is madness.'

'Come on,' Jennifer says impatiently, and behind Mike's shoulder I see her gesture towards the table for us to take our seats. 'Let's eat. We don't want it to get cold.'

Mike lets me go at his wife's command and races back over to his seat at the table. I'm confused by his immediate greeting, considering the emails and texts I'd just read. He wouldn't act like he cared if he had something to hide – or is he overcompensating?

As Zara and I trudge into the dining room, I choose to sit opposite Mike, hoping to have a one-on-one conversation with him. As we all sit, I glance down at the colourful place settings. The table is laid beautifully, which feels at odds with the reason why we're here today.

'Thank you, Jennifer,' Glenn says to his sister as he pulls some chicken towards him. I can't stomach the idea of eating – I don't know how he can. But he's obviously done something to pull himself together since his outburst earlier. He sits up straight at the head of the table, his shoulders back and his voice low as he declares, 'I can't believe we're here like this. But Suzie would want us to be together. So let's eat, then I can catch you up on the latest from the police.'

My ears prick up, and I want to shout across the table at him to tell me now, but he avoids my gaze, and everyone else follows his command. They reach for the dishes lining the middle of the table – even John, who is forced into a conversation with Glenn.

Zara exchanges a sympathetic look with me over the table as she tries to place some salad on my plate. We both know that this sort of declaration from Glenn is exactly what it appears to be: an order. One that shouldn't be disobeyed if you don't want an argument. And I don't have the energy for that today.

So I push the food around on my plate as I lean over towards Mike. 'I can't believe any of this,' I say in a tight voice. I don't mean to put on a show, but trying to have this conversation has caused my throat to close up. I try to swallow the sobs that I know are building beneath the surface.

'I know, neither can I,' Mike replies over his forkful of chicken. He seems to have no trouble eating. 'And you only just got back, right?

I remember Suzie being so excited that you were coming to stay. You must be all over the place.' I wince at his brusque tone and use of Mum's nickname. And at how much he seems to know about my plans.

I try to gulp away the building tears. 'Nothing feels real about this. I keep thinking she's about to walk in.' I gesture to the hallway. 'But I know deep down she's not.'

He nods in agreement with my words as he takes a large bite and chews.

'It's like I keep looking for her. And just now,' I continue carefully, 'I went into Mum's study to have a moment – imagine her in there, you know? And I stumbled on her iPad. There was an email and message chain between the two of you on the screen. It seemed quite urgent.'

He frowns and pauses with his mouth full to stare at me. I continue. 'It looked like you'd planned to meet up last night. I guess I want to understand what Mum's state of mind might have been like – how she could have been so distracted for this accident to happen?' I don't mention the letter. I want to see if he will tell me of his own accord – if he even knows about it.

He doesn't respond for a moment, as though he's taking his time to think through his response. He finally swallows, clears his throat and says in a too-measured voice, 'I'm not sure what you read, Emily, but yeah, she got sent some stupid anonymous letter. It had absolutely nothing of substance in it. Probably a competitor trying to mess with her head. Nothing to worry about, and I cleared it up with Suzie yesterday.'

'So you did see her last night then?' I press, not willing to give up this easily.

'I, well – no,' he says, jutting out his jaw.

I blink at him in disbelief. I mean, the texts I read all but give an eyewitness account that he and Mum were meeting at Dover Heights. 'But I saw that you'd arranged to meet at Dover Heights?' I blurt out without thinking.

He flinches. 'And I'm saying that we didn't. We spoke on the phone instead.' He says it with certainty, but I can still hear the tight edge to his voice.

'Why?' I shoot back at him.

He taps his fork against his plate. 'What do you mean "why"? I don't have to explain that to you!'

His raised voice makes me sit back in shock. Then I notice that the rest of the table has gone silent.

'What's going on?' Glenn barks at us from the other end.

Mike turns to face everyone and smiles broadly. 'Absolutely nothing.'

My mouth drops open as two sensations rise inside of me: anger and hurt.

'It's not nothing,' I snap without thinking. 'Mike is lying about seeing Mum last night.'

'What?' Glenn growls.

'That's not true,' Mike interjects, shaking his head. 'Emily is struggling to accept this awful accident.'

That riles me. 'What?' I shout. 'All I did was ask about the email and message chain that I found on Mum's iPad – it sounded like they'd met up last night.'

'Well, and I'm telling you that I did *not* see Suzannah last night, okay, Emily?' Mike says in a patronising voice, and I have to stop myself from screaming in his face. 'If you really need "proof",' he adds in an offended voice, 'then ask Jennifer – we were together the whole evening.'

Everyone, including Mike, swivels to look at Jennifer, who is wedged between Zara and Glenn. She'd just taken a large sip of water and she chokes as Mike stares daggers at her.

'Umm, that's right,' she says, turning pink. He nods once more. 'We watched a movie,' she adds and takes another sip of her water.

I sigh and mutter, 'Alright, alright,' under my breath, ready to let this go. I am either wrong about Mike and Mum meeting up yesterday, or Mike and Jennifer are covering something up. Either way, I'm not going to find anything out right now with everyone staring at me.

Then Glenn says in a low voice, 'Emily, why were you going through Suzie's stuff?'

I flinch at the accusation in his words. 'I wasn't – I was having a moment upstairs and flicked through her iPad. *Accidentally*.'

'You shouldn't be going through her things without us all there,' he says, and as I look up towards the top of the table where he sits staring down at me, judging me in front of everyone, something snaps.

'God,' I say, thrusting my chair back to stand up. 'My mum just *died*, and now I'm getting some sort of interrogation?!' As I look around at all their shocked faces, I know I can't take being here a second longer, or I'll burst into tears.

They call after me, but I turn and sprint out of the room, straight towards the front door.

As soon as I'm outside, I realise I have no car and nowhere to go. I'll have to go back inside to get my phone and call Addie – or to ask to borrow the keys to Zara's car. But for now, I settle for walking towards the lone tree in the far corner of the front lawn and sit down heavily in front of it.

I lean against it and take comfort in its solidity as I try to breathe. Today is too much. This is all too hard. I let the light breeze ruffle over me and attempt to calm my racing heart.

After what could have been hours, a small cough makes me jump.

'Oh, John,' I say, blinking up at the towering figure in front of me.

'Are you okay?' he asks, dropping down to sit beside me.

'Well, not really.'

'Yeah – I mean, of course you're not. But is there anything I can help with?'

John is a doctor, and I understand what he's asking – he genuinely wants to help me. Unlike everyone else in there. I see the forensic look in those familiar, piercing eyes. So like but unlike my mother's.

'Not unless you can bring someone back to life,' I say wryly. He flinches at my attempt at humour. 'Sorry,' I say quickly, 'that wasn't funny – you've just lost your sister and had to be subject to that show in there.' I hang my head in defeat.

'Don't worry,' he says in his calm voice. We sit in comfortable silence for a minute. A kookaburra laughs in the distance as though mocking our one moment of peace.

'Is he,' John says slowly, 'often like that with you?'

'Who, Glenn?' I ask.

He nods, and I sigh. 'Well, we're partial to an argument – we've always had a tricky relationship even at the best of times... I don't think this little family get-together today was Jennifer's best idea.'

'No,' he agrees in that same quiet voice. 'But I'm very glad I've seen you.'

I nod; it has been such a long time since we'd last seen each other – maybe five or six years. John only moved back to Sydney in the last year, a few months before Granddad died, so he could look after him. But I know that he'd also divorced his wife last year. They'd only been married for a few years after he'd finally finished medical school and moved over to South Australia.

I glance over at him and try to study his face. He's aged a lot since I'd last seen him. He's only nine years older than me – but with the number of lines on his forehead, it looks like he has the weight of the world on his shoulders. I guess after the last few years dealing with his divorce, both his parents dying, and now his sister, he really does.

'I couldn't believe it when I got a call out of the blue from Jennifer this morning. I was on my way back from a night shift, so at first, I thought I was going delusional from lack of sleep.' He lets out a long exhale. 'I don't know how to process the loss of another member of my family,' he admits under his breath. His voice is so quiet it's almost lost on the breeze.

'I know. I guess at least she's with Nana and Granddad now.' I am about to say, 'and maybe Dad,' but I have to stop speaking as my throat constricts.

'Yes, I suppose,' he says in a tight voice. 'But it seems to be the stupidest accident. I *wish* someone had been with her this morning – maybe this wouldn't have happened.'

I can't keep it in anymore – and if anyone else would want to understand what really happened and how Mum could have been so distracted, surely it would be her brother. 'The thing is,' I say in a low voice, 'I don't think it was this morning.'

'What do you mean?' he says, looking at me with concern.

'Like I said in there.' I nod towards the house. 'It sounds like Mum met up with Mike last night at Dover Heights, and I know Glenn *says* she stayed here – but Mum told me that she was going to stay at Dover Heights last night. So what if Glenn has it wrong somehow?' I don't want to mention reading Mum and Glenn's text messages – that might be too much of an invasion of privacy even for John – but I weave in this suggestion to see his response first. 'I don't know what exactly is going on. But a lot of things seem a bit weird about this "accident" – don't you think?' I'm about to tell him about the letter too, but I decide to wait for his reaction first.

He frowns as he thinks over my words. 'I don't know, Emily,' he says finally. 'I understand the desire to try and figure out exactly how Suzannah was feeling and why she might have been so distracted, but you'll tie yourself up in knots. I've seen enough of these kinds of tragedies at work to know that sometimes there isn't a simple answer. It was an awful accident, and one that you'll never be able to get the full picture of. I'm so sorry,' he adds gently.

My shoulders sag. I didn't realise how much I'd been hoping that he might say he understood me. Or that he also thought that Glenn and Mike were hiding something.

'You're probably right,' I say. 'And the police are the experts, after all. I guess I want to know *exactly* what happened. But maybe you're right, and that's impossible...'

A ping from John's phone breaks our reverie, and he glances down at it with a frown. 'Ah, sorry, I have to go – I didn't realise the time, and I promised my friend that I'd pick them up.'

'Oh, don't worry.'

'No, I wish I didn't have to leave so soon. But you have my number, right?' I nod. 'Good, I have your new one too from your mother. So please call me if you hear or need anything. Especially if you want back up,' he says with a nod back towards the house.

'Thank you, John, I appreciate it.'

He smiles a tight smile down at me as he stands. 'I'll go say my goodbyes – but seriously, anytime.'

As John disappears through the front door, I lean back on the bark of the tree once more. I gaze up at the leaves twisting overhead and try to make sense of my muddled mind.

Why can't I easily accept what everyone else can: that Mum's death was a simple accident?

I put my head in my hands.

'Em?' I look up to see Zara standing over me. 'Oh, Ems,' she kneels and gives me a hug. A hug I probably do not deserve. 'This is the worst day. But we'll get through it.'

I know she's trying to comfort me, but her words aren't helping the gaping wound that is my heart. 'Look,' she says softly, 'Dad's just got a call from the police. They have some questions for you and need you to head over to Dover Heights. Now.'

My heart starts hammering in my chest.

Oh God, this is it.

This is the moment when they tell me it's all my fault.

Chapter Eleven

The police tape blocks out the whole street. That, and all the throngs of people milling around in front of it, trying to get a peek. There are police cars and clusters of news vans crawling all around this normally quiet suburb. I can't believe their morbid curiosity.

I see a few neighbours gathered on the lawns outside their homes, whispering to each other, shock written across their faces that something like this has happened here. I hurry past, hoping no one will recognise me. I am here for one purpose and one purpose only. To speak to the police officer in charge and answer their questions. Which, in turn, I hope will answer some of mine.

Even if what they have to ask me puts me at the centre of blame for Mum's death, I have to know. I don't care. If I did something unforgivably stupid last night, I owe it to her to find out.

I reach the top corner of the police tape and duck under, hoping no onlookers notice me as I stride towards what will always be my grandparents' home. It's a walk I have done many times, but never like this.

I'm about to reach the small front gate when I'm stopped by a police officer rushing towards me.

'Excuse me, miss,' he says, coming to a halt in front of me. I stop but rock on my heels. 'You can't come through here. This is a police zone.'

'I know,' I say, not taking a breath as the words tumble from my mouth, 'but the woman that you've found is my mother.'

He blinks back in surprise. 'Oh—'

'And I've been told you wanted me to come over to answer some questions...'

I make the most of my advantage and step forward, starting to walk past him.

He hurries to catch up with me, but this time I don't stop. He continues to buzz around me like a fly.

'Wait, let me go and find Sergeant White first. It's better if you wait back there.'

I'm about to open the gate – I know every crack on its chipped white and rusty frame; I have pushed it open without a care in the world so many times over the years. And now, here I am, being stopped by a police officer.

He rushes forward as I place my hand on the frame. 'No, stop!' he barks, causing me to jump back in fright. But not because of him.

Because of the shadow that stretches across the path from the other edge of the house. The other side leads to the back garden and the cliffs beyond.

The shadow loosens something in my memory, and I'm suddenly back here last night – but in half-darkness. And I'm seeing the shadow of a person all the way at the back of the house. And hearing that scream. *My own?*

I try to grasp tighter to the memory, to bring it out into the open. But before I can, the shadow I'm seeing right now disappears, a real-life person – another police officer – appearing in its place.

They start to move towards us down the side of the slate path at a steady pace.

'Sergeant White, I'm so sorry,' the police officer blocking my way says to the man. 'This lady says she's the daughter... I was trying to say that she should wait here.'

'That's okay, Constable Jones, she can come through.'

I can't believe it as I take a step forward and study Sergeant White's face. Because as I take a closer look, I realise with a jolt that I know this man – from a time I'd rather forget.

Chapter Twelve

'Oh my god, Ben?' I venture. Ben White. My very first boyfriend. Before I'd had a total breakdown after Mum married Glenn and broke up with him, of course.

'Emily,' he says, giving me a curt nod. But concern sparkles out from his ocean-blue eyes as he flattens his cap tighter on his head. I'm sure he's keeping tight control of his emotions in front of his team. 'I'm so unbelievably sorry for your loss.' He gestures around. 'When I realised where we'd been called to and whose house it was, I couldn't believe it.'

I shake my head. But at least I have a somewhat friendly face in this police officer, and someone I can trust running this. That has to be *one* good sign, at least, if I'm about to be interrogated.

I walk through the gates and stare up at him. He's a lot taller than he was at fifteen, and I can see a few smile lines etched along the corners of his face. But I can't concentrate on the shock of seeing him again right now. I'm here for a more important reason.

'I was told that you found something and wanted me to come over to answer some questions?' I tuck my hair behind my ears and try to keep the nerves out of my voice.

'Yes, are you okay to come round the back with me, do you think? I understand if it's a little soon,' he adds kindly.

'I'm fine,' I say with certainty. I have to face this sooner or later.

He nods and turns on his heels back down the path. I open the gate at last and follow him while the other police officer takes up his guard duty again.

My breath catches as I take in the disfigured garden. Police tape still runs across the middle, blocking the furthest brambles and trees from anyone entering. But beyond that the view looks the same. And, as always, it's breathtaking.

An incomprehensible stretch of dark blue ocean reaches out as far as my eyes can see. It sparkles like thousands of diamonds are bouncing along its surface, and overhead, I spy seagulls swooping in the windy offshore breeze.

A roaring enters my ears that has nothing to do with the ocean. It's a feeling of sheer panic as an image of my mum tumbling towards it enters my mind. Down and down the cliffs without stopping.

'I have to sit,' I manage to say as a feeling of light-headedness washes over me. I'm right next to the back porch swing now and flop onto it without another word, putting my head in my hands.

Ben perches next to me. 'I'm so sorry, Emily. Are you sure you're okay to talk?'

'Yes,' I say and shift purposefully to face him – and not the terrible beauty of that too-familiar view.

He takes his hat off and brushes a hand through his sandy blond hair. The same shade that I remember – but cut short now. Long gone are the shaggy curls of his teenage years. Now, he is the picture of professionalism, and the blue of his uniform makes his eyes look an even deeper shade of cerulean.

He lowers his voice as though he might be overhead. 'So... I don't actually have any questions to ask you.'

I frown in confusion and a wistful smile escapes onto his lips. 'When I heard from Glenn that you were in Sydney, I wanted to make sure you had an opportunity to hear it from me first that I was working on this. And give you the chance to ask me any questions directly. Plus, I wanted to see how you were doing.'

He shrugs as though anyone would do the same. I do not deserve his kindness – not when I could potentially be involved in causing this in the first place. Remembering that shadow has now made me certain that someone else *had* been here last night. Whatever anyone else in my family says.

'I... no...' I start, then falter. 'I just,' I begin, my voice barely a whisper. 'So it was all an accident then?'

He lets out a long exhale and fiddles with his cap again. 'Yes, I'm sure your stepfather has already told you everything – but with what he's told us in combination with what we've found here at the site, it looks that way. This was her last known location, according to her phone records – though we haven't found the iPhone in question. But we are as certain as we can be that she must have fallen with it on her, and since she was, well, found partially in the water, it likely fell out and was washed away. Then there are also a series of scuff marks up here like she tripped alongside a long slip through the muddy cliff edge. It...'

He's trying to phrase this as delicately as possible, and he pauses to check I'm still doing okay. When I give a small nod, he adds, 'It even looks like she tried to grab and scrabble on the edge.' He hangs his head. 'I'm so sorry, Emily. But if it helps you at all, there's nothing to suggest anything *other* than a tragic fall. You know as well as I do how dangerous these cliffs are.'

I let his words wash over me. 'So, she... she,' my voice wobbles, 'she didn't jump?' I've shied away from this thought so far – but now, being here, I have to voice the small question out loud. After everything Mum told me yesterday, and now I know bigger problems were going on with Mike and Glenn, I need to ask.

His eyes flash across at me. 'Why do you say that?'

I hold in a sob. 'God, I don't know, Ben – all this. I can't believe she would fall when I thought she knew it like the back of her hand. She's gardened in that same spot for so many years – and been fine. I found out only yesterday that she was having work problems and, I *think*, fighting with Glenn. Maybe something happened last night to make her think enough was enough.' I don't mention that *I* could be a factor, too. Blinking back tears, I look up at the tall trees in the yard opposite. Anywhere but at Ben.

'I don't know about that, Emily – but as I said, from what we can see here at the scene, she didn't give up; she fought to stay up here on the cliff. That I can tell you with the utmost certainty... As for her state of mind, and whether she was distracted by family fights so didn't notice how close she was to the edge or how bad the conditions were – well, that's not something I can comment on, I'm afraid,' he says as gently as possible. 'And it's also not something I can really investigate.'

I shake my head in embarrassment. No, of course it's not.

'Look, what happens next is that the coroner will officially determine the cause and estimated time of death. I don't think there will be any surprises, but just so you know.' Then he drops his voice low to make sure no one else overhears. 'I know this must be so hard for you and such a shock; I get it. So that's why I wanted you to come and for me to explain everything directly to you. And to give you this.'

He slips a hand into his pocket and pulls out a small card. He takes my hand in his, and for a minute, I wish he would hold it and not let go. But his touch disappears as quickly as it had come, and I realise I'm now holding the little piece of paper.

'This is my card, so if there's *anything*,' he gives me a meaningful look, 'at all that you think I should know about, or you want to talk, give me a call.'

I manage a tiny 'Thank you', even as I know everything inside me is going to break again. I'm about to say something else when my phone starts buzzing in my hand. 'Oh,' I say, glancing up at Ben, 'I should get this.'

'Sure, I better go check on the team anyway. We're finishing up here now. But remember, I meant what I said, okay.' He flashes me another smile.

I nod as he walks away and look at the caller ID: it's Addie. I stand up and duck out back towards the front gate, walking as fast as I can. It's time for me to get out of here. I answer the phone with a breathless, 'Hello.'

'Oh, thank goodness, I thought you wouldn't pick up.'

'What's going on?' I ask, confused.

‘Sorry, I didn’t want to barge in until you were ready, but I thought you’d want to hear this as soon as possible.’ She pauses as I scoot out into the street.

‘Hear what?’

Silence hits me on the other end.

‘What Rach had to say—’ She stops again.

I sigh. ‘Addie, come on – what is it? Just tell me.’ Rachel was one of Addie’s friends. I guess she’d been with the group that Addie said we’d met last night. But how is this important?

She lets out in a rush, ‘I spoke with Rach, and she knows what you did last night.’

I freeze so quickly that I almost trip over. My heart hammers so fast I’m certain it’s about to fly out of my chest. Heat instantly rises to my cheeks.

Because Addie does not sound calm, not at all.

No. She sounds utterly terrified.

Chapter Thirteen

'Can't you tell me on the phone?' I ask, my voice shaky. My vision spins.

'No, I'm sorry, Em. I have to talk to you in person. I just have to.'

So that's how I've ended up storming down to the edge of Raleigh Reserve to wait for Addie to show up.

The wind whips my tangled mass of hair around my face. Through the strands, I stare out at the turbulent ocean swell below. I feel like I'm stuck in those waves, frantically treading water and getting battered beneath again and again. Is this going to be my life from now on? Wave after wave of grief and uncertainty? What does Addie now know about what I did last night that I *don't*?

The reserve is empty for this time on a Saturday afternoon – but I guess the police tape and news vans have put people off their usual walks. That, and the unbearable wind that's started sweeping up off the cliff face.

I'm so lost in watching the frantic dance of the ocean that I don't hear any footsteps behind me.

'Em!' Addie says, and I swivel around to find she's only a matter of steps away from me now. She closes the distance in a few strides.

'Ads – what's going on?' I have a wildness to my words that match the erratic swell of the sea beyond.

She chews her lip, a frown spreading across her forehead. 'I wanted to see you in person to tell you – and to be here with you as well. It's a bit of a shock, and I didn't want you to go into a full-blown panic...'

I cross my arms over my chest as though to protect myself. I'm scared.

'Please, tell me,' I hear myself say.

And she nods once, understanding that whatever it is, I have to hear it. 'So you know how you asked me about those scratches and whether you tripped over or something when we were together?'

I nod through pursed lips.

'Well, I thought I'd be helpful and call around to see if anyone saw you fall.' I should have known – Addie has never been able to sit still. My slight annoyance at Addie's interference is squashed when she says, 'And I got onto Rach – and she has some answers...'

'What?'

'But they also lead to a lot more questions...' She crosses her arms over her chest, and I want to shake her.

'Come on, Addie,' I plead.

She looks at me with a steady expression. 'She said she found you outside the bar, trying to walk down the street, but then saw you fall over and cut yourself all down your side. She helped you up and realised you were probably too drunk to order an Uber for yourself. So she did it for you – and I couldn't believe it at first. But she sent you back here. To Dover Heights. She said you *insisted.*'

I stay silent. The wind plays havoc with my hair, slapping me in the face.

'But I said she must be wrong – because you ended up back in your hotel. Right, Ems?' she speaks softly, but I can sense the undercurrents of her meaning. She wants to know the truth.

I should give it to her.

The weight of her stare and its accusation causes my knees to buckle. I sink onto the patchy grass.

'Oh God, Ads,' I say through a shaky breath, burying my head in my hands. 'I'm sorry I didn't tell you.'

She must have sunk onto the ground next to me. Because when I look up, she's in front of me, her eyes wide with concern but also something else. Fear.

'You... you knew?' she says with a slight stammer. 'I-I thought I'd be telling you something you couldn't remember. That I could be here to help you figure out *what* happened and be here to support you in the shock.' She doesn't have to say it – I know what she's suggesting. Help me figure out if the time I was at Dover Heights could have crossed over with Mum's accident...

'I, well, I *didn't* remember anything – I still don't, really. But I looked at my Uber record this morning, and I saw that I came here to Dover Heights late last night – but then I left again. I only checked because I was trying to piece together my night, and I knew I promised I'd see Mum last night. And this morning, I thought I remembered a scream. I genuinely don't remember anything else, though – and I still can't.' A sob of frustration escapes. 'I'm so sorry I didn't tell you. I just – I just couldn't process. And I don't know what to do. Because... because...'

I tremble at what I'm about to say – at what I'll finally confess out loud to my best and oldest friend in the world.

‘What if I had something to do with it, Ads?’ I force myself to look up as I see her face contort in shock at my words. But I don’t stop. I continue doggedly as I ask the most awful question of all. ‘What if she’s dead… because of me?’

Chapter Fourteen

My terrible question punctures the gulf between us, but Addie doesn't flinch away. Instead, she takes my hands in hers.

'Emily Olsen,' she says seriously, forcing me to stare into her unblinking blue eyes. 'You are many things – but you are *not* a murderer. And I'm certain there's an explanation for everything.'

'But why did I come here last night? And why do I remember a scream?'

She shakes her head, and her fair hair tumbles down around her face. 'You're probably remembering your *own* scream when you fell over and cut yourself back in the city. Remember what Rachel told me about that? Your memories are all melding into one.'

I risk a tiny nod. Maybe she's right. Memory is a funny thing at the best of times – let alone when you've experienced an alcohol-induced blackout. The whole period becomes unreliable.

'And the police have looked all over the scene by now, right? What are they saying?' she asks.

'Well, that it's an accident – and they think it happened this morning, actually. I haven't had a chance to tell you that yet. But Glenn says that Mum went back to Merton Street last night and then came back here super early.'

'There we go!' Addie says in a happy voice, letting go of my hands now to sit cross-legged, facing me. The image reminds me of when we were kids at primary school, conferring over our latest plan for a silly game. But we're very much adults now – and what we are discussing isn't some game.

'No,' I say, wanting to correct her. But then have to admit, 'Well, yes. That's what the police think right now. But it still seems so ridiculous – because they say she'd decided to garden this morning *after* that storm. I know Mum – she would never think that would have been a good time to do that. Plus, I'm not entirely sure she did go back to Merton Street at all. Glenn's been so vague about it, and I discovered these messages on Mum's iPad that suggest they were fighting, maybe. I dunno...' I shrug. 'There are so many things about this that seem off to me. Not *just* what I might have done last night.' I say this in a rush without even pausing for breath.

'Emily,' Addie says in what must be her serious teacher voice.

My gaze had wandered off into the far distance as I'd lost myself in my jumbled thoughts. I fix it back onto her. 'Listen to me: you are in utter shock hearing that your mum's died in a tragic accident.' I try to protest, but she holds up a hand. 'No, please,' she says softly. I halt the words that had been on the tip of my tongue.

'It's only natural that you'll search for any explanation possible – even blaming yourself clearly – to try and explain how something so horrific could have happened.' She uncrosses her legs as she says this and rises onto her knees. She lays two hands on my shoulders. 'But you can't do this to yourself. You'll drive yourself senseless, chasing down things that aren't there. And I don't want to watch that happen. If the police are ruling it an accident, then that's all there is, okay. And you came here last night because even though you were drunk out of your mind, you knew deep down that you promised your mum you would. So you still came – it was instinct. You were the best and most dutiful daughter to the end.'

I realise with a sniff that I must be crying. I wipe my tears away. 'But,' I say stubbornly, not letting myself get swept into her explanation. It's not that simple – it can't be. 'I know Mum and Mike were fighting too. She received this mysterious letter, which is incredibly suspicious. *And* now, going to the house, I swear I remembered seeing a shadow of a person last night!'

Addie jumps up and walks a few steps away from me along the scratchy grass. She turns back to face me, her hands on her hips. I look up as she says in a pleading voice, 'Come *on*, you *have* to stop this. Can't you hear yourself? You're clutching at straws and chasing shadows that aren't there. None of this makes any sense.'

I know deep down that she's trying to help, but it's almost like she's slapped me. All I can see in her eyes now is pity – but tinged with exasperation. I love her for being there for me and not flinching away when I told her my deepest fear: that I could have killed my mother. But now her refusal to see how I might be thinking something else is up with Mum's death is making me feel small. And embarrassed.

My cheeks grow hot, and I'm sure I must be bright red. I feel like a child being told off.

But Addie isn't my teacher; she's my best friend. And I am a lawyer – I'll just explain it to her all over again. So I clamber to my feet to try one more time.

But then my phone starts ringing. I pull it out of my pocket and look down at the name.

Zara.

I answer it with shaky hands and say in a shallow voice, 'Hello?'

'Uh, Em,' I can hear the nervousness emanating from those two words even before she says, 'can you come home? Dad's discovered something – and well, it's not good. You better get back here quick.'

'What? Okay...'

'Hurry!' I hear a loud bang in the background, and she's gone.

I look up, startled, at Addie. Going over everything again can wait. 'I've got to go. Something's wrong.'

Chapter Fifteen

I rush through the unlocked front door, not waiting to be let in, and bellow down from the hallway, 'I'm here! What's wrong?'

Glenn appears at the top of the stairs. He looms like a dark cloud about to descend. 'Where is it?' he barks down at me as he bangs down the stairs, two at a time.

The appearance of this large, strong man thundering down the stairs towards me makes me shrink back, a little terrified.

Just as I think he's going to fly straight into me, he stops on the final step and demands, 'The iPad, Suzie's iPad. Where have you taken it?'

'What?' I repeat, not fully registering his words.

'It's gone from her study,' he retorts, scowling down at me.

'What?' I cry for a third time and repeat, 'It's gone?'

'Where have you put it?' He takes a threatening step closer to me, and I dart around him, pushing past to race up the stairs towards the study.

I have to see it for myself. And sure enough, where I'd left the iPad in the centre of the desk, there's now a blank space.

I turn around to face Glenn as he appears beside me. 'What's happened? Where is it?' I ask.

He crosses his arms. I know him well enough to understand that he thinks I am lying.

'I haven't taken it,' I protest. 'Why would I?'

His eyes narrow. 'Oh, I don't know, Emily, you seemed to enjoy snooping through all her conversations earlier. Why wouldn't you take it to go over everything later at a quiet moment?'

I'm so tired of his anger and accusations. I know he's just lost his wife, and he's looking for somewhere to direct his grief, but it can't be at me anymore. I square back up to him, crossing my arms to match his pose.

'Oh, and you don't think for a second that anyone else might have wanted to take it? How about Jennifer, Mike, or even you? What's your *problem* with me?'

He shrugs and turns away from me to hide his face. 'Well, when you're done doing whatever you're doing with it, can you bring it back?' With that, he stalks back down the stairs. I hear the front door slam, and I know he is gone.

I stand in front of the study and lean heavily against the door frame. My legs are wobbly, and I let myself slide down to the floor, curling my knees up below my chin. I sit there for a moment and hug myself into a ball, trying to take deep breaths and calm down the whooshing anger that echoes around my mind. As my heart rate calms, I consider what has happened.

So, Mum's iPad is missing, and Glenn thought *I'd* taken it. *That's* what Zara had called me back for? I shake my head. Daddy's little girl through and through – he asked her to get me back here, and I trusted her. Like a chump.

But it does make me pause.

Because someone has stolen it.

I rub my temples as an awful realisation comes to my mind. Why *would* anyone steal it?

Only if they had something to hide.

And if it's not Glenn or me who stole the iPad, then there's only one other person who knows about what I found on there.

Mike.

It feels like a knife has twisted deep inside my chest. He must have known that there was some other damning evidence. Something that I hadn't found – yet. And he wanted to take it before I had another chance to. I'm suddenly sure that it's also no accident that Mum's iPhone hasn't been found. Ben said they suspected it had washed out to sea when she'd fallen or landed. But what if it hadn't? What if it had been taken, too?

The iPad had been the only electronic item left that could have stored whatever it was that Mike didn't want to be found. I know Mum had left her laptop behind in the office because she'd told me so yesterday, but I'm sure he'd already got to that.

I think back to the controlled but undeniable panic in Mike's eyes when I brought up the email and messages and his vehement denial that he'd seen Mum last night.

A sinking feeling settles in my stomach as I realise Mike must have been lying. That both Mike *and* Jennifer were lying – because she corroborated his alibi that the two of them were together last night. But really, something *must* have happened between Mum and Mike. Something that Mike doesn't want anyone to know.

I shove a hand into my pocket and breathe a sigh of relief. The strange anonymous letter is still there – thank God I hadn't replaced it back onto the desk. It might be the key to everything. Taking it out, I scan through its contents once more.

Could whatever Mum had uncovered been something so bad that it could have led to her death, could have led to... murder? I shudder at the thought, but I have to name it.

I curl my long hair back from my face and up into a high ponytail, tying it tight with the elastic on my wrist as I trace back over all the events I know for certain.

The iPad being stolen, the shadow at Dover Heights, the scream I remember... they can't all be a coincidence. Someone else was still at Dover Heights late last night. And maybe – just maybe – rather than me being involved, was I actually a witness to Mum's death – Mum's *murder*, by Mike's hands?

But Glenn had said that she'd stayed here last night. At Merton Street. So what *did* I see then? Or is Glenn trying to cover something up... could he be in on all this as well?

My head is spinning at all the possibilities, at all the lies and secrets closing tight around me. I can hardly breathe.

Someone in this family knows what really happened to Mum. And I am going to find out who.

But I have to be careful.

Because if it is Mike – and he realises that I'm onto him – then there's only one logical conclusion.

I'd be next.

Chapter Sixteen

I raise my chin to the sky and let the morning sun warm my face. As I sit on this small park bench waiting for Sergeant Ben White to arrive, I recall how bizarre it had been calling him up last night after all this time.

Even though he'd given me his number, I could only think about the little freckly, bespectacled fourteen-year-old boy who I'd had my first kiss with. And the horrible way I'd broke up with him out of the blue a year later. I couldn't reconcile that heartbroken boy with the confident police officer I'd met.

But I knew whatever my awkward feelings I had to make the call – he'd offered to help. And I was feeling way out of my depth.

After I'd patched myself back together in Mum's study, I'd pulled his card out of my pocket and tried to call him. He hadn't answered, so I'd left a brief message.

Zara must have heard my voice because she'd popped her head through the office door. 'Hey, I've got pizza,' she'd said before swooping down to sit next to where I was crumpled on the floor.

She'd put her arm around me tight. 'I'm so sorry about Dad. He didn't tell me what it was, just to call you and get you back here. If I'd known how angry he was going to be—' She'd shaken her head, 'I can't do anything right when it comes to you, Em.'

I softened at that and responded with, 'Pizza, you say?'

She smiled. I hadn't realised how hungry and tired I was until then. I'd been running off adrenalin since I'd woken up, and I needed a break.

As Zara and I tried to chew on some slices, she asked if I'd stay here with them. I agreed. I'd already taken my bags from Addie's car when I'd left her earlier. I'd realised that it was too late to arrange accommodation elsewhere for that night anyway – and besides, it would also mean I could keep an eye on Glenn and do some more searching around the house.

Even though everything pointed towards Mike stealing the iPad, I still couldn't shake the text messages I'd read earlier between Mum and Glenn – and his erratic behaviour towards me. It was even more hostile than usual, which could be deep grief, and seeing me kept reminding him of what he'd lost – or it could be something else. Something like guilt.

Once I settled into the spare room – any trace of my 'childhood' bedroom in this house had been erased long ago – I even managed to bang out a quick message to my boss back in London to let them know what was going on. I was technically on holiday but decided I should give them a heads-up and go down the official channels to get signed off on compassionate leave.

Finally, as I was about to slip beneath the sheets, my phone rang.

'Hello, Ben White here,' he said formally.

'Oh yes, hi, Ben,' I replied. I'd been tired to the bone, but now I was wired. 'It's Emily Olsen. You said to call if I needed to speak with you...'

'Of course... what can I do?'

'Thank you... Look, I think something might have happened that you should know about. Can we meet in person?' I spoke quickly before I lost my nerve.

He hesitated for a moment – this probably wasn't regular protocol – and then replied, 'Okay, how about first thing tomorrow morning?'

I'd agreed, and we'd decided to meet here, at Blues Park.

What would he make of the stolen iPad – and would it make him rethink the assumption that Mum's phone had been washed away...?

As I wait, I watch the boats milling around on the harbour in front of me and stare up at the yawning arch of the Sydney Harbour Bridge. For just a moment, I pretend that none of this is happening, that I am just enjoying some time in the sun with my family and friends, escaping the deep darkness and cold of winter in the UK.

Who knows how much time has passed when a shadow crosses my face and I hear, 'Emily?'

My eyes fly open to see a tall, muscular man in blue shorts and a casual white T-shirt standing above me. His hair looks even fairer than yesterday in the sunshine, and the slight breeze coming from the harbour ruffles it, making him look like he's stepped from the pages of a *Vanity Fair* shoot. He looks very different out of his uniform: more relaxed and gentle.

'Yes, hi!' I say, trying to inject some lightness into my voice, though I don't know how to be bright anymore. I jump up, smoothing my crumpled sky-blue linen jumpsuit down my front. It was the first thing I'd found in my bag this morning, and I hadn't bothered with the iron. What was the point?

I tuck a stray strand of hair behind my ear and stick out a hand, going into my default client meeting mode as the only way to try and maintain any semblance of regular behaviour. He frowns but puts his hand out. As we shake, I feel his grip tighten.

And it occurs to me as we touch that my hands are slick with a light sweat. I pull it back as quickly as I'd thrown it out.

'Thank you so much for coming to meet me on your time off,' I say.

'Of course,' he says, moving to sit next to me on the bench as I sit back down too. 'It's good to see you again; I just wish it wasn't in these circumstances. I'm so sorry again about your mum.'

I nod towards him, grateful for his kind words. 'Me too,' I reply in a soft voice.

'And I'm really glad you called me.'

'Well, I'm glad it was you there yesterday,' I admit, and I manage a weak smile that he returns.

'Seriously – if I can help in any way, I'm here,' he says, and I can see he means it.

Close up, I'm struck by how this boy has changed into a man. I can still see the foundations of the face I remembered from childhood, but they've been built upon by time. I notice the little lines on his forehead and around his eyes, as well as the stubble around his jaw. While familiar, it feels so strange to see him again, but I guess that's everything in my life now – familiar settings and people, and yet everything I'd ever known has completely changed.

I decide to cut to the chase. 'So, Mum's iPad has been stolen.'

'Pardon?' he says, jolting upright in his seat and turning to look at me with a forensic stare. 'That hasn't been reported – when did this happen?'

'Yesterday afternoon or early evening – I'm not sure—'

'Right,' he says, interrupting. 'Do you think someone broke in? You should have called me in an official capacity, or 000. Someone would have come to investigate.'

'Well, that's why I wanted to see you one-on-one. The thing is... I think someone in my family may have stolen it.'

He frowns at my words. It's a big accusation to make – we both know that. But I go on. I tell Ben exactly what happened yesterday and about the strange letter and messages I discovered. I'm scared he might tell me I'm imagining things like Addie basically did when I confided my deepest fears to her. I chew on my lip as I wait for him to deliver his verdict. I hope I haven't misplaced my trust.

He cocks his head to one side as though thinking through my words and then says, 'I can see your concern, but—' and there it is already, his doubt shining through. Have I made a big mistake? 'That isn't much to go on. And,' he adds gently, 'do you think there's a possibility that your uncle might also be in a state of confusion? He's lost his friend and business partner.'

'Maybe,' I snap, kicking at the hard grass beneath my feet. I don't want to get mad at Ben, but I am starting to feel frustrated – especially after what happened with Addie. 'Sorry, I really appreciate your thoughts. It just seems weird to me.'

He runs his hands through his thick hair. 'I can understand, and I think it's important to follow an instinct, but it's also crucial to determine where that instinct is coming from.'

This sort of makes sense – he is delicately suggesting that I should examine whether this might be my grief talking. *Like Addie was trying to say yesterday*, I admit to myself.

'Well,' I say, redirecting my energies, 'I think it's something worth looking into – especially the strange letter Mum had received. That can't all be a coincidence, can it?' Then, finally, I ask the question I came here for. 'Will you help me look into all this?'

He sighs. 'Speaking as Senior Sergeant Ben White, I wish I could say yes, but unfortunately, without going through the official channels, it is difficult. And even if you did report this, there was no sign of a break-in, so it would be impossible for us to investigate on that alone.' He shrugs and looks apologetic. 'I also don't think we would necessarily look at this in conjunction with what's happened to your mum... Like I said, everything at the scene looks like she was the only one there. It would be very hard for me to convince anyone otherwise.'

My shoulders sag in disappointment, and my head drops until he goes on. 'But – show me the letter. Maybe I can do some digging. Unofficially, of course.'

I snap my head up to face him. 'Oh, Ben, that would be amazing.' He's not dismissing my concerns and still wants to help – he is just being practical about what the official channels will let him do.

I pull the now-crumpled letter out of my pocket, hesitating for a second before thrusting it into his waiting hand. I follow his eyes with mine as he scans the page. His face doesn't betray any emotion until he looks up.

'Who's Felicity Smith?' He looks at me quizzically.

'I'm not sure – that's something I need to find out. Do you think you could help with that, too?' My voice squeaks at the end of my question in hope and desperation.

He looks around us to make sure no one is close by. In the distance, children play, and parents stand idly by, chatting. 'I'll see what I can do – but I can't promise anything.'

'Thank you.' I appreciate his honesty; other than Addie, it's felt like the first honesty I've received since this nightmare began.

'Look,' he says, glancing at his watch, 'I'm so sorry, but I have to head into work now – but if I find anything out, I'll let you know.'

I thank him again as he stands and starts to walk away, his footsteps crunching on the grass. He cuts a striking picture: tall, broad shoulders and purposeful stride against the backdrop of the sparkling blue harbour.

'Hey, Ben,' I call him back, and he turns around. One more question has occurred to me. 'When will we be able to know the time of death?'

He takes a few steps back towards me, and I can see that he's thinking over his answer. 'Well, when the coroner's report comes in. But I should warn you that the *exact* time of death is notoriously tricky – especially because she was found in the water. So, they'll try to use first-hand accounts to help. I haven't actually seen the body myself; the very first officers on the scene dealt with all of that and reported back. But I know that the coroners will do their best to get as exact a time and clear a cause of death as possible. Why?' His brows furrow into a deep V.

I want to tell him that I don't believe Glenn about Mum staying at Merton Street last night – but I don't have any proof. The text messages might sound like a fight, but they're not enough. And Zara said Mum was at Merton Street last night, too. So, all I have is a suspicion deep in my gut. And I know that's not enough. Until I do have anything – if I ever do – I don't want Ben to dismiss all my other concerns by going one step too far now. Not when he's just agreed to help me unofficially.

'I think knowing that will help me process everything.' It's not a lie.

'Sure.' He nods in understanding. 'But like I said, it's going to be quite difficult because of the conditions. We have to rely on everything else we can gather, too. I'll let you know if anything comes up.'

'Thank you – for everything.'

He turns again back up the path with a wave. Around him, joggers run by, and children play on the edges of the water. If only I could be having a normal day like the rest of them.

Instead, I bring my knees into my chest and reflect on our conversation. I'd been secretly hopeful that an exact time of death would help me determine once and for all whether Glenn was telling the truth. Maybe it still can.

I let out a slow exhale and shake all the clamouring thoughts out of my head. I focus on the present: Ben is going to start helping me track down Felicity Smith. And I need to find some proof – anything that will give Mike a clear motive for stealing the iPad and being involved in Mum's death.

The only tricky thing is that I'm going to have to break into a building to get it.

And *that* is something I certainly don't want Ben to know.

Chapter Seventeen

I look up at the towering skyscraper in front of me. It's bizarre being back here – I haven't been to Mum's offices for such a long time. And seeing as Harry – my ex and Zara's now boyfriend – worked here, I'd had zero desire to ever enter it again. Not until now.

I take a deep breath as I steel myself for what I need to do. If anyone asks me, I am picking up some of Mum's belongings. Ideally, I won't run into anyone while I do my digging, though.

It's a Sunday, so I'm betting no one will be around. I have Mum's key card, which I'd swiped from her desk drawer this morning before I'd left to meet Ben.

On the way over, Addie had tried to call me. I'd seen a message from her earlier asking me how I was doing, and I'd sent her a quick text back saying I'd call her later, but I still haven't, so I guess she is checking in. I feel a little bad for ignoring her, especially after everything she tried to do for me yesterday. But I have already lied to her once since Mum died, and I don't want to lie again.

Plus, after how our conversation abruptly ended yesterday, I know she would not approve of my secret mission. I don't want her to talk me out of it. I'll call her back later when I hopefully have some proof, and then she'll have no choice but to believe me.

I take a deep breath and scan Mum's pass to open the doors, relieved to see there's no one at the security desk. I present the pass again to call the elevator to take me up to the fifteenth floor. As the doors slide closed behind me, I glance at my reflection in the mirror, studying this new me.

Everything is the same on the surface, and yet I've changed irreversibly.

Just a few days ago, if you'd told me that I'd be breaking into buildings trying to discover evidence of suspicious circumstances surrounding my mum's death, I would never have believed it. And yet, here I am.

Maybe I am acting irrationally like Addie thinks, but getting to the bottom of what happened to my mum is the only thing stopping me from collapsing into crushing grief.

I stare at my reflection in the elevator mirror: my long auburn hair is pulled back from my face into a high ponytail, and dark rings circle my cloudy eyes. I barely slept last night, the scream haunting my dreams. I'm looking at a shadow of myself.

The doors slide open to reveal the Imaginate branding. A memory of the first time I met my ex, Harry, in these halls jumps into my mind. I push that thought aside – I haven't talked to Zara properly about her and Harry yet, and I can't let that distract me now. Zara and I have established a fragile peace that I'd like to hold onto.

I walk past the welcome desk and around the back to the open-plan centre. The everyday paraphernalia of office life is strewn around – printers, pens, papers.

I move towards my mum's desk on autopilot. It is in the corner near the window, so she could look out across the skyline and down into the park whenever she needed to think through a campaign. There is a little photo of the four of us from my graduation.

We actually look happy here – Mum, Glenn, Zara and me. Like a proper family. After I'd worked through my issues with Mum and Glenn, and especially once I went off to university and wasn't living in the same house anymore, we'd all even been close for a while. Well, as close as we could be.

But I can't reconcile the Glenn in this photo with the one I am seeing now. The Glenn I've seen since the fallout with Zara, and since I decided to take the job in the UK. Maybe I'd imagined this other Glenn. I sigh, my heart breaking a little bit more, and place the photo back down, trying to refocus on why I'm here.

I rifle through the piles of papers and designs that are stacked haphazardly on the desk. Her laptop is nowhere to be seen. But maybe I can find something else here. Or hopefully at Mike's desk... From the letter, it's clear that something was going on at Imaginate.

The ding of the lift doors interrupts my thoughts.

I dive off the chair and under the large white desk as fast as I can. I curl up, and a twinge of pain twists in my knees from the uncomfortable angle. Heavy footsteps thump my way, and my heart beats faster.

I try and minimise my breathing to nothing at all, though I'm convinced the person will be able to hear my heart pounding anyway.

Please don't find me. Please don't find me...

The footsteps keep coming closer and closer, and then they're so loud I'm sure they must be right in front of me.

Oh god. What if it's Mike – and he knows I'm on to him? What if he's here to kill me too?

The footsteps stop and I hold my breath even tighter.

This is it. This is the moment I'm found.

A desk rattles in front of me as though the person is systematically searching through a drawer.

I silently twist and drop my head down so I can peer through the small gap between the desk and the floor.

I can't see their face, but the person is at the desk diagonally opposite, frantically looking for something, judging by the sound they're making.

Bright white tennis trainers; strong, stocky legs; a too-tight athletic top.

I'd recognise the back of that head and those obnoxious shoes anywhere. It's him. Mike.

But he hasn't dragged me out from under the table. So he mustn't know that I'm here. Yet.

A phone rings, and for a second, I panic that it's mine. But then I hear Mike's lazy drawl.

'Hi, sweet angel.' A pause. 'Yes, I'll be there soon – I just had to clear up a loose end on the way.' Another pause. 'Don't worry – everything is taken care of, okay. No one's going to find out.' Another jangle of the desk drawer and a sigh of relief. 'Yes, I've got it now, so I'll be there soon. Love you too, my Bel Bear.'

A pain in my leg is starting to grow, and I chance a small movement. I bang my knee into the iron corner of the desk, and I let out a muffled cry as he hangs up the phone. From under the table, I see his body turn away from the desk he'd been facing and towards my hiding place. *Oh god, he's heard me.*

I clamp my mouth shut and hold my breath. *Please turn around. Please turn around.* I beg silently.

But his feet start moving closer, one slow and measured step at a time.

My palms are hot and slippery. He must have heard me...

His shoes stop mere centimetres away from my face. Any second, he's going to throw the desk off and pull me out, kicking and screaming. My heart beats faster and faster.

But he doesn't budge. He stands there in the deafening silence.

I tense, waiting. Whatever happens, I'm not going down without a fight.

The next thing I hear is his disembodied voice above me, as though he's speaking to the desk. Mum's empty desk.

'Oh, Suze,' he says with a sigh. 'I'm so sorry about what happened. But I do wish you hadn't gone digging...'

Oh my god. It was him.

Chapter Eighteen

Everything clicks into place. Because with no one around to hear him, he has whispered this confession into the air.

But he's not truly alone. I'm here.

And now my frightened mind screams out one unending thought over and over again...

It was him. It was him!

There's a blurry flash of white as his feet turn around and walk towards the elevator. It dings, and I wait for a few more moments in the silence to make sure he is gone. I let out a huge exhale.

I emerge from under the desk, stretching out my protesting limbs, and try to stamp the pins and needles out of my foot. My first thought is relief that I wasn't caught.

The next: terror at Mike's words. Those few casual words spoken aloud, probably to the very photograph I was just looking at, have shaken me to my core. That whispered apology to Mum's photo proves he's guilty.

Weaving in and out of the desks, I look down at the one Mike had been sifting through: his own. And one of the drawers is ajar. I pull it and look inside – it's full of tiny USBs, and as I dig around, the sound is exactly like Mike's rummaging.

I know the USB I want, the one that would contain any useful information, won't be here anymore. Mike would have come here to take it away. The last shred of evidence.

But even though I missed that, I know it wasn't a wasted journey. I'm now more convinced than ever that I'm on the right track. And that Mum's death wasn't a mere accident.

I'd also overheard Mike talking to someone else who must be in on it. From the romantic bent of the conversation, at first I'd thought it was Jennifer. But 'Bel Bear' would be a strange nickname for Jennifer. *Could* it have been someone else? Mike is keeping far too many secrets to keep track of. And uncovering them will be the key.

I slip my hand into my pocket and study the mysterious letter for the thousandth time.

Tucking it safely back inside, I begin a slow walk towards the exit with one focus only in my head: I have to find Felicity Smith. She is the missing piece to unlocking everything.

I slip back into the safety of the car and drive on autopilot. Even though it's only been one day, and I've only become convinced of Mike's guilt recently, I feel like my time is running out to prove it. He's so successfully tricked everyone.

As I drive on, Addie's number flashes up on the hands free. I hesitate. Panic at Mike's incriminating words continues to override all my rational thoughts. But then I force myself to answer. I can't ignore her forever. She doesn't deserve that – she was just trying to look after me yesterday.

'Hello, Ems?' she sounds relieved, as though she'd been waiting by the phone for me to call.

Guilt runs through me. 'Hey, Ads, I'm sorry for the slow response. It's all been a little full on.' This isn't a lie, after all. But I feel bad that I hadn't let her know what happened yesterday. She must have been so worried.

'Don't apologise, just wanted you to know I'm here if you need me.' She pauses, and my chest tightens at how nice it is to hear those words.

'Thank you, Ads, I know…'

'So, what happened when you got back?' she asks with a small quaver in her voice.

I hesitate once more and hear myself say, 'Oh, only Zara being dramatic – it's fine.'

She hmms down the phone, and I can sense she's about to ask another question. But I can't talk to her any longer – not without wanting to tell her everything, and I can't risk her trying to persuade me out of it again.

'Ads, I have to go now, but I'll talk to you soon, okay – thanks for calling.' I try not to choke and hang up quickly.

Shame courses through me at my deception, and I want to scream in frustration. These days, as a successful lawyer in London, I'm normally a cool, calm and collected person, someone a million miles away from the angry and volatile teenager I'd been. But with the horrible uncertainty of Mum's death, I don't seem to be able to think straight anymore.

I remember reading somewhere that when a moment of tragedy occurs, you don't have the luxury of panic until afterwards – and I'm starting to feel like I'm dangerously close to the precipice of utter panic. I need to stop that from happening.

I pull myself together as I drive back towards Merton Street. I have to push past any lingering feelings of guilt about keeping things from Addie – and focus on who I need help from next.

And it's someone I had hoped never to speak to again. Or at least not for a very long time.

My ex, Harry. The man who caused this rift between Zara and me in the first place.

The idea of asking him for help makes me feel nauseous. But I have to. I have to because Harry worked in Mike's team – and if anyone is likely to know or remember anything about Felicity Smith, it's him.

Getting him to talk freely would be another matter. And there's only one way to do it: through Zara, his girlfriend. She can spin anyone around her little finger, and I know that she's the only person who could wheedle it out of him.

Can I trust her, though? It's a risk I'm going to have to take...

Chapter Nineteen

'So, let me get this straight.' Zara frowns at me from the hammock in the garden she's swinging in. 'You think Mike stole Suzie's iPad, and not only that, but that he's hiding a tonne of stuff to do with Imaginate from us – and possibly, very possibly, he might have had something to do with the accident? *Or* maybe it wasn't even an accident at all?'

I nod slowly – when she says it like that, it does sound absurd. This is exactly why I was scared to tell Addie. Addie is so logical, and she always sees the best in everyone.

But Zara understands our complicated family relations – so if anyone can get where I am coming from, I'm betting it's her.

She swings her feet out of the hammock. 'Right, where do we start?'

I blink in a daze down at this petite force of nature. With her hair back in her natural ringlets, she looks so delicate – though I know she's anything but.

'I – uh – you mean you'll help?' There was a part of me that thought Zara would reject me and think I was delusional. But she seems to accept my thought process completely. Too quickly? I can't second-guess everyone, though...

'Yes, of course,' she says, grabbing my arm. 'I've been thinking something was off with Mike for *months*. And Jennifer has been acting weird with me, too.' I frown at that admission. Zara and Jennifer had always been thick as thieves – if I'm being entirely honest, I've even been a little jealous of their easy aunt/niece dynamic. I never had that.

Jennifer had stepped in to support Zara in a big way after her mum had run off with her yoga instructor when Zara was seven. Since then, Zara had had little contact with her mum, who'd moved to the other side of Australia. So, I guess Jennifer was a bit like a mother figure to her. I'd never come across a time when they weren't close.

'Oh really?' I say, frowning. 'Do you think it has something to do with Mike or Imaginate?'

'Maybe.' She shrugs. 'She hasn't told me anything. But lately, she keeps cancelling on me, and every time we end up alone, she practically sprints out of the room. There's definitely something she's hiding from me.

'And maybe this is it – normally, I can read her like a book. So it must be something *big*. But I can't see her wanting to hurt Suzie. I know they had their differences, but Jennifer doesn't have a bad bone in her body. She's never said anything against Suzie, I promise you. Though if Mike asked her to keep a secret about something, I do think she would. Hmm...' She taps the side of her face as she starts to pace up and down the garden. 'If Mike stole the iPad, then, as you say, he must have something to hide. It makes you wonder if he did see Suzie that night after all...'

'That's exactly right.' And because of how much Zara seems to get it, I decide to tell her about sneaking into the office as well, and what I overheard.

'Oh my god, Em!' She doesn't sound judgemental – if anything, she sounds a little impressed. 'I didn't know you had that in you anymore. I thought you were a goody two-shoes lawyer. Also, you're right – that is a seriously creepy thing to say. God, I can't believe he'd hurt her...'

I'm relieved she believes me. 'You know I'm not one to give up on anything easily. And I can't leave this alone.'

She nods. 'Oh, I know – but seriously, that sort of trick sounds more like me and less like you!'

'Whatever,' I say, trying to keep us on track. I clear my throat at the awkward question I'm going to have to ask her. 'I think you know who I'm going to ask you to call about this – because we need someone with inside access.'

The tips of her high cheekbones colour a little as we both realise this is the first time I've referred to Harry.

She nods again. 'Yes, yes, I can do that. I'll see what—' She coughs. '*He* can tell us about it, and if he knows a Felicity Smith. Leave it with me.'

'Okay,' I say, trying to diffuse the awkward moment. Because honestly, I've also realised that I don't care anymore. What Zara did behind my back hurt at the time – but not really because of Harry. No, I knew that our relationship was long over, even before all that. As Mum had reminded me, *we were on a break*.

But it had hurt so deeply because it had broken something between Zara and me. That implicit sisterly trust that we'd grown over the years.

And that's what had wounded me most – that she hadn't told me and that she couldn't properly say sorry at the time. But now she's apologised and is trying to help me. Has she truly grown up? Can we put it in the past, after all?

'Thanks,' I add. 'Why don't you do that, and I'll make a start seeing if I can find anything else I might have missed in Mum's office?'

I'm not holding out much hope, but I at least have to try. Especially whilst Glenn is out of the house. He wouldn't approve or even believe me if I told him what I'd overheard today. He'd go straight to Mike to ask him for the 'facts' – and I couldn't afford for that to happen. Not if my life could be on the line. I was putting a huge amount of trust in Zara sharing what I'd heard with her – hoping that this would be one thing she wouldn't tell her dad.

'Yes, I'll meet you up there,' she agrees. And with that, I turn away from her and back towards the large glass expanse of the back doors.

I hear Zara say hello in a light, almost giggly tone, and I pick up my speed. I might be coming to terms with the whole thing, but it doesn't mean I have to listen to her being all cute.

My feet crunch on the pebbles in front of the glass doors, and Banjo follows behind me as I slip inside. I don't pause to give him any attention, racing through the living room and towards the stairs as quickly as I can. Who knows when Glenn might get back...

I take the stairs two at a time and finally make it into the office. I'm hit by the scent of lavender and eucalyptus once more, and all I can think of is Mum. The countless times I'd popped up here to check on her or bring her a cup of tea. Never again.

I shake my head. I have to get going. Everything looks exactly as it did yesterday – but I begin rifling through drawers, looking for any scrap of paper that might refer to a 'Felicity'. I come up with nothing.

Next, I whip out my phone as I lean against the desk. I begin to google 'Felicity Smith' and various iterations of 'Imaginate', but nothing useful comes up.

I return to searching the drawers again, in desperate hope I might have missed something. I'm sweating from the exertion by the time the door opens, and there stands Zara as pristine as ever.

But instead of the open expression that had been on her face barely ten minutes ago, she looks sombre and concerned.

'Hey,' she says, stepping into the room as she closes the door with a gentle click behind her. 'Do you want to sit down?' I'm confused by her question and soft voice – it's like she's approaching a wild animal.

'I'm fine,' I say, standing up even straighter. I don't want to be treated like I'm on the edge of a collapse. Even if it's true.

She shrugs and leans against the door, crossing her arms. The gesture is almost threatening if it wasn't for the uncertainty etched along her face.

'So,' she begins, 'I spoke to Harry.'

'Yes, and...?' I flop down onto the desk chair, swivelling around to face her. Suddenly, I am exhausted, and there's an edge to Zara's voice I don't like.

But she walks away from the door and sits down in front of me on the fraying edges of Mum's favourite antique rug. She tucks her knees into her chest, wrapping her arms around herself. She appears so innocent, looking up at me. I wonder if I've imagined her attitude.

'Look, Ems,' she says again, avoiding my gaze as she picks on a straying strand of the rug. 'Harry says he *does* remember a Felicity Smith – she was one of their accountants not that long ago. But she came and went in the blink of an eye.'

'Well, there we are! Doesn't that sound exactly like she was fired for some suspicious reason?'

She shakes her head at the floor. 'Well, no – as you know, Harry is an analyst in Mike's team, and long story short, it's quite a normal explanation. She was let go for incompetence. Apparently, she made a series of expensive mistakes for the company...'

'What! Really?' I stand up from where I'd been swivelling and sit down in front of Zara, where the rug meets the hard wooden floor. I want to force her to tell me the rest of the story to my face.

She reluctantly meets my gaze and says, 'Yeah, I know. He was shocked when I mentioned her name.'

I nod but ask, 'So why didn't everyone at the company know about it? The letter makes it sound like it was completely hushed up – and that Mum didn't know about it either.'

'Well, Em – Harry made a good point: you don't normally broadcast this sort of thing to everyone in the office. And between you and me, he did say that she'd denied it at first but later admitted she'd made a huge mistake. Mike decided they'd let her go discreetly rather than ruin her whole career over it.'

'Hmm,' I wonder out loud and start to tap the edges of the chestnut floor. 'But don't you think it's suspicious that Mum got sent an anonymous letter telling her to look into Felicity Smith, and then Mike was taking stuff secretly from the office today? Not to mention what I heard him whisper – the day after Mum's death!'

Zara continues to look anywhere but at me as she presses her lips together. Quietly, she says, 'Well, we don't know what he was taking from the office today. Also, it's his office – so he has every right to be there.'

My eyes go wide. She's done a complete one-eighty after talking to Harry. So I ignore her and stay calm, trying to fight back with logic. 'Shouldn't Mum have known about what happened with Felicity anyway?'

'Well...' She hesitates for a second before saying, 'Harry said that she did know.'

I frown. 'What, really?!' I was so certain that Mum didn't know about her, and now... 'Well, he must be lying!' I say, almost to myself – but I realise I've said it out loud when Zara shoots up onto her feet.

'Hey! No, he's not – why would he lie?'

'I don't know, Zara,' I say in exasperation, jumping up to stand in front of her. 'Maybe he's in on everything.'

She steps back in shock. 'Don't accuse him of that!'

'You're right – I'm sorry,' I say quickly. 'I was so sure... but,' I go on, thinking out loud as I begin to pace around the room, 'even if Mum *did* know about it at the time, receiving a letter like that would have made her reconsider Mike's version of events. Maybe that's what she wanted to talk to him about so urgently... and then she must have discovered something that he had to cover up. That *must* be it – don't you think?' I stop on my heels and turn to face her, expecting full agreement.

Instead, I see her shake her head in concern.

I step towards her and grab her arm, forcing her to look at me. 'What, you don't think so?' She bites her lip and looks away. 'Come on – what is it?'

'I'm worried about you, Em!' she bursts out. 'So is Harry. And from everything he said, it doesn't sound like anything secret *has* been going on. Suzie knew about Felicity, and maybe the letter was from Felicity herself, trying to cause trouble. And well, like I said, it's pretty normal that Mike went to his own office today – and maybe you misinterpreted the threatening thing you thought you heard him say too...'

My mouth drops open, but she continues looking at me with a determination I've rarely seen in her.

'Do you think there's a chance that you're trying to see things that aren't there because you want to avoid facing up to the truth – that it was an awful accident?'

It's like she's punched me in the stomach.

'What the hell, Zara?!' I fly to the other side of the room. I can't stand to be close to her for a second longer. 'Barely ten minutes ago, you were on my side, offering to help me. And now, after one tiny conversation with Harry, you think I'm imagining things?'

'What? No, Em – I'm on your side always.' She takes a step towards me. I take another back. 'It's not only Harry – talking it through with him after he explained everything made us both think the same way. We're worried about you. And I can totally see why you're seeing things this way – it's only natural for you to try and find a reason other than it being a stupid accident. After what you went through with your dad disappearing when you were a kid, I get it—'

She tries to reach for me, but I press myself against the looming bookshelf. She backs away.

'Don't bring Dad up.' I try to say it calmly, but it comes out all wobbly. 'What happened to him has nothing to do with how I'm reacting to this. There *is* something suspicious here. I know it!' I throw my hands up in exasperation, and she looks at me with patience and sorrow in her deep blue eyes. I want to chuck a book at her. I don't want pity – I want her to help me. But I can see it's a losing battle.

'It doesn't matter. You've obviously made up your mind to believe that stupid man – and well, it's not exactly the first time you've chosen him over me, so hey, I shouldn't be surprised.' A bitter laugh leaves my lips.

I know I've gone too far when Zara's face flushes bright red and her nostrils flare. 'That's not the situation and you know it.' I turn away from her towards the shelf. A photo of Mum and I catches my eye. It's a photo of us from right after we'd finished the City to Surf fourteen-kilometre running race. I was about twenty-one, and we'd wanted to run it in memory of Dad. We both hated running, but we'd got up, we'd practised, and together, we'd managed to cross the finish line. The photo is of us at the end of the race on Bondi Beach – smiling broadly, medals around our necks and our arms around each other. We'd been a team – and I'm not going to give up on her now.

'Look, I really do want to help you, Em. But chasing after Felicity, Mike and whoever else isn't going to bring her back.'

I trace the outline of the photograph with my finger. Dust gathers on the edges and leaves a smudgy trail across our smiling faces. 'Maybe not,' I manage to say in a voice so quiet I'm not sure if Zara can even hear it. 'But I have to try.'

A step sounds towards me, but I say, 'Please, can you leave me alone for a minute?' My voice is soft - the anger is gone. All that's left is grief and uncertainty.

'Of course,' I hear her say alongside the tap of her footsteps on the floor. 'Just think about what we've said, okay? Maybe it's time to put it to one side. And when you do, I'll be here.'

I nod, pretending to agree. Then the door closes and finally, I am alone.

But I don't agree. Not at all.

Because what Zara doesn't realise is that this isn't the first time some accountant has messed up and been fired at Imaginate. No, hearing this story from Harry has the distinct echoes of another one he'd told me about a few years ago – of another young woman, fired for the same reason.

I shake my head. Harry 'Mr Nice Guy' Andrews – athletic, charismatic, confident. Harry, who'd been devastated by our break but equally, didn't waste any time making a move on my baby sister. Harry, who it now seems is possibly in on whatever Mike has been up to all this time and is pulling the wool over Zara's eyes...

I finish dusting down the photograph, take it in my hand off the shelf, and wrap it close to my chest.

First Glenn, then Mike, now Harry. I'm seeing liars everywhere. Maybe Addie and Zara are right, and it's all in my head. But it might not be...

And if Harry was involved in what happened to Mum, then he will wish he'd never been born.

Now, that is a promise.

Chapter Twenty

The fan above the bed whirs on and on, trying to cool down my sticky body. I've only just woken up, but it's stiflingly hot already – the weather forecast for today predicts a scorcher. I try not to imagine the beach day Mum and I would have had if we'd been given the chance. I turn my mind over to my life back in London instead. It seems like an entire world away. I haven't told any of my new friends what has happened yet. I have no idea how to. I can't stomach the idea of calling them out of the blue with news like this. Especially when I'm still not sure exactly *what* happened yet.

I wish I could turn back time, back to a month ago when I was still there. Before this nightmare.

I don't have too many close friends yet – it had been hard to break into the London circles, and seeing as I am busy working 24/7, I don't have a lot of time for socialising. But I'd become good friends with some of my work colleagues, Rhiannon and Lucy in particular.

Rhiannon had even been so generous as to invite me to spend Christmas with her family back in Wales when she heard that I couldn't get back to Australia until January. She'd been horrified when I'd admitted I was planning on having a day at home in my tiny flat, watching

Christmas movies in my pyjamas. When she'd insisted for the thousandth time, I'd finally agreed. And that's how I found myself singing carols in Welsh for the first time in my life and learning how to say '*Nadolig Llawen*' to all her family – Welsh for 'Merry Christmas'.

It had been my first cold-weather Christmas, and I would never forget their kindness involving me in every small detail, from helping her mum cook a traditional British roast with *all* the trimmings to her dad showing me the incredible beauty of the North Welsh coast. The salty sea air had reinvigorated me after a stressful year, and on a sunny day, the beach paths that hugged the coastline even reminded me of some patches of walks along Sydney Harbour. I'd been so excited to get back to Sydney this trip and tell Mum all about it – to describe the little details in the way that's only possible in person.

A stray tear escapes down my cheek. Somehow, my thoughts had turned back to Mum again.

Forcing my mind back to the present, I lie on the bed and stare into space, thinking about Felicity Smith. Last night, I'd locked myself away in this room and searched for hours for any trace of her online – with no luck. At some point, I'd fallen asleep, crawling between the sheets hours later.

I glance at the time on my phone and see that it's eleven in the morning – far later than I'd planned on waking. My body and mind are shattered, but I have to keep going.

I know there's one place left in the house that I haven't had the chance to search properly: Mum and Glenn's bedroom. It's the last place I can think of that might have anything hidden away. I don't have much hope – I doubt there will be any secret work papers there. But I should still try.

Slipping out of the sheets, I smooth down my jumbled pyjamas and scrape my hair back from my face into a loose bun. I pad over to the window and open the blinds to look down at the driveway. Only one car is there: Zara's.

Maybe this is my lucky morning, and Glenn is out. I creak my door open and chance a peek. I don't want Zara to discover me sneaking in, either.

The landing is silent as I creep out. A row of closed doors, hiding away all our secrets. I feel jittery as I sneak down the dark corridor, my feet squishing into the beige carpet. Just as I am about to reach the end, nearly at the main bedroom that had been Mum and Glenn's room, a door flies open next to me, and I shriek out loud.

'God, Emily, why are you screaming?' Zara cries, and I turn to face her, clamping my hand over my mouth. The shock of the opening door and the shadow of her appearance out of the corner of my eye had startled me. My nerves are all over the place.

'Sorry – you scared me.' I try to stop shaking and wrap my arms around myself defensively.

'Whatever,' she responds, but gives me a wink to show she's joking. 'You're getting up late – manage to sleep okay?' She's already dressed in white shorts and a light blue halter neck that brings out the matching colour in her eyes. Her hair is straightened again, and she's slipped it back at the edges with some little butterfly clips. I could never pull off an outfit like that, but she makes it look effortless. I fiddle with my pyjama shorts and tuck another loose strand of my dishevelled hair behind my ear.

'Mmmhmm,' I say with a shrug. 'Going to go and shower now.' I start to walk down the hall towards the bathroom – like that had been my plan all along.

'Sure – you want a tea? I can't say I'll make it as good as Suzie, but I'll try.' My throat constricts a little at that thought. Mum had always loved the tradition of making proper loose-leaf tea in the mornings when we were all here.

'That would be great, thanks,' I respond with a small smile and hurry away.

As I remember the small moments of toast and tea, I am filled with the wishful thought that maybe I don't *need* to be looking into Felicity. Maybe there isn't some awful conspiracy going on. Maybe the people closest to Mum *didn't* betray her.

But then, Mike's words from yesterday float back to me. *'I'm so sorry about what happened. But I do wish you hadn't gone digging.'*

I know I'm not mistaken, even if no one else believes me. Mike had something to do with Mum's death – whether he killed her outright or they'd fought and she'd fallen. *Something* had happened.

But I'm going to tell Zara that I agree with her and that I'm going to drop everything. It's the only way to hold onto the fragile peace that we've started to have. Plus, I don't want her to share her 'concerns' with Glenn or, worse, Mike.

After showering, I descend the stairs to the living room in a loose white top and floaty navy shorts with this renewed sense of determination.

Zara is sitting on a high stool in front of the island bench when I enter the kitchen, a steaming pot of tea in front of her. The heat of the day hits me, and it seems all wrong to have a hot drink.

She doesn't notice me as I walk towards her, engrossed in her phone. Just as her screen is about to be in my sight, she turns around. 'Tea?' she asks in a bright voice, gesturing for me to sit down as she jumps up. But there's a tinge of pink on her cheek.

This feels all wrong. It is wrong because Mum isn't here, but it is also starting to feel like Zara is putting on some sort of a show. I say nothing and do as she's asked, slipping onto the cream leather stool. My legs stick to it, and I wonder for the thousandth time why Mum even bought these stools. A silly, mundane question I would never get to ask her. I grab the teapot as a distraction from the lump that starts to form in my throat and begin to pour for both of us, then I say, 'You know, I want to apologise about yesterday. I think you're right, you know – I've been trying to search for the answer to something that can't be found.'

She pauses as she flits back around the marble island bench. 'Oh, you mean it?' I nod again. Her shoulders sag in relief. 'I'm so glad to hear that. I've been wracking my brain all night about what to do next. I wanted to have a chat with you before asking Dad for his advice because I was getting so worried. But I'm so glad you've accepted it. I know how hard that must be for you.'

I give her a tight smile in acknowledgement. 'Let's start again then?'

'Absolutely,' she says enthusiastically.

'And no need to worry your dad, I don't think...'

'Definitely not,' she agrees, her attention already elsewhere. 'Milk?' she asks, opening the fridge.

'Yes, please.' I tap my finger on the countertop, watching her whirl around. And that's when I notice what's up: even with what I'd just told her, she's been looking everywhere else – except at me.

'So where's Glenn?'

She continues to fuss around with the milk. 'Hmm – we've got oat, almond, regular. What are you drinking these days?'

'Umm, regular is fine. So yeah, where's Glenn?' I repeat.

She pours the milk into my tea with a flourish, then replaces it in the fridge. Her back is to me when she says, 'So, Dad said not to mention it yet as it might upset you. But… I'll tell you anyway. Please promise not to freak out… This morning, we had a call from the coroners to let us know that Suzie's body is being released.'

'What?' I swivel around on the chair to follow her movement back across the kitchen to the toaster, where she inserts a couple of slices. 'So soon?' I ask, confused. Because if Mum's body is being released already, then this means that the coroner has decided there isn't anything suspicious about her death after all. That everything, time of death included, matches up to their expectations from the police. And it means that the police have no intention of investigating further. My heart sinks as I realise Ben would have been told this and hasn't mentioned anything to me. 'But surely the police wouldn't allow it so quickly?'

She looks up from the toaster to face me. Her blazing blue eyes pierce mine. 'Emily,' she says with a note of exasperation, 'the police have already said it was an accident – like you just agreed to, remember? They weren't investigating anything on Saturday morning, and they aren't going to now. It's a good thing that Suzie's been released to us. We'll be able to organise the funeral. We can start moving on,' she adds with a gentle smile and takes a slow slip of her tea.

I start to feel a familiar clammy sweat beginning to break out from my rising sense of anxiety.

'Okay, but what's this got to do with Glenn anyway? Where is he?' My mind is racing ahead. Perhaps if I can see Mum – I try not to think too much about the terrifying and heartbreaking prospect of what she might look like after such a fall – but perhaps if I can *see* her, I'll be able to notice something that only a daughter could. I'm not sure what that is – but I have to hope.

'Well, that's the thing,' Zara continues as she places her mug down on the countertop. 'Dad's gone to sort everything out for you. He said you didn't have to worry one bit. He's there now.'

'Wait, what? What do you mean, "he's there now"?'

'Yeah, well, you were still asleep, and he thought it would be best if he went and got everything sorted out himself at the funeral home. *She was his wife*, you know.' It feels like a repeated line, a line that Glenn had fed to her this morning. As usual, Zara is defending him, and I, once again, feel like I am on the outskirts of our little 'family'.

'And,' she continues, folding her arms with intention, 'he said he thought it would probably be best if you didn't go and see her. That seeing her body after what it's been through...' She shudders. 'That it would be a bit too much for you. And after yesterday, I kinda agree... I don't think it *would* be a good idea, Em. It would make you far too upset. And he's texted me to confirm that she isn't in a good state – so he thinks it better if neither of us go. It'll be far too confronting. He says he can organise the cremation for later this afternoon, and then it'll all be sorted for us. He's trying to look after you.' She is speaking gently, but all I see is red.

I try to keep calm. I can't lose my temper: it would prove this little idea of theirs that seeing Mum is too much for me to handle. But what I can't get over is that Glenn didn't want to tell me that her body had been released. He apparently didn't even want to consult me about Mum's wishes: he's just deciding to cremate her straight away.

Maybe it's true that he's just trying to look out for me and is attempting to take on a decisive "father figure" role. But after we clashed so much when I was a teenager, I've always pushed him far away from that. And he's never seemed particularly interested since then. So, acting like this immediately after Mum's sudden death seems like a strange time to start...

Why does he not want me to see the body?

And in that instant, a thought flashes through my mind so fast it makes me gasp, drawing a concerned look from Zara.

It's a wild thought, a completely desperate one. But I can't believe I haven't considered it before...

I've been so certain that Mum couldn't just fall from that cliff – that if she'd fallen, it was because she'd been pushed.

But now that Glenn is trying to *stop* me from seeing her body, a new idea is forming...

Another reason entirely at odds with a newfound fatherly concern over my welfare.

And that reason is because this body, this battered, frozen body lying in the morgue, is perhaps one I would not recognise. But not because it has been damaged beyond all recognition.

No.

But because maybe it isn't Mum's at all.

It hits me like a crashing wave.

She could still be alive...

Chapter Twenty-One

I'm imagining things that aren't there, I tell myself. Of course it's Mum in that morgue.

But if it's not... A small flutter of hope beats in my chest.

It was *Glenn* who identified the body, after all– no one else close to Mum had seen it. Even Ben said that he hadn't seen her.

This idea is still madness; I try to convince myself again. But, unbidden, another crucial thought skitters to the surface: Glenn has barely worked in years, whereas Mum's been running, until now, a successful company. A successful company where Mike is trying to hide something and at least two accountants have been quietly let go for the same reason. Could Glenn be working *with* him? Maybe they both needed Mum gone?

Ultimately, there's still a dead female body at the end of all this. Could it even be this Felicity Smith? And Mum... is she alive somewhere but too scared to come back? Have Mike and Glenn forced her to run away?

My mind whirs in a million directions, tossing everything over, considering all the possibilities.

This idea could be a total delusion. But the fact remains that Glenn is trying to now stop me from seeing my mum's body. Not only that, he wants to *cremate* her – and so destroy all evidence – before I even discover that she is at the morgue. I only know now because I happened to run into Zara this morning and then asked multiple times where Glenn was. If I hadn't, I'd be none the wiser. He's probably rushing to get it through right now...

God – what is happening?

'Em? EM?' Zara keeps calling my name.

I clench my hands into fists and take control of the sudden violent urge to scream. I want to launch myself at Zara. At that moment, I want her to hurt as much as I do on the inside. The thought sobers me, my animalistic reaction scaring me. I am starting to feel untethered, losing sight of who I had worked so hard to become. I am slipping back into my uncontrollable teenage years. The unhappy time I have been working so hard to forget by becoming a professional, poised lawyer in London.

I pull myself back together. I need to play this right to get us over there as quickly as possible. Before Glenn has a chance to hide everything away. Because I'm suddenly certain that to try and do this without me knowing, he *must* be hiding something. 'Yes, sorry... I was thinking about how that was a very thoughtful thing to do. It probably *would* be so hard.'

She bobs her head up and down. 'Exactly – that's what I thought.'

'Except...' I say slowly and tilt my head to one side to pretend like I'm considering this only now. 'I sort of feel that it's my duty to go. And see her one last time. I don't think I'll be able to move on otherwise...'

She frowns but doesn't say anything as I glance up at the time on the big kitchen clock behind Zara's head. Eleven forty-five.

'How long is Glenn going to be there?'

'Well, I think he said he hoped he could get everything sorted this morning. Then you wouldn't have to worry.'

So he was trying to get this done as fast as possible. He really didn't want me to stop him.

'Zara,' I say, leaning across the kitchen counter. 'Can I borrow your car – or can you drive me over? I *have* to see her – before it's too late.'

She wordlessly places two slices of Vegemite toast in front of me. I ignore them as she takes a bite of her own toast and chews in silence. Her eyes glance around the room avoiding my gaze.

'I appreciate Glenn's thoughtfulness.' I add, trying to stop myself from choking on the words because I need her on my side – not his for once. 'I don't know about you, but otherwise I don't think it will sink in...'

'Oh.' She finishes her toast and absentmindedly twists a tea towel that she's picked up in her hands. 'Well,' she begins, 'Dad was adamant that you shouldn't see her of all people. But I guess you're right... if you truly think it would help you with moving on.' She looks up in hope. After last night, I know this is the key. Make her think I've given up on the Felicity Smith chase and that this is the start of me accepting that Mum's death was an accident.

I cross my fingers behind my back. 'Yes, like I already told you. And now, hearing that she's being released already and that nothing has been discovered reassures me. I'm certain that seeing her will help me close this part of the nightmare.'

I must have lied convincingly because her shoulders sag in relief. 'Oh Em, that's so good to hear.' And to my surprise, she comes round to my side of the island bench and wraps me in a big hug.

'Harry and I were so worried about you last night,' she says into my shoulder, 'and so if you think this will help you move on, then I'm sure Dad will understand too. He's just trying to protect us.' She squeezes tight, and I make sure to hug her back.

'Yes, I can see that,' I reply. 'But let's get over there and surprise him. I'm sure he'll be happy to see us.'

'Sure,' she says into my hair.

I do not want her to tell him we're coming – in case it makes him speed up the process even more and forces them to cremate her before this afternoon.

I can't risk that.

Because I have to know what Glenn's trying to hide.

Chapter Twenty-Two

The funeral home is all the way across Sydney near Warriewood. *Harder for me to get to,* I think to myself.

I squeeze my eyes shut as Zara drives through the Sydney traffic. I feel like I'm racing against the clock to get there. I hope Zara didn't text him when I wasn't looking.

We drive most of the way in silence. Zara tries to engage me in conversation, telling me that Jennifer's been in touch to ask if she can do anything to help. I brush it off – I can't face Jennifer's over the top sympathy right now. Then she tries again to say that Mum's assistant, Arabella, called to say how sorry she was and that she'd offered to collect anything from the office.

'Sure,' I say, 'whatever.' I don't really care. I don't think there's anything of Mum's there I'd want. It feels like Zara is over-compensating after earlier.

She eventually gets the picture and stops talking. I stare out the window at the bright blue sky of this perfect summer's day. It's mocking me.

Finally, we are high up the northern beaches of Sydney and veering off the main roads. This area is not dissimilar to where we live, but it feels so much quieter. More laidback, with the surf just on your doorstep. But then again, everything can seem perfect from the outside but be crumbling away to pieces on the inside. I know that far too well.

Soon, we turn into a small car park outside a single-storey red brick building with large glass doors. Zara stops the car, turning off the ignition, and without the sound of the engine, it hits me how silent it is out here.

A shiver runs down my spine when I hear the sound of a warbling magpie overhead. Zara clears her throat and turns to ask me in a small voice, 'Right, umm, ready to go?'

I nod. I have to get out of this car now, or I never will. I unclip my seat belt and all but fling myself out in my efforts to keep going. Zara steps out of the car behind me, but I am already striding, almost running, towards the doors.

It feels like this is my last chance. Glenn can't stop me now that I'm here, can he?

As we push our way through the looming doors of the funeral home, it takes my eyes a moment to adjust from the brilliance of the sunshine outside. I glance around the small waiting area, sparsely furnished and all in white. I suppose this is an intentional design to keep things neutral for people in their time of distress, but I find it far too clinical.

My heart feels like it's about to jump out of my chest. All I want to do is see this body before I lose every last shred of my nerves. I can't take the suspense of now thinking that it might not be Mum.

A tall, robust woman in her late forties bounds around the corner, her silvery blonde hair pulled into a neat bun. Glenn is nowhere in sight. Thank goodness. We appear to be the only people in here. I guess that maybe they try to keep to appointment times, everything geared towards managing the unmanageable: grief.

But then, a second later, a tall, familiar figure steps out from around the same corner: Glenn. My heart sinks. Are we already too late?

The woman comes to a sudden halt in front of us as Zara, and I pause next to a large white desk. 'Oh Glenn,' she says in an overly upbeat tone for such a place, 'these must be your girls. You mentioned they were on their way.'

I bristle. Zara must have told him. I'm also not one of his 'girls'.

'I'm Deborah.' She sticks out her hand, reaching across to Zara first, who is closer. Zara looks uncomfortable but puts her hand out and mumbles, 'Zara,' as Deborah pumps her hand up and down.

'I'm so sorry for your loss,' Deborah responds in a practised tone, and I shudder. She swivels her gaze towards me, and I freeze like a deer in the headlights at the sheer force of her shiny smile. 'Ah, Emily then.' She propels her hand out, and I glance down, considering for a moment whether I could ignore her.

But before I have a chance, she grabs my hand. 'You have such a lovely Dad – he cares about you both *so* much and was so scared about how you'd both feel seeing her. But if you're sure, we've tried our very best to clean her up for you.' She smiles at me, and I feel confused and a little bit queasy. It seems like they aren't going to stop us then. Unless she's in on it all...

'He's not my father.' I mumble under my breath.

'Oh, right – stepfather,' she tinkles with a small nervous laugh. I see Glenn frowning out of the corner of my eye.

I try to understand that this is her job, but it all feels too performative. But I grit my teeth, swallow down my swirling panic, and channel my best client voice. 'Thank you, we appreciate it.'

'Of course,' she says, her eyes sparkling, and I know I've said the right thing. She wants to feel useful. I can do this; I've dealt with a million people like this at work.

'So,' she continues, addressing all of us with a simpering smile, 'as Glenn and I discussed, we think it would be best if you all go in together.' Ah, so that's how he's trying to swing it. He won't deny me now that I'm here, but he won't let me get too close either. He'll try to stop me seeing her properly...

I'm about to disagree when Glenn interjects. 'Oh yes, definitely, Deborah, I think we'll all need the support.' As a show of just that, he takes Zara's hand and squeezes it.

I bite down on my words. I can't demand to go in there alone this second – it would draw too much attention and make Glenn realise that I know something is up. I need to bide my time for the right opportunity. So, first off, I'm going to play along. Then, find the right moment later.

We set off towards the door at the back of the room. Deborah lets Glenn take us through alone. We turn right, which opens onto a dimly lit narrow corridor of unending doors. The hairs on my arms stand on end as I try not to think about all the tidied, cleaned-up bodies behind each one, waiting for their loved ones to gaze upon them. But what the living don't realise until they come here is that the people they love are no longer there anymore. All that's left is a cold, lifeless vessel.

After passing by a few nondescript brown doors without saying a word, Glenn pauses outside one, blocking the way. 'Okay,' he says, turning to us. 'If you really want to do this, we can. But if you turn around, there's no shame in that.' I frown at his words.

'I'm sure, Glenn,' I respond, crossing my arms in front of my chest.

He continues as though he hasn't even registered my tone, 'It will be quite a shock to you both to see Suzie. She...' He pauses, reaching for the right words, and he chokes up, trying to get them out. I frown.

He pulls together his emotions. 'She doesn't look like herself anymore, okay. She is very... broken,' he concludes with a shudder. It seems like it had taken him every effort to choke out that sentence, picturing what he'd already seen. But is his distress solely from losing his wife or his own involvement? Is he acting and coming up with more dramatic excuses to make us decide *not* to see the body?

'And so, if you decide to go in there right now, remember we can't get too close. I don't want you both to be left with terrible last memories of her,' he finishes, his voice ringing clear on this last sentence.

Next to me, his dutiful daughter nods, but alarm bells start ringing in my head.

Don't get too close?

The tiny kernel of hope that had formed in my chest starts to blossom even bigger. It truly might be possible that Mum is alive.

I can't let my face show what I'm thinking. So I say in as calm a voice as I can muster, 'Of course.'

He still looks uncertain. 'So, you both still want to go in then?' He must have hoped that this last-ditch attempt would have scared us off.

I loop my arm into Zara's firmly. 'Yes, we both agreed that it would be the best way to help us move on. Isn't that right, Zara?'

It's a bit of a risk – me forcing Zara to declare a side to her dad, and she fidgets next to me. But I look down at her from my extra height, and when she glances up, she must read the pleading in my eyes because she says in a trembling voice, 'Yes.'

He exhales and runs his fingers through his wavy hair. 'Okay, fine.' I clench my hands together and swallow as Glenn turns the handle at last.

Every ounce of my careful control floats away as the small, shrouded figure is revealed. Even though I'd tried to prepare for this, I feel myself break in two. I've never seen a dead body – I didn't see my father like this because his body was never found.

But as I peer into the room at the covered-up form, carefully lit and lying at least five metres away, a whisper of doubt echoes in the corner of my mind. If this body is so broken, will I even be able to tell who it is?

Chapter Twenty-Three

Glenn and Zara step forward and into the room first. They position themselves in such a way that most of my vision is blocked. I want to push past them, but as I cross the threshold, it's like I've stepped into another world – a place where the living are not welcome.

There is a feeling of eerie stillness, as though we've intruded into a holy sanctuary. The body is too far away for me to see properly, but I glance over their shoulders to see the unmoving form laid out across what seems like a dark, waist-high table. The lights overhead feel too harsh as they reflect off the bright cream walls and the stark white sheet that covers the figure. Spots appear in my vision after the contrast of the dark corridor.

But I have to push past this sense of dread and take in what I can. From what I can tell, the figure is covered up to her neck – except for her hands, which are arranged over her stomach. The body looks to be about Mum's size, but I can't see her face.

I tilt my head to one side as I try to make out her hands – Glenn hovers in front like he'd tackle me to the ground if I stepped in front of him. But I manage a side glance. And I swear all the rings she usually wears aren't there. There's something about those hands and fingers that look different to the ones I thought I knew so well.

I start to edge a bit closer, but before I can get close enough, Glenn puts out an arm, blocking my way. 'That's enough, Emily. Honestly, you don't want to go closer.'

I turn towards him, preparing for a fight, when I see Zara's face on the other side of him. She's white as the walls behind her and looks like she's about to faint.

'Zara?' I say just as she tilts into Glenn.

'Oh!' he says in alarm. Her eyelids flutter. 'Emily, help me support her!'

I grab Zara's other arm. We steer her out of the room and back into the clinical hallway.

'Come on!' Glenn pants. 'Let's get her some fresh air.'

Zara is so tiny that she's almost as light as a feather between us as we move her back out into the reception area.

'Is everything—' Deborah starts and then lets out a small cry. 'Oh no! Don't worry – this happens all the time. Quick, get her outside, and I'll get some water.'

Glenn and I steer Zara through the double doors. By this time, she's come around and walks with gentle steps between us. 'Oh, Dad, I'm sorry,' she says, turning up to face him. 'I don't know what came over me.'

We take her to the small bench outside, and Glenn sits down next to her, a protective arm around his little girl. A pang of envy hits me, but then Deborah rushes out, a bottle of water in hand.

She fusses over Zara as she hands her the bottle and begins to ask her a series of rapid questions. 'I'm first aid trained,' she says. 'Tell me how you are feeling.'

A thought dawns in a distant corner of my mind, and I say to no one in particular, 'I need to use the bathroom.'

No one pays any attention as I slip back inside.

I am going to make the most of this moment of distraction. Glenn didn't want me near the body – he'd been about to stop me from getting a closer look. I want to know why.

As I dash back through the reception, I start to wonder: did Zara faint on purpose as a distraction?

But I don't have time to consider this right now. I only have minutes to see this body close up before Glenn realises that I'm gone for too long.

So, I propel myself forward.

Because it's now or never to finally find out if this body is my mother's.

Chapter Twenty-Four

I dash back into the corridor and run until I'm face to face with that door once more. I take a deep, reassuring breath to prepare myself.

As I push it open, the cool air of the room floods over me and a chill tingles down the back of my neck. I shake as I move closer and closer to the table. My eyes fill with tears as I take in the outline of the battered body. It's hidden behind the delicate folds of the sheet. But I blink my tears back and edge closer.

With every step, my pulse races. Is this going to be her or the face of a stranger?

And all at once, I realise that it's both.

I guess I should have known that I would feel shattered at the strange unreality of seeing someone like this.

And I know now that there is truly nothing that can ever prepare you for that feeling of total devastation. For that immense feeling of the deepest loss when you see the person you loved most in the world laid out in a small, bare room. Silent, and not there.

As you edge closer, you begin to realise that the face that you once knew so completely does not seem quite *theirs* anymore. And when you inch another step, you start to notice the chalky white of the sallow complexion and begin to understand that despite the make-up the funeral home has applied to your dearest loved one, though it *is* them, it really is *not* them. Then, the creeping feeling like a fingernail streaking slowly down a chalkboard starts to spindle up your spine.

It hits me all at once – and for a moment, an awful giggle tries to escape me. I swallow it down with a shove.

Because at last, I'm close enough to properly see this eerily familiar face.

And there's now no doubt in my mind that it *is* her.

My mum.

My knees buckle at the realisation, and I fly back against the wall for support as I try to keep upright against the shock.

I'd immediately jumped to the conclusion that Glenn was keeping the biggest secret of all: that the person who died off the cliff wasn't Mum.

I'd been preparing myself for that reality the last couple of hours and had hoped that, somehow, that could be the case. Because it would mean that my mum would still have been alive somewhere out there.

But instead, in front of me is the one person whose face I know better than my own.

My mum, whose face had been full of a million and one expressions, but never this one. It is devoid of any expression, a sunken appearance etched across her features. It's like I am gazing upon an incomplete waxwork version of her, where the creator had missed out on all the important details – all the details that made her look *alive*.

I drop my head over my knees to stop myself from retching. This figure that used to be my mother is covered in gashes, which are plain to see despite the funeral home's efforts to cover them up. I *cannot* be sick in here.

I count to ten to calm my racing heart and think instead about Glenn's actions. Because he had not been lying. I have to consider the alternative then: that he was genuinely trying to protect us.

Everything feels upside down, and all I want to do is run straight out of this room. After what I'd so desperately wanted to believe, I can't make my brain comprehend that it really is her. But now that I *am* here, and it *is* my mum, I know I should make the most of this moment and pull myself together.

I need to turn back the clock to this morning – when I had completely believed in her death but *not* her accident. Despite this wild goose chase I've been on to figure out whether this was actually her body or not, the fact that this body *is* Mum doesn't change anything else.

Mike is hiding something.

He said those irrevocably damning words yesterday.

And I saw that shadow and heard a scream on that hazy night.

I stand upright against the wall and stare down at the figure once more. I remind myself that this body isn't her anymore – Mum had gone wherever we go the second she stopped breathing. But I have to examine what I can now that I'm here. Because maybe I, her daughter, might pick up on something nobody else would.

Taking a few small steps forward, I pause when I'm hovering above her. My eyes dance over her face, but I can't detect anything else that would help me.

And then I do hit on something: a small white earlobe peaks out from behind the wisp of her tidily arranged bob, and I notice that she has some earrings on. Glancing further down, I realise that she is also wearing her favourite necklace, the Tree of Life. How ironic.

I scan all the way down to her hands, so carefully folded across her torso, in an almost hug-like position. And I confirm what I *thought* I'd seen earlier before Zara fainted: her rings are missing.

A new sense of unease begins to creep up on me that has nothing to do with this room. Mum had always worn three rings: one from her parents on her twenty-first birthday and the other two on the fourth fingers of her left and right hand. One was a shiny diamond jutting out of a gold band, her engagement ring from Glenn, and the other was a thin and extremely delicate gold band with a few small diamonds studded throughout. It had been from my dad when she'd had me. And Mum had always said that one day she would pass it on.

But where are they now? She was wearing all the rest of her usual jewellery; why not also her rings, which she cherished above all her other possessions?

I frown as I consider the new possibility: had someone taken them? But why?

Chapter Twenty-Five

I say goodbye to my mum's body and head back down the corridor – Glenn and Zara will be looking for me at any moment. I hear voices, and Zara's earlier fainting episode springs to my mind. It's my only card to play. I stumble and crumble onto the floor with a thud.

Footsteps rush towards me, and a shrill cry of 'Oh God!' which could only be Deborah, mixed with the quieter cry of 'Emily!' I raise myself into a seated position to see them hovering over me.

'What happened?' Zara cries, whilst Glenn appears shadow-like behind her. He asks deliberately, 'Where did you go?'

Deborah flusters about, muttering, 'Oh dear, oh dear.'

'I think I got lost,' I murmur, 'I need some fresh air.'

Before they can ask me another question, Deborah snaps into action. 'Of course, of course.' She bends down. 'Here,' she says, offering her outstretched hand. 'Can I help you?'

I stretch my hand up and struggle to my feet as she helps me back out towards the sunlight. Though I had pretended to faint, the adrenalin that had been pumping my body through this whole encounter rushes out of me as soon as I am through the front doors and back into the unbearable shock of the sunlight reflecting off the bright tarmac.

So this time, as I stagger, it is genuine, and I am thankful to have Deborah to lean on. She leads me towards a little bench underneath the shade of a tree and I sit down gratefully.

'Oh dear, you two poor girls. I'll go get you some water.' She bustles back towards the entrance. This time, I don't shudder at her use of the word 'girls'.

I need a few moments to process everything. Really, I should be getting back to it, trying to question Glenn or Deborah immediately about where Mum's rings might have gone. But I'm so tired. As I close my eyes, I'm tormented by the waxy pallor of her face, the traumatic cuts that were visible underneath the perfectly applied makeup. Nausea sweeps over me once more.

I'm staring at the ground, lost in my tumultuous thoughts, when Zara appears next to me, a bottle of water in hand.

'You okay?' she passes it over to me. I nod, unscrewing the cap to take a greedy gulp. 'It was a lot in there,' she continues. 'It got to me too... Did you get all the time you needed, though?' I glance across at her. There's no mistaking her expression. I'm sure she knows that I dashed back in there – which means she *did* faint on purpose.

'Yeah, I needed a minute,' I say, a little flustered at this realisation.

'It was so... awful,' she begins, 'seeing her like that. I didn't get very close – but it didn't even seem like it was her. But I'm glad you got the closure you needed. That's all I wanted for you, Ems.' She fans herself down with her hand.

Ah – she just wanted to give me another opportunity to slip in so I would continue with 'moving on' and letting go of my suspicions.

'It was like she wasn't there at all,' I agree with an exhale. And I mean it – what it has solidified to me is that she is gone. There is no bringing her back.

And now I have to know about those rings.

I stand. The blood rushes fast down my body, and I sway on my feet. 'Oh!' Zara reaches for my elbow to hold me steady. 'Are you sure you don't want to rest a bit longer?'

'No,' I reply, with surety back in my voice. 'There's some things we need to discuss.' Glenn may not have been lying about it being Mum's body... but is there something else he's hiding?

I burst back through the doors of the funeral home and turn to the left to see Glenn and Deborah sitting by the desk, talking. They're bent close together, Glenn's head in his hands. They spring apart as I approach, Zara following behind.

I walk over to perch next to Glenn. He sits up straighter, taken aback at my sudden proximity.

'I'm so glad you're both doing a bit better,' Deborah starts. 'Glenn and I were finalising the next steps – but we're almost done, so don't you worry.'

'Oh yes, I suppose we have to organise all the technicalities of... a service.' I shudder at the word. I don't want to think about that. I can't mourn Mum yet until I have all the answers.

So I bluster on, redirecting the conversation towards where I want it to start. Work seems like a world away from the nightmarish reality my life has now become, but my training as a lawyer comes in handy. 'But before you finish, I have a quick question about what she's wearing?'

'What she's wearing?' Deborah's eyebrows rise. She seems genuinely puzzled, as does Zara. From the corner of my vision, I see Glenn's eyes narrow towards me.

'Yeah, you know what she's wearing right now? I couldn't see, but I assumed she was dressed under the sheet. Did you provide that outfit?'

'Oh no,' she replies, as I see Glenn's mouth start to move. 'Your stepfather provided us with everything.' Bingo.

'I see.' I flip my hair over my shoulder and cut across Glenn: 'So I guess we provided all the jewellery then, too?' I look at Glenn. He's frowning, trying to understand the trap.

He's too slow to reply, though, because Deborah responds, 'Oh no, I remember there was some jewellery sent with the body. I can double-check for you.'

'Would you, Deborah? You've been so amazing.' She beams at me whilst Glenn glowers.

'Not at all. It's my job. This one must be such a comfort to you, Glenn.' She glances over in his direction just as his face regains a neutral composure. 'Well, I'll go check the records, but I'm pretty sure it was some earrings and a necklace.'

'Oh really?' I interject before anyone else can. 'I didn't get too close a look in there. It was so overwhelming as you said it would be,' I say in a calm voice, and Deborah nods in sympathy. Meanwhile, Glenn's expression starts to get darker, and Zara's eyes begin to jump between us like she's watching a game of tennis.

'I'll be back in a few minutes,' she hops to her feet and moves as quickly as her robust frame can carry her. Once she disappears out of sight and around the corner, an ominous silence falls across the room.

Well, I won't be the one to break it. I fold my arms and stare across the other side of the room, avoiding Glenn's gaze. But soon, a growl cuts through.

'Emily,' Glenn begins in a calm but dangerous voice. 'What is this all about?'

I decide I have nothing to lose by being semi-honest – misdirection is always more believable when it has the benefit of being somewhat true.

'Well,' I begin, sitting up straighter on the uncomfortable white leather sofa. 'I want to help you sort everything out with Mum, and so part of that is knowing where all her belongings are and deciding what we'll want to... leave with her.'

'Right,' Glenn says, twirling a water bottle in his hand. 'So you want to help now? Okay, sure.' I am a little taken aback at how easy this is. Can he really not tell what I am thinking?

I am about to go further when Deborah appears around the corner and strides back across to us.

'Soooo,' she starts, a sheet of paper in her hand. 'It looks like we were only given a necklace and some earrings.' She glances down at the paper again as though to double-check.

'Oh strange,' I say. 'Glenn – you remember Mum's rings? She never took them off. Don't you think that's a bit weird that she wasn't wearing them?' I turn to Glenn and lean forward onto my knees, placing my chin in my hand to listen to his response.

He stares back at me, a small crease beginning to form between his brows.

Deborah can't deal with the stare-off, though, and tries to ask in a helpful tone, 'Well, maybe the coroners or police might have them then? Perhaps they're still looking at something?'

'No – they're not looking at anything!' Glenn declares suddenly. He seems insulted at her insinuation. And for a second, he glares across at me, a wild look in his eyes.

Deborah steps back, her mouth dropping into a small 'O' at his outburst. 'I mean,' he tries to correct his slip up, 'I checked, and she didn't have anything else on her to be returned, apparently. No rings.' He says this with a tone of finality. He stands up, his almost-giant feet slapping loudly with the impact. It's clear he doesn't want any more questions on the matter.

I'm about to try again when he stands up and puts his hand out towards Deborah to shake. 'So thank you so much for your time. But it seems like before we go on with any more plans, we need to all catch up again as a family. Can I give you a call tomorrow when we've discussed it?'

Zara, Deborah and I all blink in surprise at the whiplash caused by this statement. Deborah regains her composure first and responds in a forced breezy tone, 'Oh, of course, I totally understand. Give me a bell whenever you're ready.'

I open my mouth to say something, anything, but then Glenn strides out of the room.

Zara rushes straight after him. In a daze, I hurriedly say goodbye to Deborah. What is it about these rings that have made him so jumpy?

By the time I arrive outside, Glenn is opening his car door at the far end of the car park, Zara close behind. I pick up my pace, not wanting him to leave before we have a chance to speak. Who knows where he'll zip off to next?

When I reach the car, he has already shut the door and rolled down the window to speak to Zara.

'Hey! What's the rush?' I ask Glenn the question, but Zara chips in.

'Emily, are you okay to take the car back yourself? Dad wants me to head over to Jennifer and Mike's with him,' she asks as she throws the keys at me. 'And you can borrow it for a while if you want, actually. I'll use their spare car.'

I catch them on reflex. 'Okay, sure,' I say, taken aback. 'How come?'

'Jennifer's asked me to pop over. And Dad's going to see if he can catch Mike to chat about a few business technicalities, aren't you, Dad?' Zara turns to face him, and my ears prick up at this. I thought Glenn had zero interest in anything to do with Imaginate.

'Oh right,' I respond in as casual a voice as I can muster and swivel to face Glenn. 'What's that about? Is it something I can help with?'

'He needs me to check a few statements on behalf of Suzie. It's nothing that you need to concern yourself with.'

It sounds like yet another thing that he's trying to leave me out of. But I have to remain friendly if I want to get a straight answer out of him.

'Okay, no worries, well let me know if you do. Before you go, though, can I ask, do you really not know what's happened to Mum's rings? Just,' I go on purposefully while his face remains steadfast, 'she wore them every day, and I'm surprised they seem to have vanished...'

A flash of something mostly unreadable darts across his eyes. Is it anger? Or fear? He composes himself quickly. 'Look, I honestly don't know where they are. They're not at home, and I haven't heard anything from the coroners or police about any items left behind. So, I guess she must have misplaced them or taken them off earlier… That's all I know. But it doesn't really matter, does it? Are rings really so important when Suzie is gone?'

I bow my head. I am not sure if he is telling me the truth about this, but at least I'd heard his version of events, which I could now put to the test. So I just nod. There's no point in questioning him further. I know he won't say anything else.

'See you later, okay, Em?' Zara calls as she opens the car door and jumps inside.

'Bye, Emily,' Glenn adds, flipping his sunglasses from the top of his head over his eyes. He doesn't want me to catch whatever they might give away.

I nod as I step back.

Then they are off, a small cloud of dust from the ashy car park left in their wake.

As I watch their car race away into the horizon, all I am left with are more questions about what else they're hiding from me.

And the uneasy feeling that I'm more isolated from this 'family' than ever before.

Chapter Twenty-Six

I return wearily to Zara's old Ford Fiesta, whipping out my phone as I readjust the driver's seat. There's no time to wallow about the state of my relationship with my stepfamily. I need to get back on track after becoming so distracted this morning.

I type a quick, *Hey, can we meet?* to Ben, then start the car, pulling out of the suffocating space of the funeral home. Hopefully, he might have uncovered something about Felicity Smith, and I can also check Glenn's story about never being given the rings, too… whatever Glenn says, I know how important they were to Mum. She would *never* misplace them.

As I begin to navigate the long journey back home, I let my mind wander over the list of what I do and don't know so far. I continue to cycle through my thoughts on repeat, but as I near the outskirts of the suburbs I used to call home, my phone rings through the hands-free. It's Uncle John. Pressing the answer button, I call out 'Hello' into the empty car.

'Hello, Emily?' his voice booms, echoing through the speakers. The sudden noise against the stark silence surprises me, and I almost lose control of the wheel.

'Hey, John, I'm driving right now. Everything okay?' I keep my eyes fixed straight ahead.

'That's what I was calling to ask you,' he replies. I feel a rush of gratitude towards him. I'd barely seen him in the last few years, but in this time of need, he cares more about how I am doing than the family I've had for the last fifteen years. This family that I can't trust at all.

'That's very kind of you, John. Yeah, I'm doing okay. I'm actually driving back from the—' I take a gulp, the words getting stuck in my throat, 'funeral home. We just saw her…' I finish and try not to well up.

'I'm so sorry. How are you doing after that? Are you with Glenn and Zara now?'

'It was quite tough,' I swallow, 'but I got through it. And no, not right now. I was there with them, but they had to go to Mike and Jennifer's, so I'm on my way back to Merton Street.'

'Oh – I'm not far from yours, and I've just finished a shift. If you like, I can drop around for a quick catch-up and bring some sushi?'

I didn't realise how much I was missing someone checking in on me until his call. And after the funeral home, I could really do with a friendly face.

As we hang up, my stomach rumbles at the thought of the late lunch John will bring over. I can't stop my hunger despite everything.

When I swerve into the glittery white drive, I have a slight sense of hope in my heart at seeing John, the first I've felt in days.

I've just about had time to let Banjo out into the back garden when the doorbell rings. I rush down the hallway and open the heavy door to reveal Uncle John framed in the doorway with his sunglasses on and a white plastic bag in one hand. The heat from the steamy day rushes in around me.

I say, 'Come on in,' at the same time as he says, 'Hey, thanks for having me over.'

'Of course, thanks for checking on me,' I respond, moving us back through the hallway and into the kitchen. 'And thanks for bringing some food. It made me realise I haven't really eaten much over the past few days. I'm probably running on empty,' I admit, as I head towards the drawers to dig out some plates.

'Which is understandable,' he says, dropping the bag on the countertop. 'I feel awful. I can't even imagine how you're feeling.' He takes a seat in front of the island as I bustle around the kitchen to fill up some water glasses. 'But at least you have Glenn, Zara and the rest of their family.' He glances up at me when I fumble with the plate I have in my hand. John raises an eyebrow and asks with a cautious undertone, 'Is that not right?'

'Well…' I start slowly as I offer him the plate and walk around the kitchen to sit on the stool next to him. He removes napkins and the plastic-wrapped sushi hand rolls from the bag and places them on a plate for each of us as I continue, 'It's a little complicated, but I'm not certain they're telling me everything, you know?' His eyes widen as I fiddle with the plastic casing of the roll, trying to unwrap it to get to the hand roll locked inside.

'In what way? I thought you were all very close?'

I scoff a little at that. 'I guess I've always felt like a bit of an…' I search for the word, 'outsider. Mum was the glue that held us together, and now…' I gesture around the empty house. 'Well, we're not so close.'

John nods, and a look of understanding passes across his face. 'I get it. I always felt out of place in Anna's family.' At the mention of his ex-wife, he reddens and changes the conversation. 'And so why do you think they're not telling you everything?'

'Well,' I begin, taking a bite of my tuna and avocado roll. I chew as I consider how much to tell him. Would he react like Addie or Zara?

But he seems to really care, and he is Mum's brother. *Was* Mum's brother, I correct myself with a gulp. If anyone can understand why I'm desperate to find the truth, it will be him.

And more than anything, I am so desperate to talk about it and have someone to understand and agree with me. To tell me that this isn't all a figment of my imagination.

He has a look of such deep understanding in those eyes that are so like my mother's that I can't help it. I tell him everything. I let it all out. And by the time I'm done, it feels like a huge weight has been lifted off my shoulders.

He takes a white paper napkin and presses it against his lips thoughtfully for a moment as he processes my story.

'And now, I don't know what to do... What do you think?' I ask him, swivelling around on the bar stool to face him.

He places the napkin down and then turns his own chair towards me.

'You know, I do think there are some things going on with Mike and Glenn, and they're maybe not telling the whole story of their last meetings with Suzannah. But, Emily, there's another thing that these seemingly suspicious things could be...' He pauses, weighing up his words. 'And I'm not sure you will want to hear this either, but is it possible that their behaviour and strange actions could also be coming from grief?'

I sit back on the stool. This wasn't the reaction I was hoping for.

'Look, it's not really my exact area of medical expertise,' he continues in a slow voice, 'but I do know that grief can cause us to act in some inexplicable ways. We might even say or do some things that are out of character for a while, especially in cases like this of huge shock. It can even cause brain fog or delusions and, in very bad cases, blackouts.'

I shake my head, not sure I really want to hear this.

He carries on in a gentle voice, 'Since you heard the news, have there been any moments of time looking back now that maybe are a bit hazy or you weren't sure why you acted like that?'

I think back involuntarily over a few of my rash actions, like breaking into the office or my now delusional belief that the body wasn't going to be Mum's. And whatever that blackout was I'd had on the night Mum died... but that was different. That was *before* Mum died – wasn't it?

I've been so focused on chasing down these other leads that I've been ignoring trying to remember the rest of my night. But John's mention of the words 'grief' and 'blackout' in the same sentence sends me spiralling...

What if I *did* still have something serious to do with Mum's death? If Glenn was lying about her staying at Merton Street on Friday, then it could be possible that rather than it being a drunken blackout stopping me from remembering my night, it was actually a *traumatic* blackout? And my brain is forcing me not to remember what I've done... I don't want to consider that.

My hands are starting to shake underneath the island bench. I hope John doesn't notice.

He continues. 'So I'm not saying that Glenn, Mike or even Jennifer *aren't* hiding something; it sounds like they possibly might be. But it also sounds like maybe you're hiding a few things from them.'

Oh my god. My heart stutters for a minute – does he know what I'm thinking? He can't...

'And maybe what you're all hiding from each other are your true feelings and experiences of grief. It can be hard for us to let each other in.'

I exhale in relief and say quietly, 'Maybe...'

All of a sudden, I really want to be alone.

Because I hate to admit it, but he's starting to make some *sense*. And it's making me question everything...

'Look,' he says gently, placing a hand on my shoulder. I continue to stare into space, wondering at the possible truth of his words. 'I have to shoot off now to meet my flatmates. I'm sorry to leave you like this. I know I've gone a bit "doctor" on you – but please trust me when I say that I get what you're going through, Emily – I wish there was another reason other than just a stupid accident. I really do. Suzie was my big sister. But I'm trying to accept what the police have said – that's all we can ever know for certain now. I know it's so hard to let go and open up – but call me later, and we can talk some more, okay? I'm here for you.'

He lets go of my shoulder, and the sudden absence of his hand causes me to look up. His melodic tone was so reassuring, like a voice of reason keeping me tethered to the ground.

Our eyes lock, and I see my mum's deep blue eyes once more. 'Thanks' is all I can squeak out.

'Of course – I meant what I said – here always,' he replies, standing up from the stool. I stand automatically. 'Can I wash these up?' he says, gesturing to the plates.

'Oh no, no,' I reply on autopilot. 'I'll do them in a moment. Thanks for the sushi and talk. You've given me a lot to think about.'

We walk towards the front door. I wave a short goodbye and promise I'll call him later to check in.

But as soon as I shut the door, I know that's a lie. Because I'm scared of what else he'll be able to see that I'm hiding away. It's like he's seen right through me.

The terrifying memory of Mum's cold body comes flying into my mind, and the sobs come now, loud and wracking, as I sink to the floor, arms wrapped around myself. I feel a snuffle by my face: Banjo has come to comfort me. How do dogs always know? I wrap my arms around him and sob more quietly into his fur, stroking him as my tears subside, and I feel a quiet calm begin to descend.

And with that calm, I know I can't ignore it any longer.

I have to investigate my own blackout, too.

Because if John's mini-diagnosis has taught me anything, it's that I'm surely still a suspect.

Chapter Twenty-Seven

I don't know how much time has passed when I eventually hear my phone ping.

> *Can you meet me at six at the Seawater Pool?*
> *I don't have long.*

It's Ben. I glance at the time. Quarter past five. It seems I'd been rocking Banjo for quite a while. John's words had affected me so much.

In spite of everything, though, my heart does a strange sort of flutter at his message. I am a certified *mess*. I can't be starting to feel things for my old crush on top of everything else. But his words have taken me back. He must remember the trips our mums had taken us on to the Maccallum Seawater Pool and Cremorne Reserve. Why else would he have suggested that spot? And I can't deny it is a good feeling to have those memories of bright sunny skies, salt-sprayed skin, and picnic-filled days wash over me for a minute.

I text back:

Yes, I can – see you then.

I grab the keys. It is time for me to keep going.

'Right, what do you think of this?' I say, crouching over Banjo. 'I'm putting everything John said to one side. Processing "grief" can wait until I have some answers about the rest of my family. I'll go and see Ben first and hear what he has to say, whether he has any concrete information. Then I need to figure out how to piece together what I might have seen... or done.' I sigh wearily as I, at last, pick myself up off the ground and make my way back out to the car.

Now, as I wander along the walkway of Cremorne Reserve that hugs the edge of Sydney Harbour, all the memories of coming here as a kid with my mum and dad run through me.

I focus instead on feeling the early summer evening. The heat of the afternoon is starting to give way to a comfortable warmth, and I listen to the sounds of cicadas chirruping along the bush track. They intermingle with the distant echoes of city traffic and the happy cries of children playing in the open part of the reserve.

This really is an idyllic city. But then the reason I'm here rushes back to me. Nothing about this day is perfect.

Soon, I reach the path above the Seawater Pool, and as I am about to descend, I spot Ben sitting on a bench a few yards away, overlooking everything. He hasn't seen me yet, and I notice as I approach that he is frowning down at his phone, typing furiously.

'Hello!' I call out, approaching him from behind. He jumps and turns around, his frown turning into a shy smile. He's in blue board shorts and a white T-shirt. It suits him. His usually fair hair looks darker because it is a little wet, as though he's just gone for a swim – and I spy the beach towel on the back of the bench.

'Hey, Emily.' He gestures towards the empty space. 'Take a seat.'

'Sorry, did I interrupt you?' I ask, pointing towards his phone.

'No worries, I'll get back to it later. How are you doing?' he asks as I sit down next to him.

'Oh, you know…' I trail off, flicking my sunglasses up to the top of my head as a distraction, and turn to take in the view.

'Of course, sorry. What a stupid thing to say, a reflex.'

'Don't worry.' I turn back around, seeing the sadness in his eyes – I don't want him to feel bad. 'How are you?'

'I'm absolutely fine.' But a shadow of something passes his face and I wonder if he is telling me the whole truth. I need to stop suspecting everyone. 'You hungry?' he changes the subject, and his frown turns into a bright smile, reminding me of the boyish grin I once knew.

'Don't worry, I'm okay, I've eaten.'

'Oh,' he says, his face falling, 'but I brought some fish and chips.' He swivels to produce two Styrofoam boxes from behind him.

Now, it is my turn to grin. 'Really?!' Before we dated as teenagers, we were childhood friends first, going to the same primary school. As kids, it had become a sort of tradition that when we'd come here to play after school, we would have an early dinner of fish and chips.

I can't believe that he remembered. It has been so long ago. And after I'd broken up with him so suddenly, I'd assumed he would have wanted to forget everything to do with me.

'Of course,' he says, his face turning into a broad smile. But then it fades when he asks, 'You do remember, right? That we used to always get fish and chips?'

'Yes, I do. I just didn't think you would have,' I reply, smiling back. This is a bad idea. My emotions are all over the place, and here this man is, my first crush, being incredibly sweet. Tears prick my vision.

Oh my god, I can't cry right now. I draw my sunglasses back over my eyes, pretending that the sun is causing me to squint.

'Good. I hoped that it might be a nice memory,' he says, and I catch a little blush creeping up his neck. He passes me over the Styrofoam box and a wooden knife and fork.

'Thank you,' I reply. 'It is,' and my voice cracks. I do not deserve him being so nice to me.

He pauses mid-handing over a napkin. 'God, sorry if it was maybe a bit soon, I didn't think properly about it.'

I sniff, opening up the box to tuck into the perfect combination of greasy and delicious fish and chips. After what John had said, I couldn't finish the sushi roll. So, my stomach rumbles at the heady smell. I balance it precariously on my lap.

'No, please, it's a good memory. It's nice to think back to happier and simpler times.' And I really mean that. Everything has become so dark and complicated in my life. I miss the sunny days of my childhood more than ever. I take a big bite of the battered fish. 'This is delicious, thank you.'

'My pleasure,' he replies with a grin, and for a moment we lapse into silence. We're just two people sitting in the easy evening sun, taking in the magnificent view over Sydney Harbour. We listen to the hubbub of an ordinary day and tuck into a classic summer meal. From the outside, we would look like two people catching up without a worry in the world.

I take a deep breath, then I blurt out in a sudden rush, 'So, I went to the funeral home today... to see Mum.'

His fork freezes midway to his mouth, and he replaces it back into his box. 'Ah,' he says, turning towards me. 'That must have been tough.'

'Yeah, it really was.' I carry on. 'So I guess that means you're not investigating things anymore, now that she's been returned to us?'

He sighs like a great weight is on his shoulders. He doesn't seem surprised by my question. 'The coroner didn't find anything suspicious on the body... or anything to question the assumed time of death. Everything points to it being a tragic accident. In cases like this, we always release back to the family as quickly as possible. And I also put in a word to make sure that would be the case if nothing was found.'

'I see, so that means... that you're not looking into anything else?'

He takes another moment. I can tell he is trying to choose his words carefully. 'Technically, we haven't *officially* closed the case yet, but that's only because we're tidying up a couple of bits of paperwork. So, it basically is. And I have to prepare you: unless something drastic comes to light, we will close it away entirely.' He sighs, reaching his hands out as though to take mine, but withdraws them quickly. 'I'm sorry. I know you wanted to put together a clearer picture of her last moments. But this is all we're ever going to know.'

I turn my face away, up towards the sun, and take a second to feel its warmth on my face. I try not to feel crushed. Deep down, I know I should be happy about all this – that the police haven't discovered anything else themselves and that the case will be closed and all behind us. But I can't. Not yet.

I open my eyes and look back at him. 'I understand,' I say. 'Thank you for telling me. I really appreciate it. But...' I continue on, 'if a new lead suddenly came up, that would make a difference?'

'Well, yes, but I don't think that's likely to happen, do you?' he asks me, a line appearing across his brow.

'Perhaps it might...' I can't tell him about what I heard Mike say in the Imaginate office because I can't tell him I broke in after our last meeting. That could compromise him, not to mention the fact that I'd be admitting to breaking and entering to a police officer. No, I had to be vague about things.

'I hope you're not doing anything that might get you into trouble yourself, Ems,' he says, using my nickname to soften the seriousness of his statement. 'Or digging into finding Felicity Smith through any... dubious means. Because that's what I thought you wanted to talk to me about – and I have to say that I haven't been able to find out anything strange, and I don't think I can keep digging into it without causing a load of unwelcome questions myself—'

'No,' I interrupt to stop him worrying. I did want to ask him more questions about her – but it sounds like he's done all he can.

'Okay, good, because I wouldn't want you to get into more trouble with your family, or worse...' He stops. The last thing we both wanted was for him to be looking into something *I'd* done.

'No,' I try to reassure him. I know I'm lying, but I need him on my side more than ever. And if he can't help me with Felicity Smith, then I need him to answer my next question without second guessing my actions. 'I get it, don't worry. But what I also wanted to ask was whether your team had anything of Mum's in possession before she went to the coroners? Or if you're still holding on to anything?' I twirl the wooden fork in my hand as I wait for his reply.

'Oh,' he begins, and I look up to see that he looks relieved. For once, I've probably asked a question he is able to answer without breaking any codes of conduct. 'Well, no, we weren't holding on to anything. Like I told you, her phone wasn't found – we think it was washed out to sea. And there wasn't anything else of interest to look at. Why? Did you not receive everything that you thought you would?'

'I don't think so.'

He runs his hands through his hair, and a droplet of water flicks onto my shoulder. 'What do you think you're missing?'

'Well,' I begin, putting my Styrofoam box to one side and tucking my knee into my chest. I lean closer. 'This might sound strange, but Mum has... *had*,' I correct myself with a gulp, 'three rings. All sentimental.'

Ben nods. 'Right...' His blue eyes pierce mine. The little boy I knew was gone, and I am looking back at an intent officer searching for answers.

'And so if you never had them, and the coroner never had them, and Glenn says that they're not at home, then where can they be? She never went *anywhere* without them. She *never* took them off.' I desperately need him to understand why this is so important. Where the rings were would hold important answers – possibly to everything.

'I understand,' he says, tilting his head to one side in thought. He isn't dismissing my rambling explanations out of hand, and that already makes me feel less alone. Even though, because he's a police officer, I can't tell him *everything* I've been up to, he's the only person I've said anything to who doesn't look at me like I'm making things up. And that's something.

'Look,' he begins, 'it's a useful thing for me to know, and I'll do some digging – it's possible they were picked up by our guys to look at, checked by forensics, that sort of thing. They even might have been handed back to Glenn... but then I don't know why he would say he doesn't have them...' He muses on and tousles his hair. 'I'll let you know what I can find out.'

'Thank you,' I reply in a small voice.

'Of course,' he says. 'I really am trying to do everything possible to overturn every stone – I want to know that we did everything to learn exactly what happened, not only because it's my job, but because I want to give that to you,' he adds with a wistful smile.

All I can do is nod. I am starting to feel all choked up.

'I just,' he says in a quieter voice, 'have to stay within the bounds of the law, which I know can be a bit slow and frustrating, but bear with me, okay?'

'I get it; I wouldn't want you to have to do anything that would jeopardise your work. Everything you're doing for us, for me, is amazing.'

Ben nods. 'Now I better get going, but I'll find out what I can and be in touch soon.'

He starts to replace his box back in the paper bag it had come in and reaches over to take mine as I turn to put it away myself. Our arms brush past each other with a whoosh, and a rush of electricity runs through me. I hurry to explain away the tingly moment as just some goosebumps. He pauses, too, but regains his composure by jumping to his feet, grabbing my box and shoving it away. Whatever that weird moment was has gone in a flash.

'Alright, I'll see you soon. Make sure you take a minute to have a drink and enjoy the view.' He nods at the can of lemonade that is on the ground by our feet.

'Oh no,' I say, standing up, 'that's yours.'

'Please,' he replies so sternly that I can't think of a response. 'Just check out the ingredients and let me know what you think next time, okay?'

I am completely bewildered by this, but all I can say is, 'Umm, sure, thanks?'

He leans forward to pick the small can up and then places it in my hands. He raises a small eyebrow at me, then says loudly, 'Good to see you, Emily. I'll be in touch.'

He strides off down the path, and I sit back down. I look around, but other than the distant hum of traffic and a dog walker in the distance, the area is deserted.

As I go to open the can, I notice something scrawled on the side. I could almost have missed it, but as I am positioning it to open, I see a small drawn-on arrow pointing down.

I quickly flip the can over.

FS, it begins, and then my eyes widen as I realise that scrawled underneath is a tiny address. *No way* – he said he hadn't found anything, but had he actually provided me with Felicity's address after all? I couldn't believe it; he truly did mean it when he said he wanted to help me in every possible way.

I flip the can around again, and this time, I continue to pull open the top, listening to the satisfying fizz. Bringing it to my lips, I take a deep sip.

Clutching the can tight in my hand, I take a final look at the sweeping view before standing up and starting my own way back, certainty beating in my chest again at the thought of what I will be doing next.

It is time to get to the bottom of this and find out what Felicity Smith knows – once and for all.

Chapter Twenty-Eight

Sunlight streams through my shuttered blinds, and I wake to my alarm gasping for air. I swear I saw my mother in my dreams – just as she tumbled over the edge... I try to hold on. But the image is gone. Was it a memory or a nightmare? I don't know.

I sigh in frustration. My mind feels like it's constantly playing tricks on me. I have to focus on the concrete facts, and today, instead of chasing ghosts, I'm visiting Felicity. I jump out of bed and get out of the house before Glenn and Zara see me. I don't want to have to try and explain where I'm going.

Zara said that I could borrow her car for now, so I fully intend to make the most of that offer. I grab a muesli bar on my way out of the house and pull out of the driveway as quietly as I can. Then, I start to make my way to the other end of Sydney's northern beaches. Felicity's apparent address is an isolated place from the looks of it: up amongst the bushland that wraps itself around the edges of that topmost corner of Sydney.

As I weave out of the city and inch my way closer to my destination, driving up the coast, the bright yellow sandy beaches peek out at me.

In a huge contrast to how my morning started yesterday, I feel hopeful. Finally, I will get some answers that might help me piece everything together. But soon, my Google Maps starts to twist away from the sun and sparkling water and up to the plateau, further into denser bushland. With the ancient trees pressing in around me, everything becomes dark and oppressive. And the hope that I felt moments ago evaporates.

A chill settles down my spine as I notice the shaded light and how *quiet* it is up here. A few minutes ago, I had seen people milling around near the beach and shops. But up here, it appears to be devoid of anyone.

I can't help the little niggling voice in my head telling me that I should run and get out of here now. There must be a reason Felicity has been so hard to track, after all. I plough on, ignoring my doubts.

Soon, I've 'reached my destination', but as I slow to a stop, it's not obvious where the house is. All I can see is bush – other than an old track that juts out of the corner via a dip on the road.

I pull over just past it and shut off my engine to take stock of my surroundings. Undoing my seatbelt, I peer out through all my windows. It doesn't feel like Sydney anymore.

I take a breath and glance behind me to see the driveway. A few little weeds peek out of the earth over the roughly laid concrete. It suggests either a home that is unkempt or that no one actually lives there. For the first time, I consider that Felicity might not be at home.

Or been silenced like my mother.

My heart starts to beat faster, and I try to keep taking deep breaths to get it under control. There is only one way to get the answers I need.

And it is down that overgrown driveway and inside the house that must be hiding behind the towering trees.

The sun inches up higher in the sky as I flatten the hat I'd brought further down over my face and push my battered, old sunglasses up my nose. I didn't want to wear anything that would be memorable. But I need to look semi-respectable as well. So, I've gone for some tailored black shorts, a white long-sleeved shirt, a wide-brimmed sunhat, and sunglasses.

I try to walk at a normal pace down the road, pretending that I belong here and that I am doing a perfectly normal thing, walking up to Felicity's door.

The cicadas chirrup in their choir, sounding much louder out here in the dense bushland than down in the city. The sun beats down, and the dry grass crunches underneath my feet. If I wasn't so completely freaked out, it could almost be peaceful. Instead, this place gives me the creeps.

As I walk down the driveway, I am covered by the shade of the trees above me – they block out both the sun and the way back to the road. A magpie caws as my eyes adjust, and the little house comes into sight.

It's tiny – a one-storey bungalow with four squat windows and a blue wooden door – dwarfed by the overhanging trees. I am unbearably close to the front door now. How am I even going to explain myself? I reach the front door, and I hover there, uncertain.

It hits me that this is a terrible idea. What was I thinking, turning up on a stranger's doorstep? But not only that: I'd assumed that Felicity Smith was the crucial piece of the puzzle in figuring out *why* Mike had killed Mum. But what if that wasn't true at all? What if Felicity had been involved too?

I'd never even considered that.

I stumble on the little step, frantically trying to turn around. But I spin so fast, causing me to trip and fall straight down to the ashy, dry grass. I cry out, feeling my ankle twist as I hit the ground.

I look up, back towards the front door. Maybe I wasn't too loud. Maybe no one heard me. But to my horror, the door opens to reveal a small woman hidden in shadow.

Whether I like it or not, I am here, facing Felicity Smith. And I have to decide what story to tell.

Chapter Twenty-Nine

'What on earth?!'

A shocked voice cries above me in a broad Australian accent. Still feeling terrified, I put my head in my hands and shake it from side to side, trying to steady my swirling mind.

'Well, wait there then, I'll get some water.' Footsteps float away, padding over the floor.

By the time the woman, presumably Felicity, returns with some water, I've managed to ease back to my feet, wincing a tiny bit as I put pressure on my ankle. I try to put on my best smile as she offers me a glass of water. So much for the professional look I'd wanted to go for.

Her long, shiny black hair has fallen around her face, but two large dark eyes peek out from behind their curtains. The expression is not unkind, but it is defensive and confused. I notice now, standing in front of her, that in contrast to my height, she is petite, but her presence somehow takes up the narrow corridor she is blocking. I instantly get the sense that she wouldn't back down from something without a fight.

'Are you okay?' she asks with a frown as I sip the water. I, a total stranger, have arrived unannounced at this woman's house, collapsed on her doorstep, and she is asking me if I am okay?! It takes me a second to respond, nodding, 'Yes, thank you.'

As I drink, I see her starting to size me up with a cautious look in her eye. 'And so, who are you?' she folds her arms across her chest.

'I'm so sorry for this,' I croak, 'and thank you so much for the water.' I gesture at the half-drunk water glass in my hand. 'I'm, uh, looking for Felicity Smith.'

'And whose asking?' she asks in her quiet but authoritative tone, not skipping a beat. And I know: the only way I am going to find out anything from this woman is if I am completely honest. She would see through a made-up story a mile off.

And so I begin, 'I'm Emily Olsen, the daughter of Suzannah Archer, and I think – I hope – you might be able to help me.'

She shakes her head, once, twice, as if trying to discard what she'd heard.

'No,' she says more to herself than to me. 'You can't be.'

'I am,' I insist in my most gentle tone. 'And all I'm here for is some answers. I'm not sure if you know, but Mum... Suzannah... is dead. I'm trying to get to the truth of what happened.'

As I get a closer look at her face, I realise she doesn't look much older than me. Her complexion is smooth as cream silk. And it goes even paler at my words. She moves to clutch the door handle. It looks like she is about to slam it in my face.

'Please,' I cry out, reaching my hand out to try and stop the shutting door. 'All I want is the truth. I don't mean you any harm, but she was all I had. I have a couple of questions,' I say desperately as my voice cracks, and I can see the door slowing down its shutting momentum.

Felicity peers out at me, her face in shadow around the half-closed door. But finally, she says in a whisper, 'Come in, quick then.'

She opens the door a fraction. I nod my thanks and shuffle inside. It shuts with a thud behind me.

I follow Felicity without a word down the beige entry. Boxes line the hallway, and I wonder if it's because they'd just moved in or they're about to move out. There's not a photograph or decoration to be seen, so I watch her instead. I notice for the first time that she's wearing an overlarge jumper and shorts. Outside, it would be far too hot for that outfit, but stepping inside her home feels like walking into the cool shade, and I try to pull my shirt further towards my wrists.

I enter a small, open-plan kitchen and living area. But though it is tiny, with shabby grey sofas and a small walnut dining table that has seen better days, everything is spotlessly clean.

Hovering at the entrance to the room, Felicity pauses by the kitchen cabinet, turning to face me. 'Look,' she begins in a voice barely above a whisper. 'I don't know how you found me or what you want from me. But I don't think I can help you.' She shakes her head. 'Your mum was always kind to me, so I'll hear you out – but I really can't risk anything more.'

She glances up to the wall opposite the kitchen cabinets, and there I see one picture of Felicity with a boy. He is about her own height but can't be more than thirteen.

I nod as she pauses, turning to gaze intently at the photograph with a sigh. Looking back at me, she says, 'We've just moved here... How did you even find me?'

I avoid the question and instead say, 'Did you send a letter to my mum last week, the day before she died?'

She crosses her arms as she leans back on the small dining table. 'What letter?'

I look into her opaque eyes to try and see if I can guess whether she's telling me the truth. 'The one that warned Mum to look into what happened to you.'

Felicity freezes still as a statue, then shakes her head again as I dig into my pocket – and drag out the note. I wordlessly take one step closer and hand it over.

She scans through its contents. I try to watch every tiny change of expression on her face, but when she looks up, there's only one overriding one: total shock.

'Oh my god,' she says, 'who sent this?' she looks genuinely frightened and glances up at the photograph of her boy on the wall. 'Why is someone trying to bring me into this? I left so quietly...' she adds in a whisper.

'I don't know. But that's what I want to know, too, Felicity. Something must have happened at Imaginate to make you so scared.' She looks away from me, avoiding my gaze. I continue doggedly. I will not give up now that I'm here.

I glance around this room – at the emptiness of it, and then back at the woman standing across from me. She shrinks back, appearing almost childlike. 'Please, can I at least ask why you've moved?'

Felicity bristles at my words. I know I'm probably asking too much. But then she stares at me and says, 'You look just like her, you know. I can't believe she's dead. I had no idea...'

I tuck a strand of hair behind my ear self-consciously. 'It happened a few days ago… and the day before she died, she received that letter telling her to look into your dismissal. So I had to come looking for you. I'm sorry, it's clear you don't want to be found. But you see, I don't think her death was an accident.'

Her eyes widen. My next questions fly out. 'How much does Mike Cowper have to do with you leaving Imaginate? Please, can you tell me?'

At the mention of his name, all the colour races out of her face. *This* is what I'd come here for. Felicity had a story about Mike, and I had to convince her to tell me.

She shakes her head. 'I-I don't think I can help you. I-I can't be involved.' Her bottom lip begins to wobble.

'Please, Felicity,' I try again. 'I promise that whatever you tell me won't leave this room. But you understand what I'm doing here. My mum is *dead*, and I think Mike has something to do with it. I need answers about how your story might fit into all this. Please – I need to know what happened to her.' My voice cracks, and I point over at the photograph she'd stared at on the wall. 'Your boy – wouldn't you do anything for him? And wouldn't he do the same for you?' I know it's a low blow, but I'm desperate.

She wrings her hands in front of her. 'I really am sorry for your loss. But I'm so scared. Everything I've done is to protect my little family, you see…'

'I understand, Felicity, but please.' I almost choke on my last word, my throat tight with emotion. I don't know what more I can say to convince her.

Her face crumples, and I see a singular tear escape from the corner of her eye. 'Seeing you here in front of me asking for help… I recognise you from the lovely photograph on your mother's desk. We didn't talk much – but in the few conversations we had, we'd share stories of our kids. She'd ask about my son, and I'd ask about you. She was very proud of you, you know.'

I blink back the tears that rise to the surface.

She gulps as she looks around the room, filled with boxes, and maybe it's seeing her life in a state of disarray that helps decide it for her. She pushes up off the side of the table where she'd been leaning and stands up straight as she says, 'You're right. If you think me sharing this story will help, I will tell you. Especially if you suspect your mum's death has anything to do with Mike Cowper. It's about time I try to be brave.'

She gestures behind her towards the sofa and coffee table tucked into the corner of the room. 'Sit down, and I'll make us some tea. Jamie will be back in about an hour, so we have until then.'

Felicity strides off into the kitchen area of the room as I say, 'Thank you,' and make my way across to the sofa.

I stare out of the window at a tangle of trees. When she first moved here, Felicity must have hoped that this house would protect her from prying eyes. But she should have known that trees in the Australian bushland are never safe. There is always the risk of furious fires that could flare at any moment from the smallest spark. And it feels like by turning up here, I might have set her carefully concealed life ablaze.

CHAPTER THIRTY

My feet tap up and down on the wooden floor, impatient for Felicity to return. At last, she walks over with a tray laden with biscuits, a pot and some mugs. I take the proffered cup wordlessly. All my attention is focused on her.

She meets my gaze with a look of quiet determination as she begins. 'Well, I'll start by saying I've worked very hard to get to where I am today. To be able to have a life I never dreamed was possible when I was growing up on the other side of Australia. When I first left my tiny home town, I was still a teenager. I hadn't come from much, but I moved to the city and found what work I could to get by. But soon enough, I got into the wrong crowd... then I found out I was pregnant. It was a huge shock, and I thought about giving the baby up – I was only nineteen and with no one to help me; how could I possibly look after a child when I was barely looking after myself? But when he was born, I knew that I couldn't do it. He changed something in me, and my little Jamie also made me realise that I had to run away from his father. Or he'd end up like him...' She shudders involuntarily at the memory.

I'm stuck to the spot, lost in her words. The strange similarity to Mum's own story and how I was born surprises me. I had been an unexpected arrival for Mum and Dad, who were fresh out of high school when they discovered Mum was pregnant. At least we had always been supported. It didn't sound like Felicity had that luxury. No, it sounded like she'd had the complete opposite.

She gazes through the windows once more as if she isn't telling her story to me now but out into the world. And since she's started, it is all spilling out of her in one long tumble.

'My parents didn't want anything to do with me either. So I left without a trace, disappearing into the masses of Sydney. And I knew that if I were to create the life I wanted my baby to have, then I needed to find myself a good living and a stable job. I began by cleaning houses, but I had always been good with numbers, and one of my clients was an accountant. I plucked up the courage one day to ask her how she'd become one. She helped me find some classes, and I managed to pay my way through school in the evening. It took me a long time, but I finally qualified. I managed to pick up work here and there until I eventually built up quite a good freelance portfolio. We were secure, no one could find us, and we could start living the life I'd always dreamt of. It should have been perfect...' She pauses and sighs.

I clear my throat. 'That sounds like an incredible story. Your son must be so proud of you.'

She turns back towards me and looks almost surprised to find me there. 'Yes, well, wait until I finish. Because I wished for too much, and it was all too good to be true...

'About a year ago now, I did some freelance work for Imaginate. And that's how I met Mike... and your mum.' She pauses as her warm brown eyes meet mine. 'I didn't have much to do with your mum as Mike was in charge of the finances. He was so kind. He showered me with compliments and told me this was some of the best work they'd ever had. I should have known better... but he was the first man that had ever seemed interested in my mind as well as my looks. He made me feel seen. It was the final day of my current job, and I was finishing up in the Imaginate offices. Jamie was having a sleepover at a friend's that night, so I didn't have to rush off. I'd lost track of time, and I was finishing up when a voice whispered in my ear, "Someone knows how to impress the boss." I'd jumped out of my skin and turned around so fast in my chair. He caught my arms as I spun, halting me right in front of him. "Whoa there!" he'd flashed that sparkling smile at me, and I tried to calm my racing heart. I'd let out a small laugh at the joke, and he joined in. We started to chat, and I found myself relaxing.' She shakes her head and clutches the pillow next to her.

'Then he suggested we get a drink. I should have said no, of course, I should have said no. But I thought no harm could be done by having one small beer. I was wrong. He took me to the most beautiful bar I'd ever seen. It had a rooftop with epic scenes across Sydney's skyline, and one drink turned into two, into three. We were having so much fun, and I got carried away. I should have seen the kiss coming – once it happened, I should have stopped it all there.

'I tried to make it a one-time thing, but he was persistent. I knew it was wrong. I knew he was married. But I couldn't help myself... I'd never felt this way before. It was like a sickness!' She suddenly jumps up from the sofa, throwing the pillow hard across the room. I sit back in shock at her violent reaction. She doesn't even notice as she starts to pace, her long dark hair swishing around her back. Then she turns to look at me desperately, anguish written across her face.

'The next part is going to be hardest to tell,' she mutters softly as she sinks back down into the cushions like a deflating balloon. 'You have to understand, I loved him. I really loved him. Or I loved the person I thought he was. You see, he started to become like a father figure to Jamie... and he promised me everything. But the one thing he didn't promise was to leave his wife. Yet. He said he couldn't; she was very unwell and needed his help. At first, I thought that was true... he said for now, he could buy Jamie and me a place and create a new life for all of us to be together a little further up the coast. It would be easy, he said. And for a little while, I let myself live in that fantasy. But there was something niggling at me. Something buried deep in the back of my mind... And I only discovered the truth because I was packing to move. For him,' she says with a bitter laugh.

'I found my accounts – the very first ones I ever did for Imaginate. I was feeling sentimental, I guess, so I went through them again. And what I saw made my blood run cold. I hadn't thought twice about it at the time; it seemed normal when I didn't know Mike or the business from a bar of soap, but amongst everything, there was a collection of line items for an "office" space and a flat *down* the coast. I knew it could be a coincidence – but I thought it a bit strange. I could have pushed it to one side, but then I saw his wife. I'd been doing some more freelance work for Imaginate, and she popped into the office one day out of the blue. I could tell Mike was furious to see her. Apparently, there had been some sort of family emergency, and she needed Suzannah. It was only then that I was told by another colleague that your mum was married to his wife's brother! – I had no idea. They didn't exactly big up the family connection. I guess I'd never asked. But from that moment, I realised he'd been lying about his wife's sickness. Then, I couldn't help but wonder what else he might have been lying about to me. I decided to do some digging…

'First, I enquired casually with someone who had worked there for a while if they knew about any other offices. They did not, which seemed very suspicious. So next, I decided to go on a little road trip. I went all the way down to the address of the "work flat" – and you can probably already guess what I found.' I can hardly breathe.

'She was pretty, I'll give her that. And she opened the door to me with a bright smile. I wanted to scream in her face. But then a child jumped out from behind her legs. A miniature version of Mike. And I turned and ran. I couldn't face her. And besides, my anger shouldn't be directed at her. But at him. I know I wasn't some innocent in all this – I'd started an affair with a married man after all! But I thought I was special to him,' her voice cracks. 'He was the only man that had ever made me feel special in my whole sorry life. And it was all a lie. I didn't know what I was going to do, but I was furious.

'He was coming over that night. We'd arranged it weeks ago; it was when his wife was on a "health retreat", and I'd organised for Jamie to be at a friend's. I knew that this was the moment for me to bring it up. It was now or never. I wasn't sure what I was going to say, but I thought we could get everything out in the open. I was desperately hoping that there was an explanation. Maybe whatever he'd had with that woman was all over. Maybe his wife had been sick but had recently recovered, and he hadn't had the chance to tell me. Maybe this was the moment he would finally choose me. Just me.

'I was so naïve. When he arrived, he was full of smiles; he'd even brought some flowers and wine. I couldn't believe that this man who'd made me feel so treasured was capable of all this.' She's facing me but not looking at me. Instead, she's staring hard at the space next to me on the sofa. A chill runs down my spine.

'We sat on that very sofa, in my old little flat back in the Inner West, sipping our wine. I should have left it.' She shakes her head. 'But it all blurted out. Everything I'd discovered and suspected. I thought he'd halt me, tell me it was all a mistake. Instead, he went deathly still as he listened. When I was finished, you could have heard a pin drop. Then he laughed. Laughed in my face! He told me what a clever girl I'd been, piecing everything together, and that's why he loved me. He said he was sorry he hadn't told me the whole truth about his wife and Jacinta, but at least now I knew – and wouldn't that be easier anyway? I couldn't believe my ears. He tried to take my hand and bring me in for a kiss, but I pulled back in disgust. Then I screamed at him, "How can you tell me you love me when you've been lying to me the whole time?" He tried to placate me, but I couldn't stop. I demanded that if he wanted to be with me, he had to leave his wife and assure me that whatever happened with Jacinta was all in the past. That it was finally time for him to make a choice...

'But he shook his head. He told me he was sorry but he couldn't. It wasn't his fault that he loved so many people... now it was my turn to laugh. He didn't like that. He went red, but I carried on and asked if the others even knew about me. His silence was a clear answer. This Jacinta might know about his wife but not about me. And I bet that the wife had no idea about either of us. My head was swimming. "I let you in," I said hopelessly. "Jamie adores you. He looks up to you..."

'Perhaps it didn't need to get as bad as it did. But then Mike said that nothing had to change. He still wanted to be part of our lives and carry on with all the plans that we'd made. But I'd have to accept the rest of him... I almost considered it. I almost said yes. Then I'd seen that photo over there out of the corner of my eye.' She points to a small picture frame to the right of my shoulder: it shows a younger Felicity and a small boy of about four. They're both grinning up at the camera happily. You'd never have known how she'd struggled to raise him.

'And that's when the rage hit me. Not just at Mike, but at myself. How could I have been so stupid as to let my son create a role model out of this man? Introduce him into our lives when surely I'd known deep down that it was always going to end in tears? I'd been foolish and irresponsible. I'd created this whole mess. And I realised that it had to stop. For my boy, I couldn't let this go on. So I tried to stay calm as I asked Mike to leave. I told him that it was over. And I should have left it there, I should have. But an image of all the friends I'd made at Imaginate sprung into my mind at that moment. And especially one of your mum. It made me so angry to think about how unfair it was on all of them that this man had not only once but constantly used company money to line his own pockets and for his selfish purposes. I couldn't bear the thought of him continuing to slowly bring the company to the ground. And now I knew the truth. As the accountant, it was my responsibility to report it as well. If I didn't, my whole livelihood and reputation would be at stake too. It had to stop. So I told him so. I said

I'd leave his wife and Jacinta alone – I'd keep our affair a secret – but he had to make good on the money he'd stolen from the company, or I'd have to do my due diligence and report him.

'That's when his composure left him. He stood up, a fire burning in his eyes, and he said how *dare* I make demands on him when he'd offered me the world.' She squeezes the pillow tight again. 'He's a big man, and suddenly, he loomed over me. It brought back terrible memories of my father, of a time when I was growing up I'd rather forget... I thought I'd left all men like that in my past. But I guess I'd unknowingly been once again attracted to the violence I'd been running from since I was small. Instinctively, I'd shrunk back. But then I heard a voice in my head telling me to stand up and fight. That I wasn't a little girl anymore. So I did, I screamed back. I told him he'd broken my heart and that saving my reputation and his company was the *least* he could do. He didn't like that, not at all. I should have seen it coming, but I was too carried away screaming back. I didn't see the foggy, vacant gaze that I should be able to recognise from a mile away. I didn't see his hand come flying at me until it was too late.' She unconsciously touches her lip as though she can still feel the impact of his fist. And I can't bear to hear what she'll tell me next...

Chapter Thirty-One

My heart is beating so fast I'm surprised Felicity can't hear it. I feel so guilty. I'd known about Mike's temper after the day I saw him and Mum fight all those years ago. But I never thought he'd be *violent*. I don't know why I'm surprised after I'd been suspecting his involvement in Mum's death this whole time.

Felicity carries on, her eyes shiny with unshed tears. 'The sofa caught my fall. Which I thought was lucky at first. Until he grabbed the back of my head and forced it to one side.' The tears start to slide down her face.

'You don't have to tell me the rest.' I speak urgently; my voice comes out hoarse after being spellbound by her story.

'No, I do,' she says defiantly, clearing her throat. 'He started whispering in my ear. The most *horrible* things. The exact words that he knew would hurt me the most. That I was weak, that I was trash, that I'd been so lucky to ever be with someone like him in the first place. And then he said, "Why do you think you were even chosen to be our accountant? Because you were clever? No, it's because I knew you were desperate. I spotted that you had a past that you'd rather keep hidden. Both from your future employers, I'm betting, but also from your little boy." And then he whispered the one name that turned my veins to ice. The name of Jamie's father. A name I'd hoped I'd never hear again.

'You see, he'd also been violent *and* part of a criminal gang. I'd been lucky to escape at the time. I'd changed our names and hoped I'd hidden us so well that he'd never find us again. Because if he did, I knew he'd never let us go or forgive me for running away with his child. I don't know how Mike had discovered his name, but the very fact that he knew it meant that I wasn't safe anymore. Neither of us were.

'I'd stopped struggling, frozen in fear. So he let his grip on me go; he knew he'd left his parting blow anyway. I wasn't going to say anything now, was I? Not now. My son could be in danger with a single word from him. I sat up slowly and saw that his once warm eyes were now cold as ice as he looked down on me pitifully. "This could have ended so differently, Flissy," he'd said in an almost mournful voice. Then he turned around and left without another word. And I don't know how long I sat right there, rocking myself back together.' She stops speaking as she stares into space.

'Oh my god,' I breathe into the echoing silence that fills the small room. 'I am so sorry.'

It doesn't seem nearly enough, but I don't know what else to say. Nothing could make what Mike had done okay.

This poor woman – she's already been through so much in her life – and look at what my 'family' has done to her now. She clears her throat and looks me straight in the eye. 'I was terrified. So I did what I'd always done: I ran away. I swept everything under the rug and left Imaginate as quietly and quickly as I could. I was halfway through a job for them, but I had to get out of there. I don't know what story Mike told to smooth it over with the team. I knew I was being a coward in running away. But I couldn't risk it – no matter what, I couldn't risk anything happening to my little boy,' she pleads with me.

'You don't have to explain any of that to me,' I say simply.

'But I do – because the thing is, by running away and keeping all this silent, not only did I allow Mike to keep stealing money from your mum and everyone else at Imaginate, but I also kept my knowledge of Mike's cheating and violence to myself.' She runs her fingers through her hair. Anguish is written across her face.

'It's okay, Felicity, really...'

She buries her head in her hands. This woman had seemed so quietly assured when I'd first met her, but now she's in pieces. Because of my family.

I clench my fists as Felicity chokes out from behind her fingers. 'And now I'm so ashamed because I did exactly as he asked. I acted like a total coward.'

'It's okay,' I say again. 'I understand.'

She shakes her head. 'No... no,' she stammers out, 'there's something else. Something that you need to know. Because he said something else to me in that horrible moment. He said he'd do *anything* to protect his position and what he built. I'd been so terrified at all his other threats that I hadn't thought about what those words might have meant for anyone else. But now... now with what you've said has happened with Suzannah... If your mum found something out that threatened him...' She leaves the words hanging in the air between us.

I know what she's trying to say. Mike is desperate and dangerous, more so than I ever could have suspected. If he hurt and blackmailed

Felicity for threatening to uncover his lies, what might he have done to Mum if she had the power to do the same?

I feel sick to my stomach, but I know, at last, that I've discovered a vital piece of the puzzle. I'd suspected for a long time that Mum had found out something about the business that Mike didn't want her to know. And now I know exactly *what* that is. I wasn't imagining everything because here Felicity is, living proof of Mike's secrets. And now I'm certain he killed Mum for them…

I jump to my feet. 'It's *Mike* that needs to answer for all this. For everything he's done.' I say this with such venom in my words that she glances up in shock, clearly not expecting this strong response from me.

'But – but you must blame me… if I'd spoken out, your mum, she might still be alive…'

My heart breaks at that, but I know I can't blame her. What else could she have done, with not only her life but her boy's life on the line? And would anyone have believed her anyway? It would have been Felicity's word against Mike's.

'No,' I say with meaning. 'Don't blame yourself – this is all Mike, and you've given me his motive and proved that he's a violent and manipulative man who would do *anything* to keep his secrets hidden. And I'm going to make sure that he'll never be able to hurt anyone ever again.'

'Really?' she replies, her voice coming out in a whisper.

'Yes – Mike will be locked away for what he's done.' I say loudly. It's a promise.

She looks up at me in slight wonder.

'Felicity, thank you – you didn't have to tell me your story, and I'm so grateful that you trusted me enough to.'

Her story has helped piece everything together. Mike is a fraud, a liar, a violent man, and, I'm certain, a killer. All I need to do now is prove without a shadow of a doubt that it was him by placing him at the scene – and get him to admit to everything.

I stand up. 'Thank you, Felicity, truly,' I say, walking towards her as she sits still, exhausted from the shattering emotion of telling her tale. She glances up at me and raises herself slowly.

'It's the least I could do now after I'd been such a coward. Thank you for forcing me to tell my story. I'm so sorry for your loss – but your mum would be proud...'

'I promise you, I will bring him down for everything he's done to you. For everything he's done to Mum. And then you'll be safe at last.'

Another tear rolls down her cheek. I look away as my throat constricts.

We walk towards the front door, and Felicity opens it. I blink at the bright sunlight. It feels like an eternity has passed since I tripped at the threshold.

We glance at each other as I pass through the door. Turning my head to face her, I nod in acknowledgement and whisper a final goodbye. At the end of the driveway, I look back to see her small figure silhouetted in the doorway. She raises a hand in a wave and shuts the door.

I have to stop Mike, not just for Mum but for Felicity.

And before he can hurt anyone else...

Chapter Thirty-Two

I stride back towards the car, ignoring the small twinge in my ankle. As I emerge out of the shade of the trees, I let the hot midday sun beat down on my hair. I don't replace my hat to cover up. Because in stark contrast to my earlier fear, I don't care who sees me now – I am a woman on a mission. It's clear to me after talking to Felicity that Mike is guilty. Her story, alongside what I heard him say when he thought no one was there in the office on Sunday, makes me certain he killed Mum for what she knew.

Now I know exactly what Mum must have found out, and hearing how he threatened Felicity into hiding everything, I am sure without a shadow of a doubt that it was no accident that Mum fell off that cliff. No. She was pushed – by him. I just have to prove he was there now.

And only two people are standing in my way of that: Jennifer and Glenn.

Both of them have provided Mike with alibis for being at the scene – depending on the *time* of death. Jennifer said Mike had been with her all night; Glenn said that Mum had stayed at Merton Street on Friday night and then gone to Dover Heights on Saturday morning. Who was lying? Or were they both?

As I slip into the car, I slam the door shut behind me. The weight of Felicity's tale falls heavily on me.

I let out an audible scream of frustration.

In some ways, it feels like I've taken two steps forward and one step back. Because without proof of Mike's guilt at Dover Heights, I have nothing.

In my gut, I know that Jennifer is going to be the key. And if she knows nothing about these affairs and second families that he's kept so well hidden, then that might be how I can get her to open up. But why would she believe me without seeing any proof? I know I could have asked Felicity for some evidence of their affair – but she seemed so terrified, and I didn't want to bring her into any more danger than she was already in. I'd have to prove it to Jennifer another way... without Mike realising what I'm up to. Because if he does, I know I will be next.

Thinking back to that terrifying moment in the office, I try to remember his words on the phone. What was that strange pet name he used... 'Bel Bear'? I'd never heard him call Jennifer that. After hearing Felicity's story, it makes me sure that Mike must have a new affair on the go...

The name suddenly rings a bell. I think back to my last conversation with Mum and what Zara had said about *Arabella* going to sort the rest of Mum's stuff out at the office. I hadn't been properly listening in either situation – but could 'Bel Bear' be 'Ara*bel*la'?

I start the car, and as I drive away, I feel like I am on the edge of a precipice. I could tumble at any moment; my only chance is to stay one step ahead. And for the first time, I feel like I am.

As I drive, I call Addie. It's long overdue, and I pray that after discovering something tangible like this, she'll help me if I ask. I hope I can take a risk on her because I need a favour.

'Hey, Ads,' I say as soon as she picks up on the second ring.

'Yeah, hey!' she says breathlessly. 'How are you going? I've been so worried about you.'

I feel guilty for a second about not being in touch. 'I'm sorry – I didn't know what to say after—'

'Em – no,' she cuts me off. 'I wanted to apologise for the other day. I feel like I haven't been there for you at all. If you're worried about what happened to your mum, then I should have believed you and helped you, no questions asked. I'm sorry if you've felt like you haven't been able to trust me or speak to me the last few days. I want you to know I'm here.'

I'm silent for a moment as I process her words. They are what I've wanted to hear for so long. 'Thank you – that means a lot. I have been holding back from you a bit because I've been worried about what you'd say.'

'That's what I thought,' she jumps in. 'And I'm so sorry.'

My heart soars at her words. It feels so good to have her back.

'Don't worry about it now – I know you were just looking out for me too. *But*, I do have something to tell you... and I need your help.'

'Go for it!' she says.

As I start the long journey back into the city, I update her on everything from the last few days – including the latest with Felicity.

'Oh my god,' Addie says breathlessly when I'm done. 'Oh my god, I cannot believe you've had to go through all that alone!'

I flinch. 'No – honestly, I had to work through a lot of it myself anyway,' I rush to reassure her.

'I can't believe it! And we need to lock Mike away *now*.'

'I know,' I say, 'and I have a plan. So can you do me a favour?'

'Anything.'

'Good. Because I need you to go to the Imaginate building and then follow him, see where he goes and if you can discover anything about his possible affair with Arabella.'

'I'm on it,' is her immediate response. 'I'll head over there right now, and I'll let you know if I spot anything.'

'Thank you,' I say with a sigh. It feels so good to have someone helping me *at last*. I knew this was something I couldn't ask Ben, a police officer, to do. And I couldn't tail Mike – I'd be recognised. But Addie knows what he looks like, and if there's any chance of catching him with Arabella, it would be through seeing if they slip off somewhere after work. If I can get proof of an affair to show Jennifer, it will be far more convincing.

I press my foot down harder on the pedal, eager to get back into central Sydney. Even though I'm devastated by Felicity's story and terrified of being caught by Mike, my fear is far outweighed by something else: determination.

I'm willing to do whatever it takes to bring him down once and for all.

Chapter Thirty-Three

I head into the city. If Addie texts me with any sort of update, I want to be nearby. By the time I get there and eventually find somewhere to park, I'm ravenous. Felicity's house is far out of central Sydney, and it is late in the afternoon now, well past a normal lunchtime.

As my stomach grumbles, I keep walking, thinking everything through. I'm beginning to convince myself that regardless of whether Addie finds any proof or not, I'll speak to Jennifer. I feel like my skin is crawling with impatience. I can't get through another day knowing Mike is still out there swanning around after everything he's done. But I'll give Addie the rest of the afternoon. I can just about manage that.

I wander the streets until I find a busy tapas bar on George Street and take a seat. All they're still serving are some small plates, which is fine – but what I need most of all is a glass of wine. I hope it will calm my frayed nerves. I down it as I impatiently watch the world go by – people wait for trams and rush down the street, oblivious to the manic thoughts that continue to swirl around and around my mind.

'Another glass, miss?' a waiter asks, and I nod wordlessly as I look down at my phone. It's almost six, and still no word from Addie. I don't think I can hole away in here forever. I tap my finger on the edge of the table. I'll have to contact Jennifer soon...

And then Addie texts me.

He's left the office alone. But another woman (OTT dressed!) left like five mins before him. He looks like he's heading that way too – away from the city and towards Surry Hills. I'm on it.

Imaginate's offices were near Elizabeth Street, by Hyde Park in Sydney. If Mike was heading to Surry Hills, then it meant that he wasn't planning on coming back towards the North Shore – where he and his wife lived in Greenwich. And if he was going in the same direction as another woman...

I quickly text back and ask her to share her location for an hour. She does, and I race to follow her pin.

I pay and start to rush through the city. In only about five minutes, Addie's pin stops, which means Mike must have gone inside somewhere – I hope. I weave my way through what feels like thousands of people finishing up work for the day and almost push them over in my haste.

Eventually, I find where Addie's pin must be. She's not out front, so she must be *inside* the brown brick building in front of me. It looks like one of those sophisticated wine bars transformed from one of the old warehouse buildings. I'm sure it has endlessly high ceilings and soft, intimate lighting. *The perfect date spot.*

Time ticks by, and soon, I can't bear it any longer. Unable to help myself and hoping my big hat and sunglasses that I still have on me will do enough to hide my identity for now, I creep along in front of the window.

As I peer through, it looks like hundreds of people are sitting around laughing and drinking – but no one who I want to see. I sigh and step back. Just as I'm walking back across the street, I feel a pull on my arm.

I almost trip over and look up in shock. It's Addie. 'Em! What are you doing? They're about to come out.' She drags me away down the other end of the street. I tuck behind her as two people emerge from the bar.

They're not touching, but as the woman stumbles in her tottering high heels, she grabs onto the man's arm for support and lets out a tinkling, silly laugh that I can hear from here. He looks down at her with a smarmy grin I'd recognise anywhere. Mike's.

My stomach flips, and I tuck my hat tighter over my head.

We don't dare to speak until they disappear further down the road.

'Oh my god,' I breathe. That was too close. 'So you saw them together?'

She nods and drags me further down the street and away from the direction they went. 'But a picture... I needed a picture...' I stammer. Without that, what proof did I have?

Addie smiles and unlocks her phone to show pictures of the two of them. One close up and smiling, the other of them kissing.

'Thank you,' I whisper as she texts them to me.

'You're welcome,' she replies with a flick of her hair. We carry on walking briskly down the street until we find another wine bar where we can talk. We head inside, and when we at last sit down with two glasses in our hands, she says, 'So what are you going to do now?'

'Talk to Jennifer.' I take a quick sip of my wine and then pull my phone out of my pocket to send a message. 'It doesn't look like Mike and Arabella will be separating anytime soon. I have to show this photo to Jennifer tonight. Maybe then she'll help me prove that nothing Mike's said about Mum's death can be trusted... It's the only thing I can think of to do next.'

Addie nods enthusiastically, but then a frown forms across her brow. 'Yeah... I think that's the right plan. But just be careful, okay? Don't give everything away about what you've found out about Felicity until you're certain she's on your side. Just in case Jennifer's somehow involved too...'

I twirl the stem of my glass as I consider her words. I knew that Jennifer and Mum clashed sometimes, but I never thought she would be capable of *killing* her. Then again, I didn't expect this from Mike either. 'Hmm. Maybe you're right – but Jennifer is so proud. I'm certain she wouldn't have stayed with Mike if she'd known about all these affairs. I'll be careful, though.'

I start to fiddle with the edge of the tablecloth when my phone vibrates, sending my hand skittering towards it. Turning it over, I race to read the message across the screen.

It's Jennifer. Confirming that it's just her at home tonight. Perfect.

I look up at Addie as her eyes go wide with understanding.

It's now or never.

Chapter Thirty-Four

I turn onto Jennifer and Mike's cul-de-sac. There's only one way back out of here: the way I came. The shady streetlights unnerve me as I drive past the large homes that are elegantly dotted behind high walls.

I park right outside their house. If anything happens, then the car is a sign for all to see that I am here. *Except if they were to move it*, a little voice within me whispers, but I push it aside – it's not helpful right now.

I try to reassure myself that at least Addie knows where I am. After I'd received Jennifer's message, we'd settled up quickly at the bar. She'd made me promise to contact her later, or she'd call the police. I'd tried to gather up as much strength as I could from the hug she'd given me when she'd said goodbye. Addie seems to be the only person I can trust right now...

Now, getting out of the car on this deserted suburban street, I inhale the scent of eucalyptus on the warm summer breeze, trying to take comfort and strength in it. But all it does is make me think of Mum.

Locking the doors behind me, I tuck my key inside my shorts pocket and march up to the house. The automatic sensor lights come on, making me see white spots at the sudden glow. But the light settles, and the next moment, the door in front of me opens to a surprised Jennifer.

'Emily?' she asks. 'Is everything okay? I was surprised by your message.'

I consider starting with a lie and just saying, *Of course*, but decide that the only way to get this off on the right foot is to be truthful.

'No,' I say. She looks taken aback. I suppose it is a shock for anyone to ever answer 'no' to that question. We're so trained to respond with a 'yes', even if we're hurting deeply inside.

'Oh, darl,' she drawls, and I can't help feeling the hairs on the back of my neck rise.

'I know how tough it is right now for you. Come on in.' She opens the door wide, and I realise she probably assumes I've come over because I'm in despair about Mum. Which I am, but I'm holding that tight in a ball and focusing instead on my despair over all the lies that are being told.

I nod and walk in, following her through the entryway straight into the open-plan kitchen. 'Go on and sit down in the lounge,' she calls behind her as she herself moves into the kitchen. 'Wine?'

I nod. I need more alcohol to get through this conversation.

I turn left towards what Jennifer calls the 'lounge', but that does not do it justice. The large open archway that separates the kitchen and the 'lounge' is bright and airy as I walk underneath it and into a spacious room with three huge plumped-up sofas and an ornate glass coffee table with styled coffee table books placed on the shelf underneath. A glossy rosewood piano frames the other corner, which sparkles in the soft light. Looking past the richly designed interior, the floor-to-ceiling glass doors are open, welcoming in the glistening and unmistakable shimmer of the ocean and, in the distance, the city lights. It is a breathtaking spot right on the water in Greenwich. But clearly, it has not been earnt by Mike and Jennifer. Now I know how he's been stealing the company's money...

I turn around as Jennifer enters, carrying two glasses of nearly translucent white wine. The glasses look slippery and shiny from the cool liquid.

'Oh, have a seat,' she says, turning to manoeuvre a couple of coasters onto the pristine glass table.

I take a seat with my back to the view, facing towards the door. I want to be the first to know if Mike comes back home – and have a direct path to the exit. I take the proffered glass of wine and take a long, cooling sip.

'So, darl.' There it is again. I grit my teeth and bring the wine to my lips again instead. 'Mike won't be back until late tonight. So it's just us two girls. How can I help? Or if you want a hug or to cry, I'm here.'

God, she is being *so nice*. Is it because she thinks I finally need her? Is she really a decent person who I've been pushing away all this time, determined *not* to like her? I thought Glenn's family had always seen me as an unnecessary extra. Maybe I'd been wrong.

But I push it out of my mind.

'No,' I reply, and her face falls, her expression switching back to confusion. 'I'm here about something else... something that I thought you should know straight away.' Her brow furrows as I pause again to take a gulp of wine. The glass is already almost empty.

Jennifer's eyes clock my almost-finished glass. 'Right, so what's that?' Her voice has taken on the edge that I am used to. This is the Jennifer I know, and immediately, I feel more able to carry on.

It seems gentler to start with Arabella's story. And it's the only one I have proof for, anyway. 'So, there's no easy way to say this. But I just saw Mike with someone, as in *with someone*.' I stress the words so there'll be no misinterpretation of my meaning. 'I'm so sorry to tell you, but I thought you had to know.'

She shakes her head, disbelieving. 'What?' she says, her question catching in her throat. 'No, surely not,' she says, more to herself than me. Then she looks up quickly. 'Who? When?'

'Tonight – and ugh, with his...' I cough. 'Assistant, Arabella.'

She buries her head in her hands. I'm not sure what I'd been expecting as a response when I told her, but I don't think I was expecting this. Her shoulders shake as sobs wrack her body. Or so I think, as a moment later, I hear a strange, strangled sound. It can't be... but it sounds like a laugh.

She flicks her head up, removing her hands from her face to reveal an almost maniacal smile as she cackles. This is *not* what I was expecting.

'That bastard.' Throwing her hands in the air, she spits out, 'I bloody knew it. I *knew* he was hiding something from me. Whenever I mentioned the tiniest thing, he's always, *always*, somehow convinced me that I was overreacting and *imagining things*,' she emphasises every word.

'But NO,' she cries out, pointing her finger directly across at me. 'NO, I was right, I was bloody *right*. And you can back me up.' Then, all of a sudden, her uncontrollable rage at the situation turns to actual sobs, and she retreats back. 'Oh God, what am I going to do now?'

Putting down my now-empty glass, I rush over to her. 'Don't worry,' I hear myself saying. I chew my lip in concern. If this is her reaction to only Arabella, then how on earth is she going to react to hearing about Felicity and Jacinta? And Jacinta's little boy...

'You'll be okay. You'll be absolutely fine,' I hear myself saying, patting her back in a smooth circle. 'You have a right to everything that he owns. I can help you.'

I might not be a family lawyer, but I can find someone we can trust to work with. I will help save Jennifer from Mike. She's as much a victim of his as Felicity and my mum. Now, I am beginning to piece together a complete picture of Jennifer: a lonely, bored and ignored housewife who has been pushed away and gaslit by her husband for years. A woman desperate for a family and close friends.

I suddenly realise why my rebuffs over the years might have hurt her so much, and I feel a deep shame bubble in me. But I'm here now. I can fix this. And hopefully, as the truth continues to come out about her husband's deceptions, Jennifer will be on my side – and she can help me prove what really happened to Mum that night.

Chapter Thirty-Five

I head to the kitchen and pour Jennifer another glass of wine, topping myself up at the same time. I glance at the bottle and decide to tuck it under my arm for good measure as I carry everything through to the lounge. God knows we need it. Especially if I'm going to tell her the rest...

Jennifer is reeling in shock at the news, stroking a cushion that she's folded in front of herself as she moves from muttering, 'That bastard, I knew it,' to a steady stream of, 'God, what am I going to do?'

She's in a state of distress like I've never seen her, and I should help her digest the news. But I also know, selfishly, this will be the best chance I have of getting her to be honest with me about what else she knows – if anything. Her reaction to Mike's affair makes me think that she's suspected something for a long time. What I don't know is whether that is just infidelity or something else, too.

'I'm so sorry, Jennifer,' I say again, passing her the topped-up glass of wine, which she takes gratefully. I take a deep breath as I say at last, 'There's more...' I don't mention Felicity's name. I don't think it's necessary to drag her in until I know what Jennifer is going to do about

Mike's betrayals. But I tell her that I suspect there's been more than this one affair over the years.

She buries her head in her hands and says in a muffled voice, 'I shouldn't be so surprised.'

Then she looks up and adds with a sniff, 'There were the signs... over and over again. He had frequent work trips and late events. Initially, I didn't think anything of it. But one time a few years ago, I swear I smelt someone else's perfume on his shirt. I convinced myself I was imagining it... maybe it was just the hotel scent? Then it happened again... and I thought it even smelt the same. So I started asking him for a few more details about his trips and work. At first, he was pretty open, but then he grew impatient with me. He made me feel guilty for even insinuating that he wasn't being entirely honest. He'd say, "I've worked so hard to give you this life. I stayed by your side even when it became clear we'd never be able to have children. I bring you back little gifts from every trip and call you every day. What more can I do?"

'I felt even worse after that. You might not know, but I suffered a few miscarriages in my thirties. I had complications that meant I couldn't carry a baby to full term.' Tears shine in her eyes as she thinks back. 'Mike supported me through everything, even at my lowest. Eventually, I made peace with it and threw all my maternal instincts into helping raise Zara when her awful mother disappeared. I guess that's why I found it hard when your mum came into the picture at first – I'd been that little girl's everything for a while, and then she had a new stepmother. Anyway,' she sniffs noisily, and I pass her a tissue from the box sitting in the middle of the coffee table. She accepts gratefully.

'I tried to forget about my worries. I was so lucky in so many ways, and whenever Mike *was* with me, he was always loving and happy. But then, in this last year, he seemed to grow more tired and stressed. God, I should have *known*. I should have demanded answers. But I was too scared... I didn't want our life, this life,' she looks up and around her at her beautiful home, 'to shatter all around me.'

'I can understand that.' I move to sit down next to her, but not too close, either. I want to give her some space to process. 'It was a total shock to me too.' Before all this, the Mike I'd always known had been the life and soul of any party. A funny, larger-than-life guy. The only doubt I'd had about him was when I'd seen him lose his temper at Mum that one time. But now, after all the stories I've uncovered about him, I'm confident that the man I'd known was a total stranger to us all.

'Exactly,' she says in a low voice. 'Mike is the perfect doting husband, the devoted brother and boss. Everyone's best friend. No one would have believed me. About an affair, or anything else, would they?' She downs the rest of her wine in one. I top it up.

'Really?' I ask, jumping on this opening. 'Do you mean...' I hesitate, trying to find the right phrase, 'about *this*? Or is there anything else?' Does she mean she suspects his other affairs or something to do with what happened to Mum...

'What do you mean?' she asks, and her eyes skitter away from mine. I think I've hit a nerve.

'Oh, just from what you said, it sounded like you didn't only mean an affair...'

She doesn't respond. I take the opportunity to fill her glass up again. I get a rush of shame at my tactics, but I need to find out the truth.

I prompt once more. 'Jennifer, please, what do you mean by that?'

She turns to face me, and she looks like she's weighing up something in her mind. 'Look,' she says, her cheeks start to redden. 'I don't know exactly what it is, but I'm certain he's hiding something else too. Maybe it's connected to his affair, but it's also something to do with Imaginate.' She turns away and tucks her bushy hair behind her ear as though she's trying to hide her face from me.

'So you do suspect he's been hiding something else?' I say in a low, almost dangerous voice. I'd been told repeatedly by her, by all of them, that I was being ridiculous to even suggest that there could be anything suspicious in Mum's death. And here she is, slowly admitting that all this time, there *was* something suspicious going on...

I wasn't losing my mind after all.

I could be mad at her; I could shout her down. But I can't let that cloud my judgment. Not now. Not when I am on the precipice of answers. It takes all my legal training and patience not to scream at her. What I needed to find out now is if she really *knows* anything. And if so, whether she has any proof.

'I...' A slight sob escapes her lips. 'I don't know.' Her voice is full of fear.

My heart fills with sympathy. For years, Mike might not have been outwardly aggressive to her, but he's been making her doubt herself over and over again. Throughout the years, she'd had to make herself ever smaller to fit herself into his demands and what he wanted, never speaking up against him. I'd seen enough cases like this when I'd done a rotation in family law during my training.

'Jennifer,' I say in a soft voice, placing one hand on her arm. 'You don't have to say anything more if you don't want to. I understand. We can take a minute.' I really want her to keep speaking, but I can also tell she is in a state of distress, and I know it isn't right to push her further. Mum wouldn't want me to cause her to break down.

'No. I have to start being braver. I have to tell the truth.' she says, with a determined shake of her head. And in that moment, a strange similarity between her and Felicity flashes through my mind. Who also made the choice to stand up at last and tell her truth.

'Because honestly, Emily—' She turns to look at me, her eyes ablaze. 'I lied. I wasn't with him on Friday night.'

Chapter Thirty-Six

'What?' I say, my voice almost a scream. 'You both *lied*?! So he *was* with Mum that night?'

She shakes her head. 'I don't know his exact timings, but he wasn't with me. In fact...' She wraps her arms around herself in total anguish. 'It's possible he didn't come home at all. He – he said that he'd got back very late on Friday and hadn't wanted to wake me, so he slept in the spare room.' She pauses as she takes in the shock in my eyes.

'I know I should have questioned him then. But lately, I've started to become scared of his reactions. He's always had a temper and could quickly fly off the handle and then be contrite the next second. We all know that about him, though, and his apologies more than made up for the anger. He was never violent. Then, a few months ago, there was that one time he lost it at me. I'd got back from a spa weekend and asked him what he'd been up to. I hadn't thought it would descend into a huge fight – but it did. And that's when he hit me. He was so remorseful after, and he promised never again. But ever since, I've felt like I've been walking on eggshells and trying to figure out my next move.

'So when he suddenly said in front of you all that we'd been together on Friday night, I was too scared to contradict him publicly. He had *that look*. I panicked and agreed with him. I lied on reflex.' She grabs my hand with her spare one. I pull it immediately out of her reach.

'I know that's no excuse. But, Emily, please,' she says, a desperate whine on the edges of her voice. 'You have to believe me – I didn't mean to cause you any harm. And now I'll tell you everything I do know.' She gulps. 'You see, he did tell me that he'd seen Suzie at some point on Friday – before we knew what had happened to her. But after we lied to you, I forced myself to ask him why he wanted to lie – and he said we were being kind. That it wouldn't help to tell you that he'd seen her that day. He said he could see a wild desperation as you questioned him – and that if you were told he was with her, you'd clutch at it and see a conspiracy when there wasn't one. And Suzie's accident had happened on Saturday morning anyway. He said there had been enough tragedy – that we should all come together. And he convinced me. Like he always bloody does... Oh god,' she cries.

'What about Saturday morning?' I ask, my question cutting through her sobs like a knife. 'You say you never saw him Friday night and that he *said* he stayed in the spare room not to wake you. But when did you see him *that morning*?'

She looks at me with wide eyes as she absorbs my meaning, registering what exactly I'm asking. And what I'm accusing him of.

'No... no. It couldn't be. He... he would never.' Jennifer claps a hand over her mouth in complete shock as she shakes her head from side to side. And then she lets it slip down her face as she whispers, 'I-I didn't see him until at least eight or nine o'clock that morning, I think.' She shakes her head again, trying to remember. 'He... he said he'd been on a run to clear his head after a big night with Suzie. But, oh my god!' She almost screams, 'He was covered in mud!' She starts to rock herself on the sofa in a state of shock. 'I – I didn't want to consider that possibility. It was an accident. Suzie's death was an *accident*!' She tries to say it loudly as though to convince herself. But every syllable is tinged in desperation.

'Let's go,' I say, standing up with an outstretched hand. 'We have to go to the police *now*. I can call Ben – I mean Sergeant White – he'll be able to help us. Take down your statement, and we can go from there.'

'I-I...' She looks up at me. 'I can't. No... it can't be true.'

'Come *on*, Jennifer,' I say, my voice growing harsh. 'He's lied to you – he lied to all of us. He *must* be hiding what really happened between him and Mum! You've said it yourself already – he's started to act erratically and become violent. Look – I know this is hard to accept as the truth, but we owe it to her. He has to explain himself to the police. Come on – can't you see that?' I snap out that last question. But I know my words have had an impact. Her expression hardens.

'You're right,' she says, a note of determination in her voice. 'I've been cowering in the shadows for too long. I didn't used to be like this, you know. I think I was stronger, braver.' She turns to look at me, tears glistening on her cheeks. 'Maybe I can be again.'

'You absolutely can,' I say, taking her hand in mine. I glance down at my watch. Nine o'clock. Will Ben be free? I want him to hear this now before Jennifer loses her momentum again. I need someone else to hear that I'd been right – and to stop Mike. 'Let me call Ben and see if we can meet him.'

'Now?!' she asks, fear mixed with determination etched across her tear-streaked face, and I know I've made the right decision. She is fuelled by sorrow, shock, anger and wine, and I need her to speak *now*.

'Yes – every second counts.' And I don't let her protest as I hop up and run out onto the balcony that extends straight from the living room to make the call. The call that I hope will change everything. Because we have to get to Ben first – before Mike comes home and gets to *us*.

'Ben?' I say into the phone as he answers with a quick 'Hello' after the third ring. He sounds distant, which I hope means he's in a car and not too far away.

'What's up?'

'I need you to talk to my aunt Jennifer straightaway. Mike's been lying about everything that happened on Friday and Saturday morning – and she can prove it.'

A moment of silence echoes down the line. Then he responds, 'Okay, really?' He sounds surprised but not dismissive, which I appreciate.

'Yes! Can we meet now?'

'Well, umm,' he hesitates, then adds, 'Yes, okay, I can. Where are you?'

'Greenwich.' I give him the address.

'I'm over near Paddington, so with any luck, I'll be there in 20 minutes.'

'Hurry,' I say, glancing down at my watch. Mike should still be out for a few more hours, and then when he arrives here with any luck, Ben will be ready and waiting to arrest him. 'Thank you.' I manage even as my throat feels thick with emotion. This might be it. Answers at last.

'Of course, I did say call me for anything – but you think this is actually *something*?'

'Yes,' I say with certainty. It might not be everything we need to prove it was Mike, but it's a start. And then Ben will be able to get him talking.

'Okay, well, hang tight, and I'll be there as soon as I can.'

The line goes dead.

I take in the city twinkling in the distance. I tilt my head back to the stars above and imagine Mum up there, looking down on me. *I'm getting there,* I whisper into the sky as I steel myself to go back in. Just twenty more minutes and there would be a statement, there would be some *proof*. I wasn't going crazy.

Taking a final deep breath, I turn around to see Jennifer jumping off the sofa, her glass of wine still clutched in her hand.

And that's when I hear it: the unmistakable sound of a key turning in the lock.

Chapter Thirty-Seven

'It's Mike!' Jennifer leaps up off her seat with a high-pitched screech, turning around to face me with an expression of horror on her face. I emerge from the balcony to the living area. It is a matter of seconds until he'll be in the room.

'Don't worry,' I whisper to her in a voice full of more calm than I feel. I need to stop her from panicking. We can get through this. 'Ben is on his way. Let's keep him occupied until he arrives – he doesn't have to know anything is up yet. He can't read our minds.' I add for good measure.

She looks terrified as I take her arm and steer her back to the sofa, where I resume my position next to her.

My mind is racing. Do I confront him? No, Ben is on his way. But what if Jennifer doesn't speak or say anything to him with Mike around? Then I'd be back to square one. Worse, I'd be in danger, and so would Jennifer.

My heart pounds in my chest, and panic causes my breathing to turn shallow. This man, if what I suspect is true, is a murderer. A lump forms in my throat, and I rub my sweaty palms on my shorts.

Next to me, Jennifer is still as a statue. Maybe I should try and get her out of here? But I can't think straight anymore. I'm confused by the alcohol and the stress. Everything seemed to have clicked into place seconds ago, and now I'm frozen to the spot.

Before I have another second to think, Mike steps into the room, appearing in the archway of the door. He looks the same as always – a crisp white shirt, a neat jacket, shiny, perfectly styled hair – and yet for the first time, I see him in a new light, as a man that is much taller and stronger than me, than us both. A man with a curated appearance who is hiding something sinister on the inside. I grasp my glass tighter.

'Hello?' he says to us both, a question in his voice as he spies me. It's a strange sight to see us both together after all. Knowing as he does that, Jennifer and I normally don't get on. 'What a surprise to see you here, Emily.' He doesn't say a *nice* surprise. I can't blame him, even if he doesn't know what I'm really doing here; he does know that I've suspected him of something since I first found the iPad – and the letter. And as my thoughts turn to that piece of paper scrunched in my pocket, I realise I still don't actually know who sent that...

I flick my attention back to the imposing man in front of me. 'Uhh, hi,' I manage, placing my half-finished wine back onto the table. I stand to face him on reflex. I try to make my voice sound normal, but it comes out in a high-pitched squeak.

Out of the corner of my eye, I see Jennifer shrink further into the sofa. When I don't say anything more, he takes another step into the room towards us. I can't help but take an automatic step back.

His brow furrows. We're being too obvious; it's clear that there's a shift in the atmosphere from him walking into the room. He can sense the finely held tension. I've always been a terrible actor.

'So... this is a little catch-up?' Mike ventures as he moves closer. I spot Jennifer covering her face with her hair, and his gaze flicks over to her, trying to work out what's going on. I try to turn his attention towards me instead. I can't let him get to her.

'Oh yes,' I lie, walking towards him. My mind is screaming to me, 'RUN'. But I step in front of Jennifer to block her from his full view. 'Just realised I hadn't seen Jennifer properly for ages, and when Zara said she'd been over recently, I thought I'd swing by.'

'Zara is here too?' he glances around him as if expecting to see someone hiding in the shadows. I can tell that he's on alert, though he won't know why.

'She's... gone to get some more wine from the shops,' I lie again, surprising myself. And I start to feel more confident. Then, I hit on an even better idea for how to get us out of the house.

'In fact, she just called me.' I gesture to the phone in my hand. 'She said that the bottle shop she went to had closed, but there's a nice bar next door, so we should head over to meet her. So yeah, let's go, Jennifer.' I don't want to draw any more notice towards her, but I need her to pay attention now and get out of the house.

I glance behind me. Jennifer is still frozen to the spot, unblinking – and staring straight at him. How could I not have seen the signs and spotted her fear and deference towards Mike all this time? I hadn't been paying attention, focused on my own determination not to let her in. I'd been lost in the delusion that she and all of Glenn's family didn't want me. Time to fix that later; I just have to get her out. I reach out a hand and place it on her tense shoulder, giving her a gentle shake to snap her out of it.

She looks terrified. Then she blinks and seems to finally register my words. With a look, I try to tell her that this is our way out. *Come with me.* I try to make her see the meaning of my words.

At last, she nods and stands on trembling legs, carrying her wine glass carefully in one hand. I take her elbow and begin to walk slowly. I notice she keeps her gaze averted from Mike, who is still looming in the entrance to the living room. His hands on his hips. Our only exit is blocked.

I look into his ice-blue eyes. They stare us down, assessing every gesture. 'I see,' he says, drawing out the 'ee' sound like he is really weighing everything up. Or rather, weighing up his next move. 'Is that right, Jennifer?' he asks, directing the full force of his gaze at her. We are only a few feet away now, having started to make our way across the room.

She freezes at his voice with its ever so slightly threatening tone and his broad, imposing stance. It must be the exact combination of so many moments that she'd experienced a thousand times. Would she have the strength to break away this time?

I see her move before I hear it. She raises her hand in the air, and the glass she is holding disappears from view. The next second, an almighty crash.

The thrown glass, along with the last remnants of wine, shatter against the wall, centimetres away from Mike's head.

This was *not* part of the plan.

Chapter Thirty-Eight

I duck, as does he, and we both turn around to face her in utter shock.

'You BASTARD,' she screams, throwing her now empty hands up in the air. Then she points one accusing finger at him. 'How DARE you? How DARE you show your face here after what you've done!' Spit flies from her mouth as she screeches at her husband. She looks like a woman possessed, fuelled by long-held rage and quiet resentment.

Mike stands up on shaky legs. He'd ducked on impulse after hearing the glass shatter behind him. His brows are knitted together in deep confusion. He looks like a man losing control of a situation for the first time in his life.

'Jennifer,' he tries to say, putting his hands up to placate her. He speaks in a matter-of-fact tone. 'What are you talking about?' He takes one step towards her, carefully, like he is approaching a wild beast.

'You stay right there,' she throws back at him. He pauses, his hands frozen in the air.

'I *know* what you've been doing... sleeping around, lying to my FACE, again and again, making me think I AM the crazy one. When really no, you're the piece of scum who goes around sleeping with their secretary. *Their secretary*,' she screeches for extra emphasis. 'Who does that? How totally *unoriginal.*' She laughs in a wild cackle again, but it is devoid of real mirth. There is nothing funny about this situation.

And I'm stuck in the middle of it all.

'Who told you that?' Mike says in a low voice, full of danger. Then his eyes fall on me. And I know, just *know*, that he is making a promise to himself that he will destroy me for this.

'Emily,' she says instantly, not giving a thought now she is on this roll about the repercussions of that simple statement for me. 'And don't even *bother* trying to deny it. She saw you today. She says she has *proof*.' Jennifer's voice breaks with that last word. She is starting to wobble.

Mike stares daggers at me, and Jennifer goes on before he can interrupt. 'So don't even start, who *knows* what else you're lying about, how many affairs you have littered everywhere. All I know is that it's plenty, and I don't want to be part of your deceit anymore. I'm going to the police and I'm going to tell them that you asked me to lie for you about meeting Suzannah on Friday night. I have no goddamn idea where you actually were over those hours or where you were on Saturday morning, and I'm tired of it. I can't trust a single thing you say. You're going to have to explain where you were, and you can do that to the police!' she cries with total finality ringing out in her voice as though she has, at last, emerged triumphant from a long war.

She starts to move towards the door, done with her outburst and wanting to complete it with a dramatic exit. But it isn't so simple. As Mike, and all of the six-foot-four bulk of him, moves quicker.

He swallows up the arch and blocks her way.

His face is reddening, almost purple, but his voice comes out calm, clear, and menacing. 'Now, what do you mean by that?' It's like I'm not even in the room. His intense stare is locked on Jennifer, and his tall frame makes her look even smaller.

She doesn't shrink back, though. Instead, she says, fuelled by her rage and the wine, 'You heard what I said. Now move out of my way!'

Jennifer tries to push past him, but in a flash, he grabs her wrist and pulls her back to a sharp stop. She loses her balance and tumbles to the ground with a shriek. I rush forward to help, kneeling beside her.

'Are you okay?' Terror creeps into my voice.

Mike doesn't seem to care that his wife is crumpled on the floor. He kneels down in front of her.

'Are you sure you want to do that, dearest?' he says. 'What were *you* doing at that same time? Can you prove it?'

Then his gaze crosses to mine, and he says with menace straight at me, 'And do you really want to test me, Emily?'

I jump back to my feet in spite of myself. *Coward.* But there's a dangerous edge to his words that makes me want to run for my life. And forces me to wonder whether he *does* remember seeing me on Friday night...

Jennifer cradles her wrist in her hand; the force of Mike's pull and then her fall must have strained it. She glares up at him. 'I don't care. At least if the police start questioning you about this, they might uncover other *lies* in your past, of which there are many, I'm sure. Especially that big one you're hiding about *Felicity...*'

'You bitch,' he spits, and out of nowhere, I see a hand fly across, hitting Jennifer, and she crumples down to the floor.

For a moment, he looks as shocked as I feel. He jumps back up and stares at his hands, but soon, the wild fury in his icy gaze returns, replacing his horror. I'm terrified.

'Jennifer,' I cry as I push past my fear and help her back to her feet, one side of her face now bright red and already swelling. She puts her hand to it as if surprised to feel the consequence of the pain. I guess she's been feeling the pain on the inside for so long that it's a shock to see it outwardly manifested.

'You coward,' she mutters, more to herself than anyone else. 'You think you're such a big shot. That you can control everyone and everything around you. But you're nothing, and now everyone is going to find that out.'

That's when he lunges, and I yell, jumping back on impulse. Jennifer flies backwards at the force of his second slap.

'Stop!' I bark at him, trying to push him away, but he's too heavy. At least it distracts him for a second as Jennifer manages to run around to the other side of the sofa. I don't see it when he throws his arm back. The contact with my chest forces me backwards. I cry out in pain as my already injured ankle twists. I fall hard to the floor, hitting the back of my head at the same time as the impact knocks all the wind out of me. I try to breathe and pick myself up as I hear another scream. But I am so dizzy now from the pain and my tumble that I can't make out whose voice it was, whose scream.

I can't breathe.

And that's when the thought enters my terrified mind: are we going to make it out of here alive?

Chapter Thirty-Nine

I think I'm imagining things. I hear someone screaming 'STOP, STOP' over and over again.

I gasp air back into my lungs. I manage to open my eyes and lift myself back up.

And there is Ben, holding a struggling Mike's arms behind his back as Jennifer cowers behind the sofa.

Mike stops resisting, his fit of rage fizzing out as Ben keeps him pinned. 'Mate, stop. Calm down, calm down,' Ben says in a strong, practised voice. This isn't the first time he's had to deal with an incident like this.

Mike says too fast, 'I'm fine, alright, I'm not going to do anything.'

'Okay,' says Ben. 'But I'm going to put these handcuffs on for your own safety.' Mike grumbles, but Ben, with an imperceptible movement, whips out the cuffs and places them around one hand and then the other. Then he tells Mike to take a seat.

Ben surveys the scene, me in one corner and Jennifer in the other, hiding behind the sofa. I stand up and wince at the pain in my head and my ankle. Jennifer is also starting to rise from behind the sofa, an unmistakable bright red handprint on her face. She does everything possible not to look at Mike.

'Are you okay?' Ben says to both Jennifer and me. I nod, and Jennifer shrugs, in total shock at what has ensued over the past twenty minutes. He doesn't seem convinced. 'What happened?'

I open my mouth to speak. But before I have a chance, Mike speaks up from his spot on the sofa. His hair is all over the place, and his face is blotchy.

But he must have realised his predicament and is trying to get his story in first. 'Just a little family disagreement, that's all. You know how it is sometimes.' He tries to smile his bright, unwavering Cheshire cat smile up at Ben.

But Ben is having none of it and, ignoring him, turns to Jennifer. 'Mrs Cowper, you can tell me what happened. You're safe now.'

I don't know if it was Ben's tone or the sudden use of her surname that switches Jennifer's attention, but she says with venom, 'I am *not* Mrs Cowper anymore. Call me Jennifer.'

'Okay then, Jennifer, what happened? How can I help?'

'You can arrest him,' she says. 'He assaulted me. Take him away.' And with that, she turns her back to him and walks out of the room onto the balcony.

'What?! What?!' screeches Mike from the sofa. 'You can't listen to her,' he shouts at Ben. 'She's delusional. Emily will tell you, won't you?' He swivels his gaze to me. God, he must be desperate. As if I would ever help him.

'He assaulted her,' I say to Ben as Mike continues to rage his innocence. 'And it wasn't the first time. I can back that up. You might also want to ask him further questions about where he was on the day Mum died. It turns out he wasn't with Jennifer, and he had gone to meet Mum on Friday night. And no one knows where he really was on Saturday morning,' I say meaningfully, meeting Ben's gaze. A look of understanding passes between us.

Find out where he was and what he did to Mum, I will to him. And then I walk out of the room and take a step onto the balcony after Jennifer. Mike continues to scream behind me. I hope that Ben will be busy dealing with him for a while.

Because I now have a very important question to ask his wife...

In all the confusion of the last few minutes, I almost missed it when Jennifer threw Felicity's name at Mike like a grenade.

With an icy feeling settling in my stomach, I take a few steps away from the inside lights and plunge into the darkness waiting outside.

Because I purposefully avoided telling Jennifer Felicity's name when I mentioned Mike's suspected affairs. But if Jennifer already knew about her, then has everything she just told me been one big lie?

Chapter Forty

I pick my way around the tidy pot plants that line the edge of the balcony. There are no lights on out here, only the distant glow of the city in the far distance. I move slowly, both because of the pain in my body but also because I'm approaching Jennifer cautiously. It feels like after what's transpired, she could get spooked and run. I have no idea what state I'll find her in.

But she has to tell me what she knows about Felicity. Why hadn't she mentioned that she knew who she was before Mike had arrived? She made it seem like she didn't know any of the details of Mike's affairs and secrets... but this makes me wonder whether she really does. Why would she have lied?

She is sitting on the outdoor sofa in the corner of the balcony with her back to me. Her curly hair sticks out at all angles, and as I get closer, I can see that her knees are tucked up to her chest, her arms wrapped tight. She stares straight out over the water and into the distance at the city lights beyond. They shimmer in a distant haze, twinkling like far-off stars.

'Hey, Jennifer,' I say in a soft voice as I stop next to her and touch her on the shoulder, 'can I get you some help? Are you hurt?'

She flinches but shakes her head and continues to stare into the distance. As I take a seat next to her, I see that she's staring out blankly. Though she has one of the most beautiful views in the world in front of her, she is unseeing, lost in her thoughts.

Not knowing where to begin, I venture, 'Ben will sort him out. You don't have to worry about anything right now.' This is a platitude, but I want to at least attempt something reassuring. I don't want her to feel frightened of me – at least not until I get the truth out of her.

'At least all this won't have been for nothing now,' she mutters under her breath.

'Sorry, what do you mean by that?'

Then she turns to me with a sad smile spread across her face.

'Emily, thank you for freeing me.' I can't quite make out her eyes in this dim light, but I swear they look hollow.

'Of course, I already suspected so many of these secrets,' she says in a matter-of-fact tone. 'But I had no way of proving it. Every time I tried to mention it to him, he would shut me down and tell me I was imagining things. He would even start to get angry,' she adds in a quieter voice. 'I didn't think I'd ever be able to find a way out. And now you've saved me. At last.'

'Oh, I—' I start, trying to brush off her thanks. But then she buries her face in her hands and lets out a low groan.

'No,' she says through the gap between her hands. 'I'm not done.' Her voice catches in a sob. 'I did something terrible. And I don't think you'll ever forgive me.'

'Tell me, Jennifer,' I say, pulling her fingers away from her face. Inside, another light switches on, and her face becomes better illuminated.

Anguish is written across every line, but I force her to look straight at me. And all I can see is pain.

'Okay – I...' She crosses her arms into her chest as she directs her gaze away from mine and back out towards the calm night. 'Well, I'll try and start from the beginning. You have to understand—' She turns and grabs my hands tight. 'I felt like I had *no* choice. None at all. You can see now why I was too scared to confront him. I didn't know how to get him to tell the truth. Which is why I did what I did.'

'Please, Jennifer.' My voice comes out harsher than I intended.

'So,' she starts as she lets go of my palms. 'I didn't tell you the whole truth earlier.' She sits up a little straighter in admittance. 'Because you see, I've suspected for quite a while that he'd been using the business somehow to hide his secrets. I didn't know how. And without the proof, I'd never get anyone to believe me.' She pauses for a minute and looks away.

'What?' I ask, hardly daring to breathe or interrupt her train of thought.

She leans back in her seat and looks up at the sky as though searching for strength. 'I started to suspect that he was having an affair with someone at work. You see, last year, he had started to go on even more "business trips" than usual and was staying out later at the office – or so he said. I tried to catch him out by asking questions, but he *always* had an answer. And one of his answers was that he was on a deadline trying to finish off the accounts. I guess that wasn't a lie,' she adds with a bitter laugh.

'I tried to question him, but he continued to bat me away. When I asked too many, he lost his temper and said I was being totally paranoid.

I became scared to push him any further. I knew he wouldn't tell me anymore anyway. But I couldn't help but start to suspect that whoever he was holed up working on the accounts with might be the key...'

She sighs. 'So I'm not proud of it – but I got your old flame, Harry, to talk one night when he and Zara dropped by. We had a few drinks, and I started to flatter him. I told him how often Mike said he was doing an amazing job and that I hoped he wasn't keeping him too late working on those accounts. Something like that... he laughed off the last part, saying that no, that was the accountant's job to go through all that. I did some digging online and managed to connect an accountant to Imaginate on LinkedIn: it was Felicity. But she didn't have a photo, which I thought was very strange. I knew I had to see her myself to decide if I was on to something. So I fabricated a reason to go into the office during the day when I knew Mike had been working late regularly again on the "accounts". And that's when I saw her. Sure, she was one of the few faces in that office that I didn't recognise. But that's not why I knew it was her. She was entirely his type. Pretty, petite, dark features and pale skin. Just like me when I was younger. Before I got old and put on so much weight.'

She looks down at herself and I instinctively start to refute her claim, but she puts up a hand to stop me. Looking more closely at Jennifer's face now, I can see those small similarities to Felicity. The same warm caramel eyes and dark hair. However, Jennifer's is curly in comparison to Felicity's straight, long locks. Jennifer wasn't overweight, but she was curvy and soft. Mike had clearly been whispering things in her ear for many years to make her think that way.

'And, of course, Mike was furious to see me. So that gave the game away a bit as well.' She hunches over and crosses her arms across her chest. 'Later, I tried to ask him about the new faces in the office, but he shut me down again. He lost his patience and *almost* hit me. After that, I tried to force it out of my mind. I was scared about what would happen if I pushed him again. So I tried to convince myself I was being silly, and for a short time, it worked. Until that weekend I told you about. When he became so furious, he did actually hit me...'

My mind works quickly, and I suspect that weekend was the very same one when Felicity confronted Mike about all his lies.

Jennifer tucks her hair away from her face. 'For a week or so, I was frozen in shock at what he'd done. But after that, I decided that enough was enough – I should track this Felicity woman down to ask her and stop being such a coward. And it was time I got my ducks in a row. I had to try and be braver. I had to gather up the strength to leave him. But when I began to search for her again, I could find nothing about her online – it was like she'd never existed.'

She starts to rock now. 'So I didn't know *what* to think anymore, but I was *convinced* that Mike must know something about her sudden online disappearance. But no matter what I tried, I couldn't uncover anything more about what happened or any of her old contact details without direct access to the files he kept locked away at Imaginate. So I came up with another plan.' She crosses her arms tighter around herself and refuses to look me in the eyes.

Alarm bells start ringing in my ears.

'I sent your mum a letter.'

Chapter Forty-One

I can't quite believe what I'm hearing.

As she carries on, I notice that her hands are trembling and she tucks them around herself. 'I sent a note to your mum telling her to look into Felicity Smith, knowing that there was no way she wouldn't investigate. And I was certain, knowing Suzannah, that she'd get to the bottom of it. That way, she would uncover the affair, the lies, whatever else Mike was hiding – and he'd have no way of denying it. And, of course, if it didn't work, it couldn't be traced to me either. I couldn't afford for him to find out. I didn't want to imagine how angry he'd be. I thought it was a fool-proof plan.'

My mind spins as I try to process everything she's said. I press my fingers against my forehead to try and make it sink in.

'I'm so sorry.' Despair drips out of every syllable. 'I truly never thought it would turn into this! Your mum had always been so much braver than me. And I convinced myself that if Mike was hiding things from her at work, she deserved to be the one to uncover it. You see that, right?' She grabs my hands and pulls them tight, trying to *force* me to understand – I can't get away even if I want to. My hands become sweaty and tight, mimicking the state of panic I am starting to feel in the rest of my body.

'Oh, Emily,' she says, tears falling freely down her face now. 'You have to believe me when I say that I never thought he would go so far. That he would actually *kill* someone.' She whispers the awful words as though she can still hardly believe it's true. 'I would never have sent it if I'd known it would lead to this... When I heard the news on Saturday morning about what happened to your mum – I couldn't believe it. At the time, I really did think it was an accident. Surely, I told myself, it was a coincidence that I'd sent the letter two days before and now she was dead. But then I heard what you said to Mike at lunch.'

She tries to take a deep breath, her words becoming choked in her distress. 'And so I wasn't honest with you earlier. The truth is that I wasn't only scared of Mike's wrath if I didn't go along with him and back up his story – no, I also panicked for myself. I was terrified of Mike finding anything out...

'So later, when I confronted him about why he wanted to pretend he hadn't seen Suzie... I did question him a bit. But not enough. I didn't want us to talk about the letter. He's always been able to read me like a book, and I knew that if we spoke about it in too much detail, he'd be able to tell I was hiding something. And then I was too scared to say anything to you or anyone else... but now I see that I've been in total denial.

'I should have considered the possibility sooner that Mike had done something to Suzannah. Of course, I should have; I knew Mike was manipulative and, more recently, violent. But it was so much easier to accept the police's explanation that it had been a tragic accident.'

She covers her face. 'I persuaded myself that if there was anything else suspicious about her death, they would have found it.'

Her voice breaks at that, and she struggles to continue. My throat is so full of choked tears that I can't speak even if I want to.

'I-I,' she stammers, 'I still don't know if he did it on purpose or if it was a terrible accident. You saw for yourself how he snapped.' She says it as though she can't quite comprehend it. 'But I'm so sorry, I'm just so *so* sorry for not speaking up earlier.' The sobs start to take over her body.

'I'm sure you'll never forgive me. But I wanted you to know the whole truth... Even if that means I'm in trouble with the police too.' She looks up at me through her tear-streaked eyes. 'Because if Suzie's death wasn't an accident... if Mike had anything to do with it – then it's my fault too. I sent that letter in the first place. I'm the reason why she's dead.'

Chapter Forty-Two

My skin feels hot and prickly all over. My mind is screaming. It is like my brain is malfunctioning and can't compute.

Jennifer sent the letter. *Jennifer sent the letter!*

She is the one who set this horrific chain of events in motion.

I could forgive a lot of things – Jennifer had been beaten down by Mike for so many years. He'd cheated, lied, and gaslit her constantly. I can see that she'd felt like she had no other choice but to send it. I could understand that.

But her letter, paired with the fact that Jennifer *knew* that Mike had lied about meeting Mum that day. And that she never let herself consider for even a second that there was a chance he could have turned violent...

Jennifer had even implied that I was being ridiculous for suggesting that someone close to Mum could have hurt her.

Then I remember the terror in her eyes when Mike hit her earlier.

Maybe she really *has* been in her own sort of haze of fear and denial since Mum's death. She might well have come forward on her own soon enough when she'd plucked up enough courage.

Whatever the outcome of Jennifer's damned letter, it wasn't her fault that Mike had lost his mind and killed Mum. That was still all Mike. And I couldn't lose sight of that and blame Jennifer for an act of desperation in an impossible situation.

I might not be able to entirely forgive her yet. But at least she'd been brave enough to tell me the truth at last. 'Look...' She sits up straighter to hear what I have to say. 'A lot has happened today. Let's talk about it more later. But Mike's actions were *not* your fault. I wish you'd told the truth at the time, but you've told me everything now. And so long as you do the same with the police, then we can all start to move on.' I blink fast to stop the tears from falling.

'Oh, Emily.' The colour rushes back to her face, and she wipes at her tear-stained cheeks. 'Do you mean it?'

I nod slowly, and I'm certain when I say, 'It's what Mum would want.'

She bows her head and accepts my words.

As we stand up to go inside, I hope this nightmare will be over at last.

***

Whilst we were on the balcony, Ben arranged for back up, and when they arrived, they arrested Mike for assault. Ben let me know that they'd bring Jennifer and me in tomorrow to give statements and that he would be handing everything over to the homicide team, who will begin to work on the case for Mike's role in Mum's death. It could take a bit of time, but Ben felt certain they'd be able to go back and gather more proof now that they had Jennifer's testimony.

For the moment, it is over.

It's extremely late by the time I arrive back to Merton Street and crash out. But for the first time in days, I feel a little bit lighter. At least the truth behind Mum's death is going to come out at last...

Jennifer decided that she wanted some time alone to process it, so she is staying at her house tonight. We agreed that she would come over tomorrow, and we would speak with the rest of the family then. Right now, it is late, and there would be enough time to explain everything to Glenn and Zara.

The house is dark. Zara had texted to say she was staying at Harry's, and I assume Glenn will be fast asleep. I sigh. Hopefully, the revelations of tonight will change their attitudes towards me, and we can all start to heal and move forward. I know deep down that perhaps they've been acting so strangely due to their own grief. It's affected us all in different ways – like John had said to me yesterday. Was that really only *yesterday*? So much had happened. I'd have to find a time to talk to him tomorrow, too.

As I creep up the stairs, all I can think about is my bed. I glance at my phone before I plug it in to charge – there's a last message from Addie, full of relief that I'm okay and to call her in the morning. I manage to send a quick thumbs up as I collapse back onto the pillows. And then I pass out, lost in the oblivion of dreams.

I feel awful when I blink my eyes open the next day. There is a pain in my stomach, probably from intense hunger and a deep headache from dehydration. I stumble downstairs and gulp down a large glass of water.

The ache in my stomach subsides, but I still have a thumping headache from where I hit it yesterday. I rummage in the usual medicine cabinet for painkillers.

I sit down, nursing my head as I chew on some crackers. Slowly, the dull thumping in my skull begins to ease. And it's when my brain clears that it hits me: the house is silent. Where's Glenn? And even Banjo? It is all quiet.

I glance up at the oven clock, which says ten o'clock. I sit up, astounded. It can't be that late. I turn around to look at the decorative wall clock that frames the other wall, and sure enough, it says the same time. Perhaps Glenn has taken the dog out for a walk, but for some reason, a strange panic begins to enter my bones. This doesn't feel right after last night. Where has Glenn gone...

Wincing at the pain in my head and the ache in my ankle, I begin to hobble up the stairs again, listening hard for any sound.

I inch towards Zara's door first and knock. There's no answer, so I take a little peek in. It is dark and empty. She definitely did stay at Harry's last night, then.

My head continues to pound as I inch along the corridor. 'Glenn?' I call out down towards the other end of the house. No answer.

'Glenn?!' I try once more, a little louder as I move towards the very last room. The hallway feels like it is shrinking in on me, but I will myself on.

Still no answer.

I have to see if he is here. I have to tell him and Zara about Mike before Jennifer does, or worse, the police. They should hear it from me.

I pause in front of the door, hesitating, and then I try to shake away my continued headache and knock on the door. No answer. I knock again, a tiny bit harder.

Then I slowly inch the door ajar. As it swings open, the light blinds me. The curtains are wide open, flooding the room with light. Disorientated, spots play in my vision as my eyes adjust.

It has been many years now since I have been in this room, but there is hardly anything familiar about it. It isn't only that there is new furniture – a large king bed sits to my right, with matching bedside tables, and a tastefully chosen rug sits over wooden floorboards.

But it's also that it is so sparse and clean. Where were Mum's favourite lamps, which I knew she kept in here, or her favourite pictures on the walls? Instead, I notice that there are a lot of faint shadows where pictures had recently hung. Then I clock the side of the bed that must have been Mum's – it's spotless. Had Glenn got rid of everything that reminded him of Mum already? I wanted to keep as many reminders of her as possible. It seems so cold to hide them away, but he might grieve differently, I remind myself once more. Perhaps having these reminders of Mum around him all the time had been too overwhelming the last few days.

Either way, he isn't here, and I will have to go and track down both him and Zara another way. But as I turn to go and find my phone to call them, I spot something on Glenn's bedside table.

One small jewellery box. I frown. It seems out of place in the sparseness of this room.

And then another thought crosses my mind. I never got the chance to search this room. And in the haze of my recent discoveries, my questions about where Mum's rings had gone had flown out of my mind. With Mike's arrest, we had our answers about what caused Mum's death... didn't we?

I tiptoe over, hardly daring to breathe.

Reaching down, I pick up the tiny box, smaller than the palm of my hand.

I slowly lift the lid and drop it like I've been burnt. Three rings tumble out and across the room.

These are Mum's rings.

The ones Glenn swore he didn't have.

Chapter Forty-Three

I watch in shock as the rings twist and twirl around on the floorboards. They come to a final stop by the foot of the bed.

My breath is coming out short and sharp.

I thought everything had been cleared up about Mum's death – that it had all been Mike.

But now...

I stoop and pick them up. There is no mistaking it: these are the rings that Mum had always worn. The shiny diamond engagement ring from Glenn. The small white gold band with the solitary emerald from Nana and Granddad. And the thin, gold band with the small diamonds studded throughout that was from my dad. I had studied that ring my whole life. It had always been there on Mum's hand. And yet, here they are.

Glenn had *assured* me that the jewellery Mum was wearing at the funeral home was all that had been returned to him. And that he had no idea where these rings were. Yet here they were... the proof of his lie shining out in all its ironic beauty in the palm of my hand.

He hadn't exactly been hiding them out of sight. But I guess he'd never expected anyone to go creeping around his room.

But why would he have lied about keeping the rings?

My stomach twists. Glenn must know something more about the day Mum died than he is willing to admit. I thought I'd figured it all out, but now, what is the *whole* truth?

I clench the rings. The shock that I'd felt a moment ago is now replaced by cold, hard anger. I need, *I deserve*, an explanation from my stepfather. Replacing the rings back into the jewellery box, I decide to take them with me. Both for safekeeping, and proof of his lies. Then, I storm out of the room, slamming the door behind me with an almighty bang. It is time for Glenn to be honest with me at last.

I try to call him, but no answer. I send him a text telling him to call me back urgently.

I text Zara instead. I have to find him – and fast. I thought I'd uncovered everything, and now I can't stand to go another day without knowing.

I change in a flash into gym shorts and a top. My new-found mission has helped my headache disappear and I decide to call Ben – he will know what to do. But his phone rings and rings to voicemail. I scream, exasperated.

I throw myself down on my bed and stare up at the ceiling, trying to figure out what to do next or who to call to track him down. When my phone starts to ring, I automatically answer even though it's an unknown number. I'd assumed it was Ben calling me from the police station.

'Hey,' I say down the line, 'Ben, I need to talk to you. I've found the rings – Glenn had them all along. He's been lying to us about something, too.'

'Oh hey, Em, it's Addie here,' a familiar voice says.

'Ah hey,' I say with an edge of disappointment. It's not that I'm not happy to hear her voice, but it's not the one I was hoping to hear.

'Sorry,' she says, 'calling on my flatmate's work phone, I've lost mine somewhere. Just wanted to check in on you this morning.'

'Thanks, Ads,' I say, and there's no denying the sigh that escapes my lips.

'What's up? Are you alright? What happened last night? All you said was that you were okay and you'd catch me up today... but it sounded like everything was sorted?'

'No!' I shout and tell her everything that's happened in a rush, including everything last night and what I discovered in the house.

'Okay, whoa, whoa, slow down!' she commands, breaking through when I take a moment to breathe. I try to get it under control as she says practically, 'What can I do?'

At that same moment I feel my phone vibrate and bring it away from my face to read a quick text message back from Zara:

I think he's at Dover Heights – why?

'Ads, I've got to go. I know where Glenn is – at my grandparents' house.'

I am now solely focused on finding him, reaching him and *demanding* answers. He will not be able to escape without telling me everything, once and for all.

'Okay, Em, is that a good idea... I think you should hear—'

But I don't get to hear what Addie thinks as I've already hung up. I don't want to hear it. I just know I have to get there and see him.

A confrontation between Glenn and me is long overdue.

Chapter Forty-Four

As I begin my drive through the streets of Sydney, the heavens open, and a deluge comes pouring down. Thank God I still have Zara's car. I put the windscreen wipers on max, and I squint through the rain to keep myself on track. This weather is reminding me more of London than Sydney right now...

The roads are quiet. Not many people want to brave the downpour. When it rains in Sydney, it *pours*, and I almost feel the car shuddering under the heavy storm.

At last, I arrive in Dover Heights and pull onto the driveway outside Nana and Granddad's house. I'll always think of it like that. I take a moment to look up at the old-fashioned house, now out of place amongst so many new luxury mansions that have popped up over the years. I guess that soon enough, this house would turn into one of those, too. I assume that John would continue what Mum had started and want to sell, providing Glenn and I agreed to it.

I sigh. I remember the idea Mum had admitted to me once in a quiet moment. She hadn't wanted to let go and liked the idea of maybe buying John out and doing it up herself one day. But we never had the chance to have a proper conversation about it, and now we never would. This has been the house of her childhood, the one constant in my childhood, too. The one home I felt like I had after Dad died and my whole life turned upside down. But now, instead, it was the house that had taken away everything.

As I consider what could have been, the rain starts to ease off. My only opportunity to run to the house. Throwing open the car door, I rush underneath the awning and then towards the front door. I try to peer in through the window to see if I can see any movement. I can't, but Glenn must be in there somewhere.

I wonder if the spare key is still hidden under the pot plants around the side gate. Mum had told me about it years ago. I should have remembered it on Friday night, but I was too drunk. It all comes back to me now, though – she used to sneak out as a teenager and leave a spare set in her secret spot. I smile at the idea of Mum sneaking in and out of this house as a teenager.

The rain is beginning to get heavier again, and I look up to spy some storm clouds rolling in from over the ocean. I need to get inside.

I scurry around, making my way down the long and overgrown path towards the gate at the end. Where I'd seen the shadow and heard that scream... If only I hadn't been so out of it – maybe I could have stopped what inevitably came next.

Finally, I spot a collection of pot plants and other decorative garden ornaments. Slipping down, I find the key and head to the back door.

It opens with a click, and I'm hit by a sense of déjà vu.

The back door goes straight into the living room, and it could be the exact same scene as my childhood. To my left is a collection of snug sofas and leather armchairs, all huddled around an old box TV. The video cassette is still plugged in, and next to it sits a series of large rectangular videos stacked up on top of each other. To my right is an alcove that cuts straight through to the kitchen. If I shut my eyes, I can almost taste the scent of Nana's freshly baked cookies.

I remember all the times I'd rush in through the back and hop up onto my tiptoes to try and see over the window into the kitchen. Now I look straight through – and it's deserted.

I take a step further forward, and my foot scuffs on the edge of the rug that separates the kitchen from the back of the living room sofas. It's been rotated a little strangely to one side, as though someone pushed it there. Probably Mum as she was packing stuff up. The room is littered with haphazard piles and boxes in corners. I try to ignore it.

I wander further into the familiar room until the sofas are behind me, and all that's in front of me is the small mahogany dining table and chairs. I let the memories wash over me, even as I feel the tears start to fall.

In that corner next to the china cabinet, I'd taken my first steps, according to my mum. And on that dining table, I'd tackled my homework – my granddad calling out from that sofa the answers to maths questions I needed help with.

I take another step and find myself in the hall off the kitchen, and then in another few paces, I'm looking into another room. The room that housed me through some of the best and worst times of my life. *My* room.

The pink wallpaper is still on the walls. I don't think my grandparents ever imagined Mum and I would end up living with them for as long as we did.

My faded posters are there, a mixture of floral paintings and punk and boybands. A testament to a confused childhood. My old Victorian doll's house is in the same spot. It had been Mum's when she was a girl, Nana had proudly told me. I remember playing happy families for hours with her within the walls of that pristine three-storey house. If only real life could be as simple as a doll's house.

My old schoolbooks and sketchbooks remain piled on top of my small white desk, probably in the exact spot I'd left them all those years ago. And next to it, my old wooden single bed. The chequered sheets are long gone; my old bed seems to have become a collection place for pillows and throw cushions instead.

A few empty boxes are in the very middle of the room. Mum must have begun sorting out my room as her next project before everything had happened.

I'm exhausted. The house is silent – Glenn obviously isn't here. I close the last few steps, sit on the edge of the bed, and try to imagine Mum's last moments.

I fall sideways onto the bed and scream into a pillow.

Yesterday, I thought I'd discovered the whole truth about her death...

Now I don't know.

I grab the pillow and throw it across the room.

I'm expecting to hear a satisfying but soft thud. Instead, I hear an almost metallic *whack* as it falls to the ground next to the desk.

I sit up in confusion, standing up swiftly to make my way over to the pillow. Rummaging inside the case, my hand locks onto something rectangular.

And in one smooth motion, I take it out.

It's a phone.

But not just any phone. I flip it over and see the iconic case: a picture of Mum, Banjo and I.

This is *Mum's* phone.

The phone Ben said they assumed had been on her at the time of her fall and got swept out to sea.

So what on earth is it doing here?

Chapter Forty-Five

I need an iPhone charger – fast.

If Mum's phone was here – not lost like the police had assumed – then maybe there's some final proof on there, which will help lock Mike away. And there might be answers as to why Glenn had lied about the rings. If he didn't admit the truth immediately when I confronted him at last...

There has to be something – or why else would she have hidden it?

I race around every corner of Nana and Granddad's once-cosy home, finally finding a charger in the kitchen. I plug in the phone and then pace the room. It's been out of battery for days, so I know it'll take a while to wake up.

I'm so distracted by my find that I almost miss the rustle from outside.

Glenn.

I duck my head out of the back door, but I can't see anything through the hedges or hazy sky. The rain has stopped, so I walk out, calling Glenn's name as I go.

Beyond the brush of the trees and brambles, I can just make out the stormy waters and the cliff edge.

I'm drawn there, even as I see a storm cloud on the horizon. I think I see some movement, so I trip out over the grass and towards the brush.

I duck around the biggest hedge but stop before I'm too close to the edge. I don't want to go too far.

I'm still about ten feet away from the drop, but as I stare out at the swirling ocean and the craggy cliffs in front of me, I find myself taking one more step forward. I haven't been out onto this part of the garden cliff since what happened. And being here, I find myself trying to understand *how* she could have fallen. What would have been the last thing she'd seen?

I'm so lost in my thoughts that I don't hear the approaching footsteps. A hand touches my shoulder, and I jump back, dangerously close to the precipice.

I manage to keep my balance as I turn around, fully expecting to see Glenn. But instead, I see a very surprised Uncle John.

'John! What are you doing here?!'

He looks confused by my question. 'Glenn and I are meeting here a bit later to discuss estate agent business. But I've come a little early – I like to check on the house when it storms. Especially after what happened in the last one.' He's referring to Mum, I know. I step further away from the edge. 'I thought I saw some movement over here, so I came to check it out. You should be careful near the edge,' he adds.

'Of course – you're right,' I say, taking another step away from it.

'What are you doing here anyway?' He's wearing a baseball cap, and he tucks it tighter onto his head as another gust of wind races past.

'Oh, I—' I tuck my hair behind my ear. 'I was looking for Glenn – I thought he was going to be here.'

He shrugs. 'Not for a little while...'

'Well, let's go in – I have to tell you about yesterday,' I say, grabbing his arm to turn us in the direction of the house. 'And guess what I just found inside?!'

Suddenly, I'm pleased that John has found me. Not only do I feel better that he'll be here when Glenn eventually arrives, but he – Mum's brother – will be as excited as me about what I've found.

'What?' he says, a smile slipping across his face in a bemused expression.

The ocean roars behind us, so my words end up coming out as more of a yell. 'Mum's phone! I'm charging it up right now. The police thought it was lost. But maybe it will be able to give us some more proof – wait till I tell you about what else I've discovered since we spoke on Monday.'

I take another step forward, but John has stopped in his tracks, and I come to a slamming stop, too.

'John?'

His face has gone white – but maybe it's the light. The storm cloud from over the ocean has moved, and it's almost directly above us.

'I—' he starts, shaking his head. 'Nothing, sorry, just thought I heard a car pulling up.'

'I don't think I did?'

'Maybe Glenn has arrived – you should go round the front to check and ask him about those rings you found straight away. Get those answers,' he says distractedly with a wave of a hand. 'And I'll go in and make us a cup of tea, then we can look at that phone together.'

The wind roars behind me, and in the distance, a thundercloud cracks.

'Yeah, okay,' I agree, starting to walk. But then a thought crosses my mind, and I pause mid-step, blurting out, 'Wait – how do you know about the rings?'

'What do you mean? You told me about them?'

I think for a minute. 'No…' I begin slowly. 'Well yes… I *did* tell you that the rings were missing on Monday, but I never told you that I *found* them. That happened barely an hour ago.' I cross my arms. 'How did you know that?'

He tries to shrug it off. 'Oh, just a guess then, my mistake. Go and see if that's Glenn – and I'll head inside.' He ventures one hand out, angling it to the sky. 'It looks like it's starting to rain again.'

He tries to start walking again, but I refuse to budge. 'The only person that I've told about finding the rings so far is… Addie,' I whisper more to myself than him as the realisation dawns.

I start to shake my head in disbelief and step towards him to demand an answer. 'Tell me, John, how do you know I found them? How do you know Addie?'

He shakes his head. 'Look, Emily, I really don't know what you're talking about.'

The rain is starting to fall heavier overhead, but I don't care. I'm exhausted. I can't deal with yet another family member not telling me the truth. 'Stop lying to me, John! I'm so sick of everyone lying to me.'

'Trust me, you don't want to know,' he says, his voice as low as the thunder overhead.

But I can't let this go. My best friend in the world is sharing my deepest secrets with my uncle. How do they even know each other? And why would she do that? The betrayal is starting to hit me hard. I thought she was the one person I could *trust* in all this.

'Tell me how you know Addie,' I demand again.

He sighs and turns back to face me.

And suddenly, his expression is unrecognisable. Those eyes that I thought were just like my mother's are now as hard and fathomless as the dark grey churning ocean below the sharp cliffs.

'It's not important,' he says calmly. 'Promise to let this go, and we can leave it at that. No more questions asked. Addie's been trying to look after you...'

But even as he says it, I watch as he steps further around. He's blocking my path to the house.

The rain continues to splatter down overhead. I don't want to let this go – but at the same time, I can feel the rain soaking my clothing, and I want to get inside.

'Fine,' I say. 'I'll drop it for now. But let's get that phone then.'

I try to take a step past him, but he mirrors me. I realise that I won't be able to get past him until he *lets* me.

'Umm – John?'

'Emily. That's another thing that I think you should let go.' At first, I think he must be joking, but there's no mirth in his blank expression.

'What are you talking about?'

'I think,' he says, taking a step towards me, the rain coming down harder, 'we should forget you even found this little phone. Do you think you can do that?'

I shake my head in confusion, moving back and away from him in surprise.

He takes another small step towards me and grabs me by the hand. Too tightly. 'Please,' he looks down at me, 'I really don't want to hurt you.' He doesn't look too upset at the prospect, though. It's more like frustration.

I try to wriggle out of his grasp, but he holds tighter. 'What do you mean you don't want to hurt me? Why would you hurt me?'

He leans down to whisper in my ear as the wind roars around us. 'I think you know why.'

The hairs on the end of my neck stand up as I look up at him in horror.

The truth hits me at last, and I try to scream, but my three tiny words come out barely louder than a gasp as they rasp out of my throat.

'You killed her.'

Chapter Forty-Six

'You killed her,' I say again, more loudly this time. 'Why?' I scream at him, trying to shake out of his grasp. 'Why would *you* want to kill her?'

I'm desperately hoping someone will hear me. But I know my cries are barely audible over the roar of the ocean and the now full-blown storm.

No one can hear me. And no one else would be out in a storm like this.

So he smiles slowly like he has all the time in the world. There's no escape. And he knows it.

He hasn't said a word. He hasn't admitted openly that he killed my mum, his sister. But I see the truth the instant I look into those terrible eyes.

'I don't know anything,' I say over the howl of the wind, trying a different tactic. Anything to get away. And then I see his derisive grin. *He's enjoying my fear.* A flash of anger rises in me. How dare he?

I lose it.

'So, *Uncle John*,' I cry in my own mocking tone. 'What really happened that day? Tell me!'

'Well,' he begins slowly, 'it was very similar to this situation we find ourselves in now, really. Your mother, like you, stumbling upon something that she really shouldn't have.' He sounds exasperated, as though his actions were all Mum's fault. And now also mine.

'What was that?' I manage to spit out, though there's ice in my heart as I clock how close I've unconsciously moved towards the edge. Only about seven more steps, and I'd be scrambling.

'She always *was* too clever by half, *always* the favourite with Mum and Dad... By the time I came along, I was entirely unwanted,' he adds, now his tone dripping in bitterness.

I try to interrupt. 'John, come on, that's not true...'

'Give me a break, Emily, you know exactly what it's like. You became a sibling no one wanted when you stepped into Suzannah's perfect new family. And it was the same for me. Only, I was the *unwanted* younger child, and *you* are the unwanted older one.' I'm offended by his words, but they also hit a nerve. Mum was only eighteen when she had me. An accident, really, but I know that Mum and Dad loved each other. They made it work. They *loved* me. I knew that. It would all have been different if Dad hadn't disappeared when I was ten.

'John, come on, Nana and Granddad *loved* you too.'

He scoffs. 'If that was the case, they had a funny way of showing it. When my perfect older sister got knocked up with *you*,' the venom seeps from his tongue, 'I was only nine! My sister should have been moving out of the house, going to university or whatever, but instead, everything became focused on her again and *you*, her *precious* baby. It should have been *my time* to be their favourite. But I wasn't. I was swept under the carpet yet again as they did everything possible to help out Suzannah, you and your dim-witted dad.'

'Don't say that about my dad!' I screech, lunging towards him. But he grabs my wrist with one swift move, holding tight. Anger swirls in his eyes, and for a second, I think he's going to push. But he doesn't, and he lets go as though my touch has burnt him. He keeps holding his ground. There's no way I can get past.

'Oh, come on,' he chuckles. 'He decided to leave the house that day even though there was a storm warning issued... Did you know that? Or did no one tell you that, either? It was his own fault that he got into that accident.' He takes off his cap and runs his hands through his hair before replacing it. 'How was I ever supposed to save him?'

'What are you talking about? No one knows what happened to him...' Adrenalin courses around my body, my pulse racing at his words.

'Well,' John says, cocking his head to one side and slicking his hand back to dash away the water drops. 'That's not strictly true. I guess it's only fair I tell you now... your father drowned. I should know. I saw it happen.'

'I don't believe you! Dad's body was never found!' I scream at him. Why would I believe a word of what he says? But then again, if he's telling the truth about what he did to Mum...

'Suit yourself,' John shrugs. 'Anyway,' he continues in an almost singsong voice over the now-thunderous rain. He's clearly enjoying his story now. 'Suzannah had always been the perfect child, even when she got herself knocked up!' He shoots a scornful glance at me.

'Wait,' I say, trying to stop his tirade, 'I don't understand. Dad... Dad is really dead?'

He looks shocked at my interruption. Like I'd broken the spell of his performance. He sighs and says in a bored tone, 'Yes, dear Emily. He really is dead. I'm sorry if you harboured any silly little hope over the years. I saw it – but I couldn't tell any of you. People would ask why I didn't try and save him. But I wasn't about to get myself killed because your dad was an idiot... No, obviously not.'

My mouth gapes open in horror as I try to register his words. John ignores me and carries on. 'Where was I? Oh yes, Dad always berated me; nothing I did was ever good enough, *nothing*. So then I tried to get their attention...' I'm struggling to follow his train of thought. All I keep thinking is that he killed my mum... and pretty much killed my dad, too, by letting him drown. *Oh God.*

I try to force my mind to focus on the present. I could process what he just admitted about Dad later. If I survived to tell the tale...

First, I have to listen and try and find a way out of this situation.

In the midst of my whirling memories, I reach for a vague one of John in high school, Mum, Granddad and Nana muttering about how they were worried about him as he got into drugs and the rebellious crowd.

'Well,' he continues, 'when that didn't work, I cleaned myself up. Got perfect grades, got into med school – but even then, Suzannah was the star.' John puts on a high-pitched voice as he mimics my Nana's tone, '"Wow, your own business, and it's doing *so* well – that's incred ible."'

'What are you talking about? They were *so* proud of you becoming a doctor,' I say, trying to distract him with some flattery. Maybe it would work...

'Well, they never told me ONCE,' he retorts venomously. 'I became a *doctor* for my goddamn fool of a father. Even after your stupid dad got himself killed, they didn't care about what I did. His disappearance was *such* a distraction...

'I had a big fancy wedding, married the woman I thought my dad would adore, but then that all fell apart too after only *ten months* of marriage – ten months! Well, as you know, I lost everything. Did you know I had to move back home because of that? Mum was already gone, and Dad constantly called me a failure. A *constant failure*. Suzannah kept saying, "Dad's sick; he doesn't mean it." But I knew he did. All he could say when he saw me was that he was so disappointed in me, and he'd ramble on that I needed to work harder.'

I find it hard to imagine Granddad saying those words... but then again, I remember Mum saying that his illness had changed him in so many ways. Living in London, I guess I hadn't seen him often enough to notice.

John shakes his head, almost regretfully, as he continues. 'I had to make it stop. All he was doing was wasting away, spouting hatred. He was going to die sooner rather than later... So I started to give him a bit of a helping hand.'

My mouth drops open, and I flick the water away from my face. 'You killed him too?!'

'No,' he says. '*Well*... truthfully, I never intended for it to end quite like that. I was just helping him slip away a little quicker than normal.

But what did he have to live for anymore? He was wasting our time and holding onto our inheritance until he eventually passed away. I was doing him kindness, really.

'He was near the end, I could tell, and so out of it most days. I didn't think he could remember anything I was telling him, or that's how it appeared. So one day, when I was so bored at yet another day passing by, I whispered that little secret to him – about your dad – just to see if he would react. And *nothing*. Not a peep. So I laid off upping the doses – I was convinced that he was about to take his last breaths. I should never have stopped, though.' I can hardly bear to hear what he did next.

'Because instead of doing the decent thing and *dying*, what do you think he did? He tried to cut me off! I thought he was out of it, but that whole time, he'd been fooling me... I found a letter from his solicitor. He'd enquired about changing his will – the crafty bugger! To remove me and give everything to you and Suzannah. He obviously *had* heard everything I'd said in my rash test. So enough was enough. I helped him along to his final resting place very swiftly after that, that's all. Before he had a chance to go through with those changes. Because that inheritance was *my* right – for putting up with him for my whole life!'

My jaw drops. Had I heard him correctly? He carries on with an elaborate sigh, water streaming over his cap. He has to shout to make himself heard. 'It should have been left at that, you know. No one else needed to get hurt.' He shakes his head, and a look almost like sadness passes his face. I'm sure it's an act.

'But Suzannah found a copy of the letter he had sent to the solicitor on Friday night when she was clearing up his bedroom. That crafty old fool, leaving a copy behind. She called me up right away to discuss it.

And, of course, I came over immediately. I tried to laugh it off – but I should have known that she'd be able to see right through me. She could tell I was lying – there was no point. *And* there was a pesky little reference to what really happened to your dad in there, too. Apparently, it said something like "my own son is a coward" – just because I didn't try and run into that raging rip of an ocean. So, I guess Suzie wanted to ask about what that meant… I knew she'd be mad at the truth. But I'd never seen her so berserk…'

He shakes his head in disbelief. 'I was quite shocked really. It was a little unfair. What would she have wanted me to do in that situation? Kill myself trying to save her husband?'

'What the hell, John! What did you do to her?' I cry.

He sighs as though this is the part of the story that exhausts him the most. 'Honestly, Emily, I didn't *intend* to hurt her. But you see, she got angrier and angrier the more I tried to explain. She said I was a murdering coward and *deserved* to be written out of the will. She was horrible – really, she was! I gave her a chance and everything! I tore the letter up right in front of her and told her we could pretend we never even found it. Nothing *had* to change. Well, she just laughed in my face and said there was no way in hell that was going to happen after what I'd done to her darling husband. She said that she'd taken pictures and was going to speak with her lawyer. It was at that point that I lost control.' He sighs at the memory.

I don't want to hear this – but I also can't stop hanging on his every word.

'I hit her impulsively. I didn't even stop to think. I was *furious*. I didn't think there would be so much force behind it. But then again—'

He tilts his head to the side as though trying to remember. 'I might have hit her more than once. Maybe I held her face down for too long... I can't quite remember how it happened now. I just saw red.

'And by the time I'd regained control, I realised that she wasn't moving... I panicked then – of course I did. What I'd done was a stupid and reckless loss of control. If I got caught, everything I'd worked so hard for would all be gone. And really, all these deaths would be for nothing. I did the only obvious thing – there was a storm coming, and her injuries looked similar to ones that you could sustain from falling from a great height. It was perfect. I slipped out here, and—' He gestures behind me and makes a whooshing noise. 'Dear Suzie just took a tumble off there.' I am frozen to the spot in horror and can't turn around. It's all I can do to stop myself from retching and throwing up.

'I'd hoped her body would be washed out to sea. But either way, I was certain it couldn't be traced to me. I was very careful to cover any evidence of my being over that night, and I was expecting that the next day, I'd get a phone call from Glenn, panicked that Suzannah was missing. But nothing. It was very strange indeed when I got a call from your dear aunt Jennifer to tell me that they believed Suzie had died that Saturday morning! I almost laughed out loud. I had no idea why Glenn was pretending like Suzannah had been with him the evening before, but it was like a gift had landed on my lap. No one would even be considering the Friday night now... except possibly you. I didn't know for sure whether Suzannah had told you anything because her stupid phone was missing. I looked everywhere in that house, and I couldn't find it.

'But I wasn't too concerned because I knew I had a back-up option – your darling friend to keep tabs on you. She'd tell me everything...'

I manage to croak out, 'Addie...?' He can't have heard me over the roar of the storm and crashing waves below, but he's watching me so closely he can read my lips.

He nods. 'Oh yes, your little friend, she *is* wonderful and quite the chatterbox. You see, it was perfect. I already knew that she was going to be with you that night when I came over here. I was a little worried for a time when she told me it turned out you *had* been here on Friday night. You know, I thought I heard a taxi when I was cleaning everything up, and I ducked out into the pouring rain to check. But all I could see when I peeked out from the shadows was someone stumbling around drunkenly in the storm at the front of the house and ringing the buzzer. The person even slipped over on their way down the steps and screamed. I hoped if I ignored them for long enough, they'd go away. I didn't realise it had been you... but Addie reassured me that you literally couldn't remember anything from that night. And well, it was like the universe had given me another gift.' He claps his hands in delight.

I shake my head. 'No!' I shout at him over the lashing rain. 'Addie would never have told you all this. She would never want to hurt me. She can't have done this...' But my mind is racing. Had Addie been knowingly helping John this whole time? And was that scream I'd been remembering all this time really just mine?

He ignores my muttered cries, adding, 'And when I heard about that iPad and managed to steal it away without anyone realising, I truly thought that would be the last thing I'd have to do to cover any possible tracks.'

'What! You took the iPad?!'

'Of course, I did. I had to have all bases covered. I was worried that Suzannah's iCloud could have connected from her iPhone to her iPad. It was a sensible thing to do. I tried to make sure there would be zero traces of what really happened that night.

'And no one suspected anything. Even you had no idea about me, did you? You were convinced this whole time that it was dear old Mike. Well, it sounds like he's no saint, either. But your mother's death is one crime he's *not* guilty of. Oh well, shame that no one will believe him now that you've done such an excellent job of convincing everyone...'

I gulp. I know that he's right.

'Well, that's all there is to it, my darling *niece*...' He curls his lips into a sickening smile. 'Look, honestly, I didn't want any of this to happen. I didn't *intend* that things would end this way for your mother and now you. Your mother should have said that she wouldn't even think about trying to change the inheritance, and well, she'd still be alive. It's her own fault that she's dead...' He sighs again in mock sorrow as he takes one step closer.

'Now it's quite serendipitous that you will follow your mum in the same way, don't you think?' He moves closer again, and I try and hold my ground.

I manage to shout again over the roar of the storm. 'You can't expect that if I fall, this will work a second time.'

'But it will, Emily. It will be even simpler than your mother. In my *expert* opinion, as a medical professional, you've been showcasing some *very* erratic behaviour since your mother died. So, for you to fall here would not be surprising in the least. Sure, people will think it's a tragedy, but they won't be shocked. They'll assume that your grief from the loss of your mum, after the loss of your grandparents and father too, was all too much. It really *is* too much for one person to bear, don't you think?'

Panic rises in me. He's probably right. I *have* been all over the place. Addie is the only person in the whole world who knows I've come here today. But if she's working with John, then she'll back up his opinion, too. She will convince everyone that I was in an unsound state of mind today...

No one will suspect.

He takes a step towards me. 'And, even if they do question anything, like you said yourself, dear Glenn is going to be here a little later. I won't show up to our planned appointment – I'll say I was called in for a medical emergency. The usual... and I just won't tell him. Then he'll be the only person that had a reason to be here today... you see, Emily. It's so easy to cover up a murder.'

His eyes flash dangerously.

I know I'm out of time.

And there's nowhere left for me to run.

Chapter Forty-Seven

I try not to glance over my shoulder – I know I'm on the precipice.

This can't be it. This can't be how my life ends.

As though someone in the heavens is answering my prayer, a huge strike of lightning streaks across the sky, and John jumps back in surprise.

My one chance to escape opens up.

I run and try to dodge past John's right shoulder. He flinches as though blinded by the light.

I think I've made it, but then I feel a sharp pull on my arm that forces me back. I stumble, wobbling, as I fall towards the edge of the cliff.

He grabs me by the shoulders and turns me as though he's about to throw me off, too. I kick out, trying for his shins, and he lets out a grunt of pain. I see his cap fly off his head. The wind catches it, and it tumbles out towards the ocean. Down to the jagged rocks below.

I wriggle out of his grasp, dropping low to the floor, and I scramble as fast as I can away from him on my hands and knees. I think I'm clear. I'm about to hop to my feet when there's a tug on my ankle, and I'm being dragged back again.

'Not so fast,' he growls out. The storm continues to rage around us.

I try to kick him off me, but he continues to pull me back along the rocky terrain. My entire body scratches painfully along the craggy cliff edge.

Scrabbling, I dig my nails into the ground, but the rain has made any remaining pockets of dirt wet and slippery. There's nothing for me to hold onto.

The next thing I know, he's grabbing my shoulders and flipping me over. Ready to pull me up and toss me over the edge.

His usually tidy hair is now soaked and black as his evil heart. Water droplets stream over his face and a wild glint mars his features.

Is this really going to be the last face I ever see?

I let out one last almighty screech at the terrifying thought. I try to writhe, wriggle and kick my way out of this – anything to escape certain death.

But the sound I hear in the corner of my panicked mind is too loud – too *masculine* to be my scream... was that John or someone else?

At the same time, I fling my eyes open, and I see John look back towards the house, away from me.

I kick out of his grasp and then, once more, hard into his chest to propel myself even further away.

Distracted, the force of my blow takes him by surprise, and he stumbles back on the slippery cracks. His arms pinwheel out as he tries to regain his balance. But it's too late.

In his haste to throw me off the edge, he's become too close to it himself.

And the force of gravity is too much to stop the inevitable as he starts to fall backwards – and off the cliff.

I let out another cry as I see his hands attempt to clasp onto the edge.

I try to get up – try to stop his fall. But by the time I scramble forward on my hands and knees to look over, I can't see anything at all. Only the storming seas below. I feel the slickness of my sweat mixed with rain on every pore. It pools on the ground at the edges of my fingertips and runs over the cliffs into the churning water below.

And then I feel another grab from behind me.

I scream.

I'm in the air and tumbling again...

This must be it, I think. And all I know is black.

Chapter Forty-Eight

'Emily, Emily!' My name is called over and over. As I start to regain consciousness, I sense the pain all over my body. And then everything comes back to me in a rush. Have I fallen? Did someone push me over the edge, too? Am I okay? Where's John?! Then I remember...

I bolt up, terrified, and a pain shoots down my spine. I fall back again, but my head doesn't hit the hard ground; my shoulders caught behind me. I look up, and I'm shocked to see Glenn hovering overhead.

'Glenn?!' Then urgently, I spit out, 'It's John, you have to get him. You have to find him. Because, because, it was... it was him. He killed Mum.' I try and pull myself up again to look around, and my stomach drops. I am now a lot further away from the edge than I remember being when John was circling me. And, behind Glenn, I can see Ben and... Addie?

Fear and confusion rush through my body once more as I realise I am shivering all over, soaked through. I glance up at the sky – and at last, the rain is slowing. The sun is trying to peak through as the clouds roll away.

Glenn sits down and puts an arm around me. 'Hey,' he says. 'It's okay, Em. It's okay, you're safe now. John can't hurt you. He can't hurt anyone ever again.'

'No! No!' I cry out, trying to jump up, but he holds me down. I point at Addie. 'She and John were working together! I don't know how or why…' and then I cry at him, standing up as I manage to get away, 'AND YOU! Why did you have Mum's rings? Why did you lie about where she was on Friday night?!'

I can see three sets of eyes staring at me through the rain, and I am sure I am making no sense. But I still don't feel safe. Not at all.

Ben rushes over to me. 'Emily, it's okay, it's okay.' He takes my hand firmly, as though he's scared that if he doesn't, I might turn around and jump off that cliff anyway. He looks at me, trying to explain. 'Addie called me. She said where you were and why she was terrified for you… We came as soon as we could. She called Glenn too…'

I shake my head. 'No!' I shout. 'She betrayed me. She's been working with John this whole time, told him everything…'

'I know, I know,' he says calmly. 'But let's get inside. You can dry off, and they can explain everything,' he says solemnly. As I take in his words, I decide to trust him. He's the only one I've had to rely on in all this. The only person I can trust completely.

So I nod once, and he pulls on my hand gently, taking me inside and finally away from that cliff.

***

'I'm so sorry, Ems,' Addie is crying. She has been since I first came back out into the small lounge room after being forced to change into the only dry clothes left in this place: Mum's gardening clothes.

She sits across from me as Ben perches between us, and Glenn paces up and down the room, refusing to sit still as we all listen to her story. The room feels warm and sticky after the deluge of the wind and rain I'd experienced.

'I didn't know he was your UNCLE – I swear!' she manages to get out between sobs. 'You know I needed a flatmate to help with the rent a few months ago, and I couldn't find anyone else. He seemed nice enough and not that much older than us. He said he'd just moved back to Sydney and had started working at St Vinnie's...' She puts her head in her hands. 'He seemed really nice and was such a good listener. And you know me, I tell everyone *everything*. I guess, yeah, in hindsight, he did want to know about my best friend in England who was about to come visit – but I thought that was *normal*! That we were becoming good friends, and he was interested in my life...'

She looks up and wipes her streaming eyes. 'And then, well... thinking back, he knew that I was with you that night because I told him – he was texting about where we were and that we might meet up. I told him that you were wasted.' She shoots me an apologetic glance. 'And then he kept asking about how you were doing the last few days, and I was far too open. And then obviously today I was *with him* when you called about those rings, and I told him without thinking as I was so worried about you...' She pulls at the ends of her hair.

'I thought he'd reacted a little strangely, but I put it out of my mind. I only called Ben because you sounded so distressed, and you'd said on the phone that you'd been hoping to speak to him, not me. He said we should come over here to find you, and so I called Glenn, too. We were all racing inside when I swear I heard you scream over the thunder. I couldn't believe it when I saw someone dragging you towards the edge... and then I realised it was John. We all cried out, and, oh God, it was only because of that distraction that you survived – we got there just in time! You almost died today because of me! I can't believe how I helped that *monster*!' Her eyes are red, tears flowing down her face. I can tell she's in total agony and shock at her unwitting role in all this.

I stand up and give her a huge hug. 'It's okay,' I say. I forgive her; of course, I do. Her only fault was being too trusting, and I can't blame her for that. John was purposefully deceitful and wrapped us all around his little finger. She breaks down once more in relief.

Ben stands up. 'Look,' he says. 'I'm going to wait outside for the back up to arrive.'

As soon as he'd managed to get me inside, he'd called in the team to assess the scene and see if anything could be done for John. But he had said it was unlikely. That kind of fall would be impossible to survive.

Now, I nod and say, 'Thanks, Ben,' shooting him a grateful look.

'No problem and the ambulance can give you a once over, too.'

I hit my head quite hard so that probably isn't a bad idea. Right now, my body is still running on adrenalin. So, I need to make the most of it.

As soon as Ben leaves the room, I stand and turn to face Glenn, mustering all the strength I can. After what I've been through, I know I can manage this.

'Now tell us why you had Mum's rings and why you lied about Friday night.' It isn't a question. It is a demand. It is time for him to tell the truth.

Glenn's face deflates under the force of my stare. He looks away and down at the ground like he is trying to stop himself from crying.

He starts in a quiet, despairing voice. 'Your mum and I had a huge fight that night. About you...' He hangs his head. 'And, well, so much more. We'd been fighting quite a bit lately,' he admits, twisting his T-shirt into a fist. 'And she left the house that night – throwing her rings at me in a huge ultimatum. She said she needed the night to think everything through and to leave her alone. So those were the messages you might have seen – I was trying to check on her and get her back.

'She didn't come back that night – obviously. But I thought she'd stayed here like she said she was going to. When I heard the awful news from the police, I didn't know what to think. Was it an accident? Had she done it on purpose because of me? So, I didn't correct anyone when they assumed that she stayed at Merton Street that night. I went along with it all... it was so much easier. And I was so ashamed...

'But Zara never realised that Suzie left after our fight – so don't be mad at her. She was telling the truth the whole time.' He looks up at me with tears in his eyes.

'Oh, Glenn—' I manage, but he interrupts me, holding up his hand.

'Let me finish, please,' he croaks. 'It all became a tangled web, and I didn't know how to admit it to you, so I lied about the rings.

'I'm sorry I was so harsh on you – but it's because I was so ashamed. I was blaming myself. I thought that somehow, because of our fight, I'd led her to this. And if I told you, well, you'd never forgive me...

Then, when you started asking Mike all these questions, I was even more terrified that if I told you the truth, you'd start looking at me in the same way. So I've been pushing you away. I found it so hard to even look at you, you know. You look so much like her,' he says as a single tear escapes down his cheek.

'And I didn't mean to exclude you from the funeral home – I genuinely thought it would be a horrible thing for you to see. I was trying to save you that pain – since I'd already caused such a mess in the first place. But I'd realised I'd done the wrong thing then, too – especially when you started grilling Deborah and me about the rings. I knew that I couldn't admit it to you then.'

He starts pacing the room again. 'And then this happened – you were almost killed! I should have believed you that something was up. But I couldn't see past the fight we'd had. I thought it was all my fault. And I never got the chance to fix it.' He slumps down on the sofa as his voice cracks. He covers his face in his hands as his shoulders shake.

I sit down and gently put an arm around him. 'Glenn – it's okay,' I say softly. And I mean it. He'd lied to me, and he shouldn't have kept what really happened from me for so long. But I understand why now. All the horrible feelings of blame and guilt that had been running through his mind the last few days since he'd heard the news. We all deal with grief in our own way, and this had been his.

'No,' he says, 'it's not. I've not been there for you when I should have. I lied to protect myself because I was so scared of what you'd say – and what everyone else would think of me. I let Suzie down.'

'You didn't,' I say again. 'Look...'

And I pass him a phone – Mum's phone. It had woken up. When I was changing, I managed to have a quick scan. The first message that opened was one she'd been typing out to Glenn but had never sent. I guess she'd been interrupted by John's arrival.

> *I'm sorry we had such a big fight. I'm over-stretched right now and taking it out on you. There's a lot of stuff going on – and I should talk to you about it and not hide it away. I'm going to stay here tonight, but I'll explain everything tomorrow. I do love you –*

His expression changes as he reads the message again and again. From despair to relief, and then to a look of such sadness that I have to look away for a minute.

'Did she really write this?' he manages to rasp out.

I place a hand over his. 'Yes, she did. And she wouldn't want you to blame yourself for what happened for the rest of your life. We all make mistakes.'

No matter our differences, I know how much he loved her. Didn't Mum and I fight that day, too? Isn't that how things are sometimes with family? You can have an argument, but then, in the next hour, everything is resolved. The terrible truth here is that none of us got our happy resolutions with Mum. She was taken too soon.

But now that we finally knew the truth, I could see that we had to try and find a way to free ourselves from all the guilt that comes with a sudden death.

So I simply say in a voice that I try to free from judgement, 'You still should have told me.'

He nods, and his gaze meets mine. Pain is etched across every line. 'I know that,' he says quietly. 'And I'm so sorry. I want to be better for you – and Zara. But I haven't been myself,' he adds, 'since it all happened. I haven't known how to act.'

I know what he means. Grief is so uncontrollable. It makes you think differently and see things that aren't there. It can bring families together or tear them apart. Ours had been ripped in two. But at least with the truth out, maybe we can start to rebuild something.

So I simply say, 'I understand,' and follow with, 'I think that maybe we should try and start again.'

He looks up at me now in hope. 'Really?'

'Mum would have wanted us to,' I reply, shrugging, but I feel a small twinge of emptiness in that sentence. Did I even have a family left anymore?

As though reading my mind, he says, 'You know that no matter what, you're our family? I've always thought of you as my daughter – and maybe that's why I've been tough on you sometimes. Maybe even tougher than on Zara, but I always knew you could make something of yourself. And look at you, in London, taking over the legal world. Your mum was so proud. *I'm* so proud,' he says softly.

I think back to all our fights and arguments over the years – but in a different light. I didn't want to try to understand Glenn when I was a kid and teenager. But I can admit now that he pushed me to be better. He tried to help me out of my self-destructive behaviour. Would I be where I am today without him? Maybe not.

The sound of pounding footsteps approaches, followed by a high-pitched screech as the door flies open. 'Where's my sister?!'

Zara rushes over to me and Glenn. He must have called her when I was recovering and changing. Now, she pulls us towards her and wraps us in a huge hug as she sobs. 'Oh my god, what happened?! Is it true?!' Her eyes flash with panic between mine and Glenn's. We nod soberly.

'Oh god,' she clutches her head, and then she turns to me. 'And Ems, I'm so sorry I didn't believe you about everything. I just couldn't deal with anything else, and I didn't want to hear it, and I—'

I wave my hand in the air to stop her. It truly didn't matter now. 'Don't worry, Zar, it's okay.' I am just relieved to have my sister back, at last. It's all I ever wanted.

She looks at me with her bright blue eyes, now filled with tears. Choking on her words, she manages, 'I was just with Jennifer, and she was telling me everything that had happened between you both and Mike last night when we got the call from Dad.' She shakes her head. 'I guess it wasn't him that hurt Suzie, but I can't believe what he did to you both last night – or what he's been doing for years to Jennifer! He's still going to pay, right?'

'He absolutely will.' Glenn chimes in before I have a chance to respond. Ben had also filled him in on all the details of what had happened between Jennifer and Mike when I was cleaning up.

Glenn has a thunderous expression on his face as he says with a growl, 'That pathetic excuse for a man will regret the day he ever came into our lives. He won't get away with everything he's done. Sergeant White said that he's sure we could work on a case for assault and fraud.'

I nod solemnly and take each of their hands in mine. Determination blazes on both of their faces, and I'm certain we're all thinking the same thing: we might not have been able to save Mum from John, but we would do everything in our power to save Jennifer from Mike.

'Yes, we'll bring him down.' I say in a quiet voice filled with promise. I give their hands a tight squeeze as we all reflect on everything that's happened and everything that's to come. As we sit together in this room, I know that whatever there is to face next, all that matters is that we are here now. We are safe, and the truth of all our family secrets are uncovered at last.

It is time for us to start healing. Because through time, all our wounds will close over – I hope.

Chapter Forty-Nine

I stand looking out over the cliff face that has claimed so many of my family's lives – next to the house that had once held happy memories for me. Now, there is nothing left but ghosts.

I'm the only one still standing from Mum's side of the family, and as though to commemorate that, the clouds that had been clearing away for the past hour suddenly break into bright sunshine. It beams out into the ocean beyond.

Everyone else is inside, but I needed a moment to reflect on all that has happened, all that has been lost, and, in some ways, what has been gained. I would never see my mum again, but at least I knew what happened to her. And at last, I knew that my dad was at peace, too.

Now that John was gone, he couldn't hurt anyone else that I loved.

Maybe one day, I'd finally find a way to heal.

I watch the dancing waves and wonder if Mum and Dad have re-united somewhere out there. A small, sad smile plays on my lips as I wrap my arms around myself.

I jump when I hear a voice behind me. 'Sorry to disturb you,' Ben says gently, walking up to stand beside me. 'I can't even imagine how you're feeling right now.'

I shrug – there is nothing I can say to express it.

We stand in amicable silence for a moment before he says, in a more serious tone, 'Well, you'll hear from us soon about the case, but please don't worry about anything for now. You need to look after yourself.'

I turn to face him. 'Thank you, Ben, for everything. I don't know if I'd be standing here without you.'

His shoulders relax, the professional demeanour leaving him for a moment. 'Don't worry about it. Just doing my job.' And he sticks his hand out to shake mine. But unprofessional or not, I ignore it and sweep him into a hug. In his arms, it's the safest I've felt since all this happened. He holds me for a moment before he stumbles back, now bright red. 'Oh, I-I'm sorry,' he says automatically.

'Don't be,' I say, 'that was all me. I really appreciate it. I don't know what I'd have done without you.' Then I add with a shy smile, 'And I hope we can see each other again, outside of this whole mess.'

'I'd like that,' he says, with that same sparkle in his eyes that I feel like I've known my whole life. 'Maybe I'll even come over to London.'

I'm not sure if he means this or not. But right now, I feel so grateful to be alive that, for once, I am a tiny bit optimistic that things will work out as they should. Mum's death, discovering the truth about Mike, uncovering John's true nature, and almost losing my own life has put everything in perspective.

'Oh,' I say in a soft voice. I look down at our hands, almost brushing, and decide to chance it. I take his hand in mine and squeeze as I look up at his beautiful blue eyes. 'I think my London chapter might be behind me now, you know. It's time for me to focus on myself, my family and the people I love for a while. After all this, I've realised that's what's most important to me. And I don't have any more time to waste.'

He smiles, bright as the sun overhead.

We stand there in silence, looking out at the horizon. For once in what feels like years, I enjoy this simple moment.

I bask in the happiness of knowing that I've been given a tomorrow. Whatever happens next, I know I'll have Addie by my side – and maybe, as I sneak a sideways glance at his dimpled cheek, I'd even have Ben.

There would even be time to build my bridges again with Glenn, Zara and Jennifer.

Because we might never be 'perfect', but after what we'd been through, we'd certainly become a family.

And I know, as I take one last glance up at the now clear blue sky, that was all Mum had ever wanted.

***

A Big Thank You

Dear reader,

Thank you so much for choosing to read *My Perfect Family*. This book is very close to my heart, dedicated to my father, who I lost in a tragic accident eight years ago.

I really hope you raced through the pages and that your jaw dropped at the twist at the end! And if you did, I would be so grateful if you could share an honest review online, and with your family and friends. I can't wait to hear what you think, and it makes a such a big difference in helping new readers to discover my book too.

I'd also love for us to stay in touch, so if you'd like to stay up to date with all my newest releases, you can sign up to my mailing list on my website, below. You will also receive an exclusive short story, absolutely free! Your email address will never be shared and you can unsubscribe at any time.

Sign up here for a free short story: www.melaniepricebooks.com

And don't forget to follow me on social media. I respond to all my messages and would absolutely love to hear from you!

facebook.com/melaniepricebooks

instagram.com/melaniepricebooks

twitter.com/melanieRprice

Thank you,

Melanie

Acknowledgements

Here we are, somehow publishing my second novel! I can't thank enough every single person that has cheered me on to get to this point. Thank you for believing in me.

My Perfect Family is especially close to my heart: dedicated to my father, Geoff Price, who I lost in a tragic accident at our home in Sydney eight years ago. I miss him every single day, but I want to thank him for always encouraging my dreams. I wouldn't be where I am today without him.

I also want to thank all of my amazing family and friends. I am so lucky to have so many supportive people around me. (Thankfully, very different compared to Emily in the book!) You got me through those darkest moments after losing Dad, and you continue to make me smile every day. You all know who you are.

A huge thanks to my brilliant editor, Eve Hall, who helped me ensure this book became a twisty page-turner, to Lisa Brewster for her epic cover design, to Natasha Hodgson and Alex Holmes for their insightful copyedit and proofreads, and Kelly Lacey for her fantastic work on my review tours, and helping to spread the word about my books!

All my love and thanks to my wonderful fiancé, Seb. Thank you for your everlasting patience, support, kindness and audio editing with both of my books. I can't wait to marry you in exactly a month from this publication!

And finally, the biggest thank you to all of my readers. I absolutely love writing these stories, and I'm so grateful to all of you for choosing to read my books. You've made my dreams of becoming an author a reality!

ABOUT THE AUTHOR

Melanie Price is the author of *The Mother-in-Law's Secret* and *My Perfect Family*. She grew up in Sydney but now lives in London. All of her books explore the intricacies of living between Australia and the United Kingdom – with twists and turns galore. *My Perfect Family* is her second novel.

Printed in Great Britain
by Amazon

39601923R00169